BORDERS®
CLASSICS

JACOB AND WILHELM GRIMM

Selected Tales

BORDERS.
CLASSICS

Please direct sales or editorial inquiries to:
BordersTradeBookInventoryQuestions@bordersgroupinc.com

This edition is published by
Borders Classics, an imprint of Borders Group, Inc.,
by special arrangement with
Ann Arbor Media Group, LLC
2500 South State Street, Ann Arbor, MI 48104

Printed and bound in the United States of America
by Edwards Brothers, Inc.

Quality Paperback ISBN 13: 978-1-58726-489-4
ISBN 10: 1-58726-489-7

11   10   09   08   07   10 9 8 7 6 5 4 3 2 1

CONTENTS

SELECTED TALES

The Golden Key

In the winter time, when deep snow lay on the ground, a poor boy was forced to go out on a sledge to fetch wood. When he had gathered it together, and packed it, he wished, as he was so frozen with cold, not to go home at once, but to light a fire and warm himself a little. So he scraped away the snow, and as he was thus clearing the ground, he found a tiny, gold key. Hereupon he thought that where the key was, the lock must be also, and dug in the ground and found an iron chest. "If the key does but fit it!" thought he; "no doubt there are precious things in that little box." He searched, but no keyhole was there. At last he discovered one, but so small that it was hardly visible. He tried it, and the key fitted it exactly. Then he turned it once round, and now we must wait until he has quite unlocked it and opened the lid, and then we shall learn what wonderful things were lying in that box.

The Frog Prince

Long ago, when wishes often came true, there lived a King whose daughters were all handsome, but the youngest was so beautiful that the sun himself, who has seen everything, was bemused every time he shone over her because of her beauty. Near the royal castle there was a great dark wood, and in the wood under an old linden tree was a well; and when the day was hot, the King's daughter used to go forth into the wood and sit by the brink of the cool well, and if the time seemed long, she would take out a golden ball, and throw it up and catch it again, and this was her favorite pastime.

Now it happened one day that the golden ball, instead of falling back into the maiden's little hand which had sent it aloft, dropped to the ground near the edge of the well and rolled in. The King's daughter followed it with her eyes as it sank, but the well was deep, so deep that the bottom could not be seen. Then she began to weep, and she wept and wept as if she could never be comforted.

And in the midst of her weeping she heard a voice saying to her, "What ails you, King's daughter? Your tears would melt a heart of stone."

And when she looked to see where the voice came from, there was nothing but a frog stretching his thick ugly head out of the water. "Oh, is it you, old waddler?" said she; "I weep because my golden ball has fallen into the well."

"Never mind, do not weep," answered the frog; "I can help you; but what will you give me if I fetch up your ball again?"

"Whatever you like, dear frog," said she; "any of my clothes, my pearls and jewels, or even the golden crown that I wear."

"Your clothes, your pearls and jewels, and your golden crown are not for me," answered the frog; "but if you would love me, and have me for your companion and play-fellow, and let me sit by you at table, and eat from your plate, and drink from your cup, and sleep in your little bed—if you would promise all this, then would I dive below the water and fetch you your golden ball again."

"Oh yes," she answered; "I will promise it all, whatever you want;

if you will only get me my ball again." But she thought to herself, "What nonsense he talks! as if he could do anything but sit in the water and croak with the other frogs, or could possibly be any one's companion."

But the frog, as soon as he heard her promise, drew his head under the water and sank down out of sight, but after a while he came to the surface again with the ball in his mouth, and he threw it on the grass.

The King's daughter was overjoyed to see her pretty plaything again, and she caught it up and ran off with it.

"Stop, stop!" cried the frog; "take me up too; I cannot run as fast as you!"

But it was of no use, for croak, croak after her as he might, she would not listen to him, but made haste home, and very soon forgot all about the poor frog, who had to betake himself to his well again.

The next day, when the King's daughter was sitting at table with the King and all the court, and eating from her golden plate, there came something pitter-patter up the marble stairs, and then there came a knocking at the door, and a voice crying, "Youngest King's daughter, let me in!"

And she got up and ran to see who it could be, but when she opened the door, there was the frog sitting outside. Then she shut the door hastily and went back to her seat, feeling very uneasy.

The King noticed how quickly her heart was beating, and said, "My child, what are you afraid of? Is there a giant standing at the door ready to carry you away?" "Oh no," answered she; "no giant, but a horrid frog." "And what does the frog want?" asked the King.

"O dear father," answered she, "when I was sitting by the well yesterday, and playing with my golden ball, it fell into the water, and while I was crying for the loss of it, the frog came and got it again for me on condition I would let him be my companion, but I never thought that he could leave the water and come after me; but now there he is outside the door, and he wants to come in to me."

And then they all heard him knocking the second time and crying,

> "Youngest King's daughter,
> Open to me!
> By the well water
> What promised you me?
> Youngest King's daughter
> Now open to me!"

"That which thou hast promised must thou perform," said the King; "so go now and let him in."

So she went and opened the door, and the frog hopped in, following at her heels, till she reached her chair. Then he stopped and cried, "Lift me up to sit by you."

But she delayed doing so until the King ordered her. When once the frog was on the chair, he wanted to get on the table, and there he sat and said, "Now push your golden plate a little nearer, so that we may eat together."

And so she did, but everybody might see how unwilling she was, and the frog feasted heartily, but every morsel seemed to stick in her throat.

"I have had enough now," said the frog at last, "and as I am tired, you must carry me to your room, and make ready your silken bed, and we will lie down and go to sleep."

Then the King's daughter began to weep, and was afraid of the cold frog, that nothing would satisfy him but he must sleep in her pretty clean bed. Now the King grew angry with her, saying, "That which thou hast promised in thy time of necessity, must thou now perform."

So she picked up the frog with her finger and thumb, carried him upstairs and put him in a corner, and when she had lain down to sleep, he came creeping up, saying, "I am tired and want sleep as much as you; take me up, or I will tell your father."

Then she felt beside herself with rage, and picking him up, she threw him with all her strength against the wall, crying, "Now will you be quiet, you horrid frog!"

But as he fell, he ceased to be a frog, and became all at once a Prince with beautiful kind eyes. And it came to pass that, with her father's consent, they became bride and bridegroom. And he told her how a wicked witch had bound him by her spells, and how no one but she alone could have released him, and that they two would go together to his father's kingdom. And there came to the door a carriage drawn by eight white horses, with white plumes on their heads, and with golden harness, and behind the carriage was standing faithful Henry, the servant of the young Prince.

Now, faithful Henry had suffered such care and pain when his master was turned into a frog, that he had been obliged to wear three iron bands over his heart, to keep it from breaking with trouble and anxiety. When the carriage started to take the Prince to his kingdom, and faithful Henry had helped them both in, he got up behind, and was full of joy at his master's deliverance. And when they had gone a part of the way, the Prince heard a sound at the back of the carriage, as if something had broken, and he turned round and cried, "Henry, the wheel must be breaking!" but Henry answered,

> "The wheel does not break,
> 'Tis the band round my heart
> That, to lessen its ache,
> When I grieved for your sake,
> I bound round my heart."

Again, and yet once again there was the same sound, and the Prince thought it must be the wheel breaking. But it was the breaking of the other bands from faithful Henry's heart, because he was so relieved and happy.

Tom Thumb

There was once a poor countryman who used to sit in the chimney-corner all evening and poke the fire, while his wife sat at her spinning-wheel.

And he used to say, "How dull it is without any children about us; our house is so quiet, and other people's houses so noisy and merry!"

"Yes," answered his wife, and sighed, "if we could only have one, and that one ever so little, no bigger than my thumb, how happy I should be! It would, indeed, be having our heart's desire."

Now, it happened that after a while the woman had a child who was perfect in all his limbs, but no bigger than a thumb. Then the parents said, "He is just what we wished for, and we love him very much," and they named him according to his stature, "Tom Thumb." And though they gave him plenty of nourishment, he grew no bigger, but remained exactly the same size as when he was first born; and he had very good faculties, and was very quick and prudent, so that all he did prospered.

One day his father made ready to go into the forest to cut wood, and he said, as if to himself, "Now, I wish there was some one to bring the cart to me." "O father," cried Tom Thumb, "if I can bring the cart, let me alone for that, and in proper time, too!"

Then the father laughed, and said, "How will you manage that? You are much too little to hold the reins." "That has nothing to do with it, father; while my mother goes on with her spinning I will sit in the horse's ear and tell him where to go." "Well," answered the father, "we will try it for once."

When it was time to set off, the mother went on spinning, after setting Tom Thumb in the horse's ear; and so he drove off, crying, "Gee-up, gee-wo!"

So the horse went on quite as if his master were driving him, and drew the wagon along the right road to the wood.

Now it happened just as they turned a corner, and the little fellow was calling out "Gee-up!" that two strange men passed by.

"Look," said one of them, "how is this? There goes a wagon, and the driver is calling to the horse, and yet he is nowhere to be seen." "It is very strange," said the other; "we will follow the wagon, and see where it belongs."

And the wagon went right through the forest, up to the place where the wood had been hewed. When Tom Thumb caught sight of his father, he cried out, "Look, father, here am I with the wagon; now, take me down."

The father held the horse with his left hand, and with the right he lifted down his little son out of the horse's ear, and Tom Thumb sat down on a stump, quite happy and content. When the two strangers saw him they were struck dumb with wonder. At last one of them, taking the other aside, said to him, "Look here, the little chap would make our fortune if we were to show him in the town for money. Suppose we buy him."

So they went up to the woodcutter, and said, "Sell the little man to us; we will take care he shall come to no harm." "No," answered the father; "he is the apple of my eye, and not for all the money in the world would I sell him."

But Tom Thumb, when he heard what was going on, climbed up by his father's coat tails, and, perching himself on his shoulder, he whispered in his ear, "Father, you might as well let me go. I will soon come back again."

Then the father gave him up to the two men for a large piece of money. They asked him where he would like to sit. "Oh, put me on the brim of your hat," said he. "There I can walk about and view the country, and be in no danger of falling off."

So they did as he wished, and when Tom Thumb had taken leave of his father, they set off all together. And they traveled on until it grew dusk, and the little fellow asked to be set down a little while for a change, and after some difficulty they consented. So the man took him down from his hat, and set him in a field by the roadside, and he ran away directly, and, after creeping about among the furrows, he slipped suddenly into a mouse-hole, just what he was looking for.

"Good evening, my masters, you can go home without me!" cried he to them, laughing. They ran up and felt about with their sticks in the mouse-hole, but in vain. Tom Thumb crept farther and farther in, and as it was growing dark, they had to make the best of their way home, full of vexation, and with empty purses.

When Tom Thumb found they were gone, he crept out of his hiding-place underground. "It is dangerous work groping about these holes in the darkness," said he; "I might easily break my neck."

But by good fortune he came upon an empty snail shell. "That's all right," said he. "Now I can get safely through the night"; and he settled himself down in it.

Before he had time to get to sleep, he heard two men pass by, and one was saying to the other, "How can we manage to get hold of the rich parson's gold and silver?" "I can tell you how," cried Tom Thumb. "How is this?" said one of the thieves, quite frightened, "I hear some one speak!"

So they stood still and listened, and Tom Thumb spoke again: "Take me with you; I will show you how to do it!" "Where are you, then?" asked they. "Look about on the ground and notice where the voice comes from," answered he.

At last they found him, and lifted him up. "You little elf," said they, "how can you help us?" "Look here," answered he, "I can easily creep between the iron bars of the parson's room and hand out to you whatever you would like to have." "Very well," said they, "we will try what you can do."

So when they came to the parsonage-house, Tom Thumb crept into the room, but cried out with all his might, "Will you have all that is here?" So the thieves were terrified, and said, "Do speak more softly, lest any one should be awaked."

But Tom Thumb made as if he did not hear them, and cried out again, "What would you like? Will you have all that is here?" so that the cook, who was sleeping in a room hard by, heard it, and raised herself in bed and listened. The thieves, however, in their fear of being discovered, had run back part of the way, but they took courage again, thinking that it was only a jest of the little fellow's. So they came back and whispered to him to be serious, and to hand them out something.

Then Tom Thumb called out once more as loud as he could, "Oh yes, I will give it all to you, only put out your hands."

Then the listening maid heard him distinctly that time, and jumped out of bed, and burst open the door. The thieves ran off as if the wild huntsman were behind them; but the maid, as she could see nothing, went to fetch a light. And when she came back with one, Tom Thumb had taken himself off, without being seen by her, into the barn; and the maid, when she had looked in every hole and corner and found nothing, went back to bed at last, and thought that she must have been dreaming with her eyes and ears open.

So Tom Thumb crept among the hay, and found a comfortable nook to sleep in, where he intended to remain until it was day, and then to go home to his father and mother. But other things were to befall him; indeed, there is nothing but trouble and worry in this world!

The maid got up at dawn of day to feed the cows. The first place she went to was the barn, where she took up an armful of hay, and it happened to be the very heap in which Tom Thumb lay asleep. And he was so fast asleep, that he was aware of nothing, and never waked until he was in the mouth of the cow, who had taken him up with the hay.

"Oh dear," cried he, "how is it that I have got into a mill!" but he soon found out where he was, and he had to be very careful not to get between the cow's teeth, and at last he had to descend into the cow's stomach. "The windows were forgotten when this little room was built," said he, "and the sunshine cannot get in; there is no light to be had."

His quarters were in every way unpleasant to him, and, what was the worst, new hay was constantly coming in, and the space was being filled up. At last he cried out in his extremity, as loud as he could, "No more hay for me! No more hay for me!" The maid was then milking the cow, and as she heard a voice, but could see no one, and as it was the same voice that she had heard in the night, she was so frightened that she fell off her stool, and spilt the milk. Then she ran in great haste to her master, crying, "Oh, master dear, the cow spoke!"

"You must be crazy," answered her master, and he went himself to the cow-house to see what was the matter. No sooner had he put his foot inside the door, than Tom Thumb cried out again, "No more hay for me! No more hay for me!"

Then the parson himself was frightened, supposing that a bad spirit had entered into the cow, and he ordered her to be put to death. So she was killed, but the stomach, where Tom Thumb was lying, was thrown upon a dunghill. Tom Thumb had great trouble to work his way out of it, and he had just made a space big enough for his head to go through, when a new misfortune happened. A hungry wolf ran up and swallowed the whole stomach at one gulp.

But Tom Thumb did not lose courage. "Perhaps," thought he, "the wolf will listen to reason," and he cried out from the inside of the wolf, "My dear wolf, I can tell you where to get a splendid meal!" "Where is it to be had?" asked the wolf. "In such and such a house, and you must creep into it through the drain, and there you will find cakes and bacon and broth, as much as you can eat," and he described to him his father's house.

The wolf needed not to be told twice. He squeezed himself through the drain in the night, and feasted in the store-room to his heart's content. When at last he was satisfied, he wanted to go away again, but he had become so big, that to creep the same way back was impossible. This Tom Thumb had reckoned upon, and began to make a terrible din inside the wolf, crying and calling as loud as he could.

"Will you be quiet?" said the wolf; "you will wake the folks up!" "Look here," cried the little man, "you are very well satisfied, and now I will do something for my own enjoyment," and began again to make all the noise he could.

At last the father and mother were awakened, and they ran to the storeroom-door and peeped through the chink, and when they saw a wolf in occupation, they ran and fetched weapons—the man an axe, and the wife a scythe. "Stay behind," said the man, as they entered the room; "when I have given him a blow, and it does not seem to have killed him, then you must cut at him with your scythe."

Then Tom Thumb heard his father's voice, and cried, "Dear father, I am here in the wolf's inside."

Then the father called out full of joy, "Thank heaven that we have found our dear child!" and told his wife to keep the scythe out of the way, lest Tom Thumb should be hurt with it. Then he drew near and struck the wolf such a blow on the head that he fell down dead; and then he fetched a knife and a pair of scissors, slit up the wolf's body, and let out the little fellow.

"Oh, what anxiety we have felt about you!" said the father. "Yes, father, I have seen a good deal of the world, and I am very glad to breathe fresh air again."

"And where have you been all this time?" asked his father. "Oh, I have been in a mouse-hole and a snail's shell, in a cow's stomach and a wolf's inside; now I think I will stay at home."

"And we will not part with you for all the kingdoms of the world," cried the parents, as they kissed and hugged their dear little Tom Thumb. And they gave him something to eat and drink, and a new suit of clothes, as his old ones were soiled with travel.

The Young Giant

A long time ago a countryman had a son who was as big as a thumb, and did not become any bigger, and during several years did not grow one hair's breadth. Once when the father was going out to plough, the little one said, "Father, I will go out with thee." "Thou wouldst go out with me?" said the father. "Stay here, thou wilt be of no use out there, besides thou mightst get lost!" Then Thumbling began to cry, and for the sake of peace his father put him in his pocket, and took him with him.

When he was outside in the field, he took him out again, and set him in a freshly-cut furrow.

While he was there, a great giant came over the hill. "Dost thou see that great monster?" said the father, for he wanted to frighten the little fellow to make him good. "He is coming to fetch thee." The giant, however, had scarcely taken two steps with his long legs before he was in the furrow. He took up little Thumbling carefully with two fingers, examined him, and without saying one word went away with him. His father stood by, but could not utter a sound for terror, and he thought nothing else but that his child was lost, and that as long as he lived he should never set eyes on him again.

The giant, however, carried him home, suckled him, and Thumbling grew and became tall and strong after the manner of giants. When two years had passed, the old giant took him into the forest, wanted to try him, and said, "Pull up a stick for thyself." Then the boy was already so strong that he tore up a young tree out of the earth by the roots. But the giant thought, "We must do better than that," took him back again, and suckled him two years longer.

When he tried him, his strength had increased so much that he could tear an old tree out of the ground. That was still not enough for the giant; he again suckled him for two years, and when he then went with him into the forest and said, "Now, just tear up a proper stick for me," the boy tore up the strongest oak tree from the earth, so that it split, and that was a mere trifle to him. "Now that will do," said the giant, "thou art perfect," and took him back to the field from whence he had brought him. His father was there following the plough. The young giant went up to him, and said, "Does my father see what a fine man his son has grown into?"

The farmer was alarmed, and said, "No, thou art not my son; I don't want thee—leave me!" "Truly I am your son; allow me to do your work, I can plough as well as you, nay better." "No, no, thou art not my son, and thou canst not plough—go away!" However, as he was afraid of this great man, he left hold of the plough, stepped back and stood at one side of the piece of land. Then the youth took the plough, and just pressed it with one hand, but his grasp was so strong that the plough went deep into the earth. The farmer could not bear to see that, and called to him, "If thou art determined to plough, thou must not press so hard on it, that makes bad work." The youth, however, unharnessed the horses, and drew the plough himself, saying, "Just go home, father, and bid my mother make ready a large dish of food, and in the meantime I will go over the field." Then the farmer went home, and ordered his wife to prepare the food; but the youth ploughed the field, which was two acres large, quite alone, and then he harnessed himself to the harrow, and harrowed the whole of the land, using two harrows at once. When he had done it, he went into the forest, and pulled up two oak trees, laid them across his shoulders, and hung one harrow on them behind and one before, and also one horse behind and one before, and carried all as if it had been a bundle of straw, to his parents' house.

When he entered the yard, his mother did not recognize him, and asked, "Who is that horrible tall man?" The farmer said, "That is our son." She said, "No, that cannot be our son, we never had such a tall one, ours was a little thing." She called to him, "Go away, we do not want thee!" The youth was silent, but led his horses to the stable, gave them oats and hay, and all that they wanted. When he had done this, he went into the parlor, sat down on the bench and said, "Mother, now I should like something to eat, will it soon be ready?" Then she said, "Yes," and brought in two immense dishes full of food, which would have been enough to satisfy herself and her husband for a week. The youth, however, ate the whole of it himself, and asked if she had nothing more to set before him. "No," she replied, "that is all we have." "But that was only a taste, I must have more."

She did not dare to oppose him, and went and put a huge caldron full of food on the fire, and when it was ready, carried it in. "At length come a few crumbs," said he, and ate all there was, but it was still not sufficient to appease his hunger. Then said he, "Father, I see well that with thee I shall never have food enough; if thou will get me an iron staff which is strong, and which I cannot break against my knees, I will go out into the world."

The farmer was glad, put his two horses in his cart, and fetched from the smith a staff so large and thick that the two horses could only just bring it away. The youth laid it across his knees, and snap! he broke it in two in the middle like a beanstick, and threw it away.

The father then harnessed four horses, and brought a bar which was so long and thick, that the four horses could only just drag it. The son snapped this also in twain against his knees, threw it away, and said, "Father, this can be of no use to me, thou must harness more horses, and bring a stronger staff." So the father harnessed eight horses, and brought one which was so long and thick, that the eight horses could only just carry it. When the son took it in his hand, he broke a bit from the top of it also, and said, "Father, I see that thou wilt not be able to procure me any such staff as I want, I will remain no longer with thee."

So he went away, and gave out that he was a smith's apprentice. He arrived at a village, wherein lived a smith who was a greedy fellow, who never did a kindness to any one, but wanted everything for himself. The youth went into the smithy to him, and asked if he needed a journeyman. "Yes," said the smith, and looked at him, and thought, "That is a strong fellow who will strike out well, and earn his bread." So he asked, "How much wages dost thou want" "I don't want any at all," he replied, "only every fortnight, when the other journeymen are paid, I will give thee two blows, and thou must bear them." The miser was heartily satisfied, and thought he would thus save much money.

Next morning, the strange journeyman was to begin to work, but when the master brought the glowing bar, and the youth struck his first blow, the iron flew asunder, and the anvil sank so deep into the earth, that there was no bringing it out again. Then the miser grew angry, and said, "Oh, but I can't make any use of thee, thou strikest far too powerfully; what wilt thou have for the one blow?"

Then said he, "I will only give thee quite a small blow, that's all." And he raised his foot, and gave him such a kick that he flew away over four loads of hay. Then he sought out the thickest iron bar in the smithy for himself, took it as a stick in his hand, and went onwards.

When he had walked for some time, he came to a small farm, and asked the bailiff if he did not require a head-servant. "Yes," said the bailiff, "I can make use of one; you look a strong fellow who can do something, how much a year do you want as wages?" He again replied that he wanted no wages at all, but that every year he would give him three blows, which he must bear. Then the bailiff was satisfied, for he, too, was a covetous fellow. Next morning all the servants were to go into the wood, and the others were already up, but the head-servant was still in bed. Then one of them called to him, "Get up, it is time; we are going into the wood, and thou must go with us."

"Ah," said he quite roughly and surlily, "you may just go, then; I shall be back again before any of you."

Then the others went to the bailiff, and told him that the head-man was still lying in bed, and would not go into the wood with them. The bailiff said they were to awake him again, and tell him to harness the horses. The head-man, however, said as before, "Just go there, I shall be back again before any of you." And then he stayed in bed two hours longer. At length he arose from the feathers, but first he got himself two bushels of peas from the loft, made himself some broth with them, ate it at his leisure, and when that was done, went and harnessed the horses, and drove into the wood.

Not far from the wood was a ravine through which he had to pass, so he first drove the horses on, and then stopped them, and went behind the cart, took trees and brushwood, and made a great barricade, so that no horse could get through. When he was entering the wood, the others were just driving out of it with their loaded carts to go home; then said he to them, "Drive on, I will still get home before you do." He did not drive far into the wood, but at once tore two of the very largest trees of all out of the earth, threw them on his cart, and turned round. When he came to the barricade, the others were still standing there, not able to get through. "Don't you see," said he, "that if you had stayed with me, you would have got home just as quickly, and would have had another hour's sleep?"

He now wanted to drive on, but his horses could not work their way through, so he unharnessed them, laid them at the top of the cart, took the shafts in his own hands, and drew it over, and he did this just as easily as if it had been laden with feathers. When he was over, he said to the others, "There, you see, I have got over quicker than you," and drove on, and the others had to stay where they were. In the yard, however, he took a tree in his hand, showed it to the bailiff, and said, "Isn't that a fine bundle of wood?" Then said the bailiff to his wife, "The servant is a good one, if he does sleep long, he is still home before the others."

So he served the bailiff a year, and when that was over, and the other servants were getting their wages, he said it was time for him to have his too. The bailiff, however, was afraid of the blows which he was to receive, and earnestly entreated him to excuse him from having them; for rather than that, he himself would be head-servant, and the youth should be bailiff. "No," said he, "I will not be a bailiff, I am head-servant, and will remain so, but I will administer that which we agreed on." The bailiff was willing to give him whatsoever he demanded, but it was of no use, the head-servant said no to everything.

Then the bailiff did not know what to do, and begged for a fortnight's delay, for he wanted to find some way to escape. The head-servant consented to this delay. The bailiff summoned all his clerks together, and they were to think the matter over, and give him advice. The clerks pondered for a long time, but at last they said that no one was sure of his life with the head-servant, for he could kill a man as easily as a midge, and that the bailiff ought to make him get into the well and clean it, and when he was down below, they would roll up one of the mill-stones which was lying there, and throw it on his head; and then he would never return to daylight.

The advice pleased the bailiff, and the head-servant was quite willing to go down the well. When he was standing down below at the bottom, they rolled down the largest mill-stone and thought they had broken his skull, but he cried, "Chase away those hens from the well, they are scratching in the sand up there, and throwing the grains into my eyes, so that I can't see." So the bailiff cried, "Sh-sh"—and pretended to frighten the hens away.

When the head-servant had finished his work, he climbed up and said, "Just look what a beautiful necktie I have on," and behold it was the mill-stone which he was wearing round his neck. The head-servant now wanted to take his reward, but the bailiff again begged for a fortnight's delay. The clerks met together and advised him to send the head-servant to the haunted mill to grind corn by night, for from thence as yet no man had ever returned in the morning alive. The proposal pleased the bailiff, he called the head-servant that very evening, and ordered him to take eight bushels of corn to the mill, and grind it that night, for it was wanted.

So the head-servant went to the loft, and put two bushels in his right pocket, and two in his left, and took four in a wallet, half on his back, and half on his breast, and thus laden went to the haunted mill. The miller told him that he could grind there very well by day, but not by night, for the mill was haunted, and that up to the present time whosoever had gone into it at night had been found in the morning, lying dead inside. He said, "I will manage it, just you go away to bed." Then he went into the mill, and poured out the corn.

About eleven o'clock he went into the miller's room, and sat down on the bench. When he had sat there a while, a door suddenly opened, and a large table came in, and on the table, wine and roasted meats placed themselves, and much good food besides, but everything came of itself, for no one was there to carry it. After this the chairs pushed themselves up, but no people came, until all at once he beheld fingers, which handled knives and forks, and laid food on the plates, but with this exception he saw nothing. As he was hungry, and saw the food, he, too, placed himself at the table, ate with those who were eating, and enjoyed it.

When he had had enough, and the others also had quite emptied their dishes, he distinctly heard all the candles being suddenly snuffed out, and as it was now pitch dark, he felt something like a box on the ear. Then he said, "If anything of that kind comes again, I shall strike out in return." And when he had received a second box on the ear, he, too, struck out. And so it continued the whole night, he took nothing without returning it, but repaid everything with interest, and did not lay about him in vain.

At daybreak, however, everything ceased. When the miller had got up, he wanted to look after him, and wondered if he were still alive. Then the youth said, "I have eaten my fill, have received some boxes on the ear, but I have given some in return." The miller rejoiced, and said that the mill was now released from the spell, and wanted to give him much money as a reward. But he said, "Money, I will not have, I have enough of it." So he took his meal on his back, went home, and told the bailiff that he had done what he had been told to do, and would now have the reward agreed on.

When the bailiff heard that, he was seriously alarmed and quite beside himself; he walked backwards and forwards in the room, and drops of perspiration ran down from his forehead. Then he opened the window to get some fresh air, but before he was aware the head-servant had given him such a kick that he flew through the window out into the air, and so far away that no one ever saw him again.

Then said the head-servant to the bailiff's wife, "If he does not come back, thou must take the other blow." She cried, "No, no, I cannot bear it," and opened the other window, because drops of perspiration were running down her forehead. Then he gave her such a kick that she, too, flew out, and as she was lighter she went much higher than her husband. Her husband cried, "Do come to me," but she replied, "Come thou to me, I cannot come to thee."

They hovered about there in the air, and could not get to each other, and whether they are still hovering about or not, I do not know, but the young giant took up his iron bar, and went on his way.

Fitcher's Bird

There was once a wizard who used to take the form of a poor man. He went to houses and begged, and caught pretty girls. No one knew whither he carried them, for they were never seen more. One day he appeared before the door of a man who had three pretty daughters. He looked like a poor weak beggar, and carried a basket on his back, as if he meant to collect charitable gifts in it. He begged for a little food, and when the eldest daughter came out and was just reaching him a piece of bread, he did but touch her, and she was forced to jump into his basket. Thereupon he hurried away with long strides, and carried her away into a dark forest to his house, which stood in the midst of it.

Everything in the house was magnificent; he gave her whatsoever she could possibly desire, and said, "My darling, thou wilt certainly be happy with me, for thou hast everything thy heart can wish for." This lasted a few days, and then he said, "I must journey forth, and leave thee alone for a short time; there are the keys of the house; thou mayst go everywhere and look at everything except into one room, which this little key here opens, and there I forbid thee to go on pain of death." He likewise gave her an egg and said, "Preserve the egg carefully for me, and carry it continually about with thee, for a great misfortune would arise from the loss of it."

She took the keys and the egg, and promised to obey him in everything. When he was gone, she went all round the house from the bottom to the top, and examined everything. The rooms shone with silver and gold, and she thought she had never seen such great splendor.

At length she came to the forbidden door; she wished to pass it by, but curiosity let her have no rest. She examined the key, it looked just like any other; she put it in the keyhole and turned it a little, and the door sprang open. But what did she see when she went in? A great bloody basin stood in the middle of the room, and therein lay human beings, dead and hewn to pieces, and hard by was a block of wood, and a gleaming axe lay upon it. She was so terribly alarmed that the egg which she held in her hand fell into the basin. She got it out and washed the blood off, but in vain, it appeared again in a moment. She washed and scrubbed, but she could not get it out.

It was not long before the man came back from his journey, and the first things which he asked for were the key and the egg. She gave them to him, but she trembled as she did so, and he saw at once by the red spots that she had been in the bloody chamber. "Since thou hast gone into the room against my will," said he, "thou shalt go back into it against thine own. Thy life is ended." He threw her down, dragged her thither by her hair, cut her head off on the block, and hewed her in pieces so that her blood ran on the ground. Then he threw her into the basin with the rest.

"Now I will fetch myself the second," said the wizard, and again he went to the house in the shape of a poor man, and begged. Then the second daughter brought him a piece of bread; he caught her like the first, by simply touching her, and carried her away. She did not fare better than her sister. She allowed herself to be led away by her curiosity, opened the door of the bloody chamber, looked in, and had to atone for it with her life on the wizard's return.

Then he went and brought the third sister. But she was clever and crafty. When he had given her the keys and the egg, and had left her, she first put the egg away with great care, and then she examined the house, and at last went into the forbidden room. Alas, what did she behold! Both her sisters lay there in the basin, cruelly murdered, and cut in pieces. She began to gather their limbs together and put them in order, head, body, arms and legs. And when nothing further was lacking, the limbs began to move and unite themselves together, and both the maidens opened their eyes and were once more alive. Then they rejoiced and kissed and caressed each other.

On his arrival, the man at once demanded the keys and the egg, and as he could perceive no trace of any blood on it, he said, "Thou hast stood the test, thou shalt be my bride." He now had no longer any power over her, and was forced to do whatsoever she desired. "Oh, very well," said she, "thou shalt first take a basketful of gold to my father and mother, and carry it thyself on thy back; in the meantime I will prepare for the wedding."

Then she ran to her sisters, whom she had hidden in a little chamber and said, "The moment has come when I can save you. The wretch shall himself carry you home again, but as soon as you are at home send help to me." She put both of them in a basket and covered them quite over with gold, so that nothing of them was to be seen, then she called in the wizard and said to him, "Now carry the basket away, but I shall look through my little window and watch to see if thou stoppest on the way to stand or to rest."

The wizard raised the basket on his back and went away with it, but it weighed him down so heavily that the perspiration streamed from his face. Then he sat down and wanted to rest awhile, but immediately one of the girls in the basket cried, "I am looking through my little window, and I see that thou art resting. Wilt thou go on at once?" He thought his bride was calling that to him; and got up on his legs again. Once more he was going to sit down, but instantly she cried, "I am looking through my little window, and I see that thou art resting. Wilt thou go on directly?"

Whenever he stood still, she cried this, and then he was forced to go onwards, until at last, groaning and out of breath, he took the basket with the gold and the two maidens into their parents' house. At home, however, the bride prepared the marriage-feast, and sent invitations to the friends of the wizard. Then she took a skull with grinning teeth, put some ornaments on it and a wreath of flowers, carried it upstairs to the garret-window, and let it look out from thence. When all was ready, she got into a barrel of honey, and then cut the feather-bed open and rolled herself in it, until she looked like a wondrous bird, and no one could recognize her. Then she went out of the house, and on her way she met some of the wedding-guests, who asked,

> "O, Fitcher's bird, how com'st thou here?"
> "I come from fitcher's house quite near."
> "And what may the young bride be doing?"
> "From cellar to garret she's swept all clean,
> And now from the window she's peeping, I ween."

At last she met the bridegroom, who was coming slowly back. He, like the others, asked,

> "O, Fitcher's bird, how com'st thou here?"
> "I come from Fitcher's house quite near."
> "And what may the young bride be doing?"
> "From cellar to garret she's swept all clean,
> And now from the window she's peeping, I ween."

The bridegroom looked up, saw the decked-out skull, thought it was his bride, and nodded to her, greeting her kindly. But when he and his guests had all gone into the house, the brothers and kinsmen of the bride, who had been sent to rescue her, arrived. They locked all the doors of the house, that no one might escape, set fire to it, and the wizard and all his crew were burned.

The Robber Bridegroom

There was once a miller who had a beautiful daughter, and when she was grown up he became anxious that she should be well married and taken care of; so he thought, "If a decent sort of man comes and asks her in marriage, I will give her to him."

Soon after a suitor came forward who seemed very well-to-do, and as the miller knew nothing to his disadvantage, he promised him his daughter. But the girl did not seem to love him as a bride should love her bridegroom; she had no confidence in him; as often as she saw him or thought about him, she felt a chill at her heart.

One day he said to her, "You are to be my bride, and yet you have never been to see me." The girl answered, "I do not know where your house is." Then he said, "My house is a long way in the wood."

She began to make excuses, and said she could not find the way to it; but the bridegroom said, "You must come and pay me a visit next Sunday; I have already invited company, and I will strew ashes on the path through the wood, so that you will be sure to find it."

When Sunday came, and the girl set out on her way, she felt very uneasy without knowing exactly why; and she filled both pockets full of peas and lentils. There were ashes strewn on the path through the wood, but nevertheless, at each step she cast to the right and left a few peas on the ground. So she went on the whole day until she came to the middle of the wood, where it was darkest, and there stood a lonely house, not pleasant in her eyes, for it was dismal and unhomelike. She walked in, but there was no one there, and the greatest stillness reigned. Suddenly she heard a voice cry,

> "Turn back, turn back, thou pretty bride,
> Within this house thou must not bide,
> For here do evil things betide."

The girl glanced round, and perceived that the voice came from a bird who was hanging in a cage by the wall. And again it cried,

"Turn back, turn back, thou pretty bride,
Within this house thou must not bide,
For here do evil things betide."

Then the pretty bride went on from one room into another through the whole house, but it was quite empty, and no soul to be found in it. At last she reached the cellar, and there sat a very old woman nodding her head.

"Can you tell me," said the bride, "if my bridegroom lives here?"

"Oh, poor child," answered the old woman, "do you know what has happened to you? You are in a place of cutthroats. You thought you were a bride, and soon to be married, but death will be your spouse. Look here, I have a great kettle of water to set on, and when once they have you in their power they will cut you in pieces without mercy, cook you, and eat you, for they are cannibals. Unless I have pity on you, and save you, all is over with you!"

Then the old woman hid her behind a great cask, where she could not be seen. "Be as still as a mouse," said she; "do not move or go away, or else you are lost. At night, when the robbers are asleep, we will escape. I have been waiting a long time for an opportunity."

No sooner was it settled than the wicked gang entered the house. They brought another young woman with them, dragging her along, and they were drunk, and would not listen to her cries and groans. They gave her wine to drink, three glasses full, one of white wine, one of red, and one of yellow, and then they cut her in pieces; the poor bride all the while shaking and trembling when she saw what a fate the robbers had intended for her.

One of them noticed on the little finger of their victim a golden ring, and as he could not draw it off easily, he took an axe and chopped it off, but the finger jumped away, and fell behind the cask on the bride's lap. The robber took up a light to look for it, but he could not find it. Then said one of the others, "Have you looked behind the great cask?" But the old woman cried, "Come to supper, and leave off looking till tomorrow; the finger cannot run away."

Then the robbers said the old woman was right, and they left off searching, and sat down to eat, and the old woman dropped some sleeping stuff into their wine, so that before long they stretched themselves on the cellar floor, sleeping and snoring.

When the bride heard that, she came from behind the cask, and had to make her way among the sleepers lying all about on the ground, and she felt very much afraid lest she might awaken any of them. But by good luck she passed through, and the old woman with her, and they opened the door, and they made haste to leave that house of murderers. The wind had carried away the ashes from the path, but the peas and lentils had budded and sprung up, and the moonshine upon them showed the way. And they went on through the night, till in the morning they reached the mill. Then the girl related to her father all that had happened to her.

When the wedding-day came, the friends and neighbors assembled, the miller having invited them, and the bridegroom also appeared. When they were all seated at table, each one had to tell a story. But the bride sat still, and said nothing, till at last the bridegroom said to her, "Now, sweetheart, do you know no story? Tell us something."

She answered, "I will tell you my dream. I was going alone through a wood, and I came at last to a house in which there was no living soul, but by the wall was a bird in a cage, who cried,

> 'Turn back, turn back, thou pretty bride,
> Within this house thou must not bide,
> For here do evil things betide.'

"And then again it said it. Sweetheart, the dream is not ended. Then I went through all the rooms, and they were all empty, and it was so lonely and wretched. At last I went down into the cellar, and there sat an old old woman, nodding her head. I asked her if my bridegroom lived in that house, and she answered, 'Ah, poor child, you have come into a place of cutthroats; your bridegroom does live here, but he will kill you and cut you in pieces, and then cook and eat you.' Sweetheart, the dream is not ended. But the old woman hid me behind a great cask, and no sooner had she done so than the robbers came home, dragging with them a young woman, and they gave her to drink wine thrice, white, red, and yellow. Sweetheart, the dream is not yet ended. And then they killed her, and cut her in pieces. Sweetheart, my dream is not yet ended. And one of the robbers saw a gold ring on the finger of the young woman, and as it was difficult to get off, he took an axe and chopped off the finger, which jumped upwards, and then fell behind the great cask on my lap. And here is the finger with the ring!"

At these words she drew it forth, and showed it to the company.

The robber, who during the story had grown deadly white, sprang up, and would have escaped, but the folks held him fast, and delivered him up to justice. And he and his whole gang were, for their evil deeds, condemned and executed.

Maid Maleen

There was once a King who had a son who asked in marriage the daughter of a mighty King; she was called Maid Maleen, and was very beautiful. As her father wished to give her to another, the Prince was rejected; but as they both loved each other with all their hearts, they would not give each other up, and Maid Maleen said to her father, "I can and will take no other for my husband."

Then the King flew into a passion, and ordered a dark tower to be built, into which no ray of sunlight or moonlight should enter. When it was finished, he said, "Therein shalt thou be imprisoned for seven years, and then I will come and see if thy perverse spirit is broken." Meat and drink for the seven years were carried into the tower, and then she and her waiting-woman were led into it and walled up, and thus cut off from the sky and from the earth. There they sat in the darkness, and knew not when day or night began. The King's son often went round and round the tower, and called their names, but no sound from without pierced through the thick walls. What else could they do but lament and complain?

Meanwhile the time passed, and by the diminution of the food and drink they knew that the seven years were coming to an end. They thought the moment of their deliverance was come; but no stroke of the hammer was heard, no stone fell out of the wall, and it seemed to Maid Maleen that her father had forgotten her. As they only had food for a short time longer, and saw a miserable death awaiting them, Maid Maleen said, "We must try our last chance, and see if we can break through the wall." She took the bread-knife, and picked and bored at the mortar of a stone, and when she was tired, the waiting-maid took her turn. With great labor they succeeded in getting out one stone, and then a second, and third, and when three days were over the first ray of light fell on their darkness, and at last the opening was so large that they could look out.

The sky was blue, and a fresh breeze played on their faces; but how melancholy everything looked all around! Her father's castle lay in ruins, the town and the villages were, so far as could be seen, destroyed by fire, the fields far and wide laid to waste, and no human being was visible. When the opening in the wall was large enough for them to slip through, the waiting-maid sprang down first, and then Maid Maleen followed. But where were they to go? The enemy had ravaged the whole kingdom, driven away the King, and slain all the inhabitants. They wandered forth to seek another country, but nowhere did they find a shelter, or a human being to give them a mouthful of bread, and their need was so great that they were forced to appease their hunger with nettles. When, after long journeying, they came into another country, they tried to get work everywhere; but wherever they knocked they were turned away, and no one would have pity on them. At last they arrived in a large city and went to the royal palace. There also they were ordered to go away, but at last the cook said that they might stay in the kitchen and be scullions.

The son of the King in whose kingdom they were, was, however, the very man who had been betrothed to Maid Maleen. His father had chosen another bride for him, whose face was as ugly as her heart was wicked. The wedding was fixed, and the maiden had already arrived; because of her great ugliness, however, she shut herself in her room, and allowed no one to see her, and Maid Maleen had to take her her meals from the kitchen. When the day came for the bride and the bridegroom to go to church, she was ashamed of her ugliness, and afraid that if she showed herself in the streets, she would be mocked and laughed at by the people.

Then said she to Maid Maleen, "A great piece of luck has befallen thee. I have sprained my foot, and cannot well walk through the streets; thou shalt put on my wedding-clothes and take my place; a greater honor than that thou canst not have!" Maid Maleen, however, refused it, and said, "I wish for no honor which is not suitable for me." It was in vain, too, that the bride offered her gold. At last she said angrily, "If thou dost not obey me, it shall cost thee thy life. I have but to speak the word, and thy head will lie at thy feet." Then she was forced to obey, and put on the bride's magnificent clothes and all her jewels. When she entered the royal hall, every one was amazed at her great beauty, and the King said to his son, "This is the bride whom I have chosen for thee, and whom thou must lead to church." The bridegroom was astonished, and thought, "She is like my Maid Maleen, and I should believe that it was she herself, but she has long been shut up in the tower, or dead." He took her by the hand and led her to church. On the way was a nettle-plant, and she said,

> "Oh, nettle-plant,
> Little nettle-plant,
> What dost thou here alone?
> I have known the time
> When I ate thee unboiled,
> When I ate thee unroasted."

"What art thou saying?" asked the King's son. "Nothing," she replied, "I was only thinking of Maid Maleen." He was surprised that she knew about her, but kept silence. When they came to the foot-plank into the churchyard, she said,

> "Foot-bridge, do not break,
> I am not the true bride."

"What art thou saying there?" asked the King's son. "Nothing," she replied, "I was only thinking of Maid Maleen." "Dost thou know Maid Maleen?" "No," she answered, "how should I know her; I have only heard of her." When they came to the church-door, she said once more,

> "Church-door, break not,
> I am not the true bride."

"What art thou saying there?" asked he. "Ah," she answered, "I was only thinking of Maid Maleen." Then he took out a precious chain, put it round her neck, and fastened the clasp. Thereupon they entered the church, and the priest joined their hands together before the altar, and married them. He led her home, but she did not speak a single word the whole way. When they got back to the royal palace, she hurried into the bride's chamber, put off the magnificent clothes and the jewels, dressed herself in her gray gown, and kept nothing but the jewel on her neck, which she had received from the bridegroom.

When the night came, and the bride was to be led into the Prince's apartment, she let her veil fall over her face, that he might not observe the deception. As soon as every one had gone away, he said to her,

"What didst thou say to the nettle-plant which was growing by the wayside?" "To which nettle-plant?" asked she; "I don't talk to nettle-plants." "If thou didst not do it, then thou art not the true bride," said he. So she bethought herself, and said,

> "I must go out unto my maid,
> Who keeps my thoughts for me."

She went out and sought Maid Maleen. "Girl, what hast thou been saying to the nettle?" "I said nothing but,

> 'Oh, nettle-plant,
> Little nettle-plant,
> What dost thou here alone?
> I have known the time
> When I ate thee unboiled,
> When I ate thee unroasted.'"

The bride ran back into the chamber, and said, "I know now what I said to the nettle," and she repeated the words which she had just heard. "But what didst thou say to the foot-bridge when we went over it?" asked the King's son. "To the foot-bridge?" she answered; "I don't talk to foot-bridges." "Then thou art not the true bride." She again said,

> "I must go out unto my maid,
> Who keeps my thoughts for me,"

and ran out and found Maid Maleen, "Girl, what didst thou say to the foot-bridge?" "I said nothing but,

> 'Foot-bridge, do not break,
> I am not the true bride.'"

"That costs thee thy life!" cried the bride, but she hurried into the room, and said, "I know now what I said to the foot-bridge," and she repeated the words. "But what didst thou say to the church-door?" "To the church-door?" she replied; "I don't talk to church-doors." "Then thou art not the true bride."

She went out and found Maid Maleen, and said, "Girl, what didst thou say to the church-door?" "I said nothing but,

'Church-door, break not,
I am not the true bride.'"

"That will break thy neck for thee!" cried the bride, and flew into a terrible passion, but she hastened back into the room, and said, "I know now what I said to the church-door," and she repeated the words. "But where hast thou the jewel which I gave thee at the church-door?" "What jewel?" she answered; "thou didst not give me any jewel." "I myself put it round thy neck, and I myself fastened it; if thou dost not know that, thou art not the true bride." He drew the veil from her face, and when he saw her immeasurable ugliness, he sprang back terrified, and said, "How comest thou here? Who art thou?" "I am thy betrothed bride, but because I feared lest the people should mock me when they saw me out of doors, I commanded the scullery-maid to dress herself in my clothes, and to go to church instead of me." "Where is the girl?" said he; "I want to see her, go and bring her here." She went out and told the servants that the scullery-maid was an impostor, and that they must take her out into the court-yard and strike off her head. The servants laid hold of Maid Maleen and wanted to drag her out, but she screamed so loudly for help, that the King's son heard her voice, hurried out of his chamber and ordered them to set the maiden free instantly.

Lights were brought, and then he saw on her neck the gold chain which he had given her at the church-door. "Thou art the true bride," said he, "who went with me to church; come with me now to my room." When they were both alone, he said, "On the way to the church thou didst name Maid Maleen, who was my betrothed bride; if I could believe it possible, I should think she was standing before me—thou art like her in every respect." She answered, "I am Maid Maleen, who for thy sake was imprisoned seven years in the darkness, who suffered hunger and thirst, and has lived so long in want and poverty. Today, however, the sun is shining on me once more. I was married to thee in the church, and I am thy lawful wife." Then they kissed each other, and were happy all the days of their lives. The false bride was rewarded for what she had done by having her head cut off.

The tower in which Maid Maleen had been imprisoned remained standing for a long time, and when the children passed by it they sang,

"Kling, klang, gloria.
Who sits within this tower?
A King's daughter, she sits within,

A sight of her I cannot win,
The wall it will not break,
The stone cannot be pierced.
Little Hans, with your coat so gay,
Follow me, follow me, fast as you may."

The Goose Girl

There was once upon a time an old Queen whose husband had been dead for many years, and she had a beautiful daughter. When the Princess grew up she was betrothed to a Prince who lived at a great distance. When the time came for her to be married, and she had to journey forth into the distant kingdom, the aged Queen packed up for her many costly vessels of silver and gold, and trinkets also of gold and silver, and cups and jewels; in short, everything which appertained to a royal dowry, for she loved her child with all her heart. She likewise sent her maid in waiting, who was to ride with her, and hand her over to the bridegroom, and each had a horse for the journey, but the horse of the King's daughter was called Falada, and could speak. So when the hour of parting had come, the aged mother went into her bedroom, took a small knife and cut her finger with it until it bled, then she held a white handkerchief to it into which she let three drops of blood fall, gave it to her daughter and said, "Dear child, preserve this carefully; it will be of service to you on your way."

So they took a sorrowful leave of each other; the Princess put the piece of cloth in her bosom, mounted her horse, and then went away to her bridegroom. After she had ridden for a while she felt a burning thirst, and said to her waiting-maid, "Dismount, and take my cup which you have brought for me, and get me some water from the stream, for I should like to drink." "If you are thirsty," said the waiting-maid, "get off your horse yourself, and lie down and drink out of the water, I don't choose to be your servant." So in her great thirst the Princess alighted, bent down over the water in the stream and drank, and was not allowed to drink out of the golden cup. Then she said, "Ah, Heaven!" And the three drops of blood answered, "If your mother knew this, her heart would break." But the King's daughter was humble, said nothing, and mounted her horse again.

She rode some miles further, but the day was warm, the sun scorched her, and she was thirsty once more, and when they came to a stream of water, she again cried to her waiting-maid, "Dismount, and give me some water in my golden cup," for she had long ago forgotten the girl's ill words. But the waiting-maid said still more haughtily, "If you wish to drink, drink as you can, I don't choose to be your maid." Then in her great thirst the King's daughter alighted, bent over the flowing stream, wept and said, "Ah, Heaven!" And the drops of blood again replied, "If your mother knew this, her heart would break." And as she was thus drinking and leaning right over the stream, the handkerchief with the three drops of blood fell out of her bosom, and floated away with the water without her observing it, so great was her trouble.

The waiting-maid, however, had seen it, and she rejoiced to think that she had now power over the bride, for since the Princess had lost the drops of blood, she had become weak and powerless. So now when she wanted to mount her horse again, the one that was called Falada, the waiting-maid said, "Falada is more suitable for me, and my nag will do for you," and the Princess had to be content with that. Then the waiting-maid, with many hard words, bade the Princess exchange her royal apparel for her own shabby clothes; and at length she was compelled to swear by the clear sky above her, that she would not say one word of this to any one at the royal court, and if she had not taken this oath she would have been killed on the spot. But Falada saw all this, and observed it well.

The waiting-maid now mounted Falada, and the true bride the bad horse, and thus they traveled onwards, until at length they entered the royal palace. There were great rejoicings over her arrival, and the Prince sprang forward to meet her, lifted the waiting-maid from her horse, and thought she was his consort. She was conducted upstairs, but the real Princess was left standing below. Then the old King looked out of the window and saw her standing in the courtyard, and how dainty and delicate and beautiful she was, and instantly went to the royal apartment, and asked the bride about the girl she had with her who was standing down below in the courtyard, and who she was. "I picked her up on my way for a companion; give the girl something to work at, that she may not stand idle."

But the old King had no work for her, and knew of none, so he said, "I have a little boy who tends the geese, she may help him." The boy was called Conrad, and the true bride had to help him tend the geese. Soon afterwards the false bride said to the young King, "Dearest husband, I beg you to do me a favor." He answered, "I will do so most willingly." "Then send for the knacker, and have the head of the horse on which I rode here cut off, for it vexed me on the way." In reality, she was afraid that the horse might tell how she had behaved to the King's daughter. Then she succeeded in making the King promise that it should be done, and the faithful Falada was to die.

This came to the ears of the real Princess, and she secretly promised to pay the knacker a piece of gold if he would perform a small service for her. There was a great dark-looking gateway in the town, through which morning and evening she had to pass with the geese; would he be so good as to nail up Falada's head on it, so that she might see him again, more than once. The knacker's man promised to do that, and cut off the head, and nailed it fast beneath the dark gateway.

Early in the morning, when she and Conrad drove out their flock beneath this gateway, she said in passing,

> "Alas, Falada, hanging there!"

Then the head answered,

> "Alas, young Queen, how ill you fare!
> If this your tender mother knew,
> Her heart would surely break in two."

Then they went still further out of the town, and drove their geese into the country. And when they had come to the meadow, she sat down and unbound her hair which was like pure gold, and Conrad saw it and delighted in its brightness, and wanted to pluck out a few hairs. Then she said,

> "Blow, blow, thou gentle wind, I say,
> Blow Conrad's little hat away,
> And make him chase it here and there,
> Until I have braided all my hair,
> And bound it up again."

And there came such a violent wind that it blew Conrad's hat far away across country, and he was forced to run after it. When he came back she had finished combing her hair and was putting it up again, and he could not get any of it. Then Conrad was angry, and would not speak to her, and thus they watched the geese until the evening, and then they went home.

Next day when they were driving the geese out through the dark gateway, the maiden said,

> "Alas, Falada, hanging there!"

Falada answered,

> "Alas, young Queen, how ill you fare!
> If this your tender mother knew,
> Her heart would surely break in two."

And she sat down again in the field and began to comb out her hair, and Conrad ran and tried to clutch it, so she said in haste,

> "Blow, blow, thou gentle wind, I say,
> Blow Conrad's little hat away,
> And make him chase it here and there,
> Until I have braided all my hair,
> And bound it up again."

Then the wind blew, and blew his little hat off his head and far away, and Conrad was forced to run after it, and when he came back, her hair had been put up a long time, and he could get none of it, and so they looked after their geese till evening came.

But in the evening after they had got home, Conrad went to the old King, and said, "I won't tend the geese with that girl any longer!" "Why not?" inquired the aged King. "Oh, because she vexes me the whole day long." Then the aged King commanded him to relate what it was that she did to him. And Conrad said, "In the morning when we pass beneath the dark gateway with the flock, there is a sorry horse's head on the wall, and she says to it,

> 'Alas, Falada, hanging there!'

"And the head replies,

> 'Alas, young Queen, how ill you fare!
> If this your tender mother knew,
> Her heart would surely break in two.'"

And Conrad went on to relate what happened on the goose pasture, and how when there he had to chase his hat.

The aged King commanded him to drive his flock out again next day, and as soon as morning came, he placed himself behind the dark gateway, and heard how the maiden spoke to the head of Falada, and then he too went into the country, and hid himself in the thicket in the meadow. There he soon saw with his own eyes the goose-girl and the goose-boy bringing their flock, and how after a while she sat down and unplaited her hair, which shone with radiance. And soon she said,

> "Blow, blow, thou gentle wind, I say,
> Blow Conrad's little hat away,
> And make him chase it here and there,
> Until I have braided all my hair,
> And bound it up again."

Then came a blast of wind and carried off Conrad's hat, so that he had to run far away, while the maiden quietly went on combing and plaiting her hair, all of which the King observed. Then, quite unseen, he went away, and when the goose-girl came home in the evening, he called her aside, and asked why she did all these things. "I may not tell you that, and I dare not lament my sorrows to any human being, for I have sworn not to do so by the heaven which is above me; if I had not done that, I should have lost my life." He urged her and left her no peace, but he could draw nothing from her. Then said he, "If you will not tell me anything, tell your sorrows to the iron-stove there," and he went away.

Then she crept into the iron-stove, and began to weep and lament, and emptied her whole heart, and said, "Here am I deserted by the whole world, and yet I am a King's daughter, and a false waiting-maid has by force brought me to such a pass that I have been compelled to put off my royal apparel, and she has taken my place with my bridegroom, and I have to perform menial service as a goose-girl. If my mother did but know that, her heart would break."

The aged King, however, was standing outside by the pipe of the stove, and was listening to what she said, and heard it. Then he came back again, and bade her come out of the stove. And royal garments were placed on her, and it was marvelous how beautiful she was! The aged King summoned his son, and revealed to him that he had got the false bride who was only a waiting-maid, but that the true one was standing there, as the sometime goose-girl. The young King rejoiced with all his heart when he saw her beauty and youth, and a great feast was made ready to which all the people and all good friends were invited.

At the head of the table sat the bridegroom with the King's daughter at one side of him, and the waiting-maid on the other, but the waiting-maid was blinded, and did not recognize the Princess in her dazzling array. When they had eaten and drunk, and were merry, the aged King asked the waiting-maid as a riddle, what a person deserved who had behaved in such and such a way to her master, and at the same time related the whole story, and asked what sentence such an one merited.

Then the false bride said, "She deserves no better fate than to be stripped entirely naked, and put in a barrel which is studded inside with pointed nails, and two white horses should be harnessed to it, which will drag her along through one street after another, till she is dead." "It is you," said the aged King, "and you have pronounced your own sentence, and thus shall it be done unto you." When the sentence had been carried out, the young King married his true bride, and both of them reigned over their kingdom in peace and happiness.

Cinderella

There was once a rich man whose wife lay sick, and when she felt her end drawing near she called to her only daughter to come near her bed, and said,

"Dear child, be good and pious, and God will always take care of you, and I will look down upon you from heaven, and will be with you."

And then she closed her eyes and died. The maiden went every day to her mother's grave and wept, and was always pious and good. When the winter came the snow covered the grave with a white covering, and when the sun came in the early spring and melted it away, the man took to himself another wife.

The new wife brought two daughters home with her, and they were beautiful and fair in appearance, but at heart were black and ugly. And then began very evil times for the poor step-daughter.

"Is the stupid creature to sit in the same room with us?" said they; "those who eat food must earn it. She is nothing but a kitchen-maid!"

They took away her pretty dresses, and put on her an old gray kirtle, and gave her wooden shoes to wear.

"Just look now at the proud princess, how she is decked out!" cried they laughing, and then they sent her into the kitchen. There she was obliged to do heavy work from morning to night, get up early in the morning, draw water, make the fires, cook, and wash. Besides that, the sisters did their utmost to torment her—mocking her, and strewing peas and lentils among the ashes, and setting her to pick them up. In the evenings, when she was quite tired out with her hard day's work, she had no bed to lie on, but was obliged to rest on the hearth among the cinders. And because she always looked dusty and dirty, as if she had slept in the cinders, they named her Cinderella.

It happened one day that the father went to the fair, and he asked his two step-daughters what he should bring back for them. "Fine clothes!" said one. "Pearls and jewels!" said the other. "But what will you have, Cinderella?" said he. "The first twig, father, that strikes against your hat on the way home; that is what I should like you to bring me."

So he bought for the two step-daughters fine clothes, pearls, and jewels, and on his way back, as he rode through a green lane, a hazel twig struck against his hat; and he broke it off and carried it home with him. And when he reached home he gave to the stepdaughters what they had wished for, and to Cinderella he gave the hazel twig. She thanked him, and went to her mother's grave, and planted this twig there, weeping so bitterly that the tears fell upon it and watered it, and it flourished and became a fine tree. Cinderella went to see it three times a day, and wept and prayed, and each time a white bird rose up from the tree, and if she uttered any wish the bird brought her whatever she had wished for.

Now it came to pass that the King ordained a festival that should last for three days, and to which all the beautiful young women of that country were bidden, so that the King's son might choose a bride from among them. When the two step-daughters heard that they too were bidden to appear, they felt very pleased, and they called Cinderella and said, "Comb our hair, brush our shoes, and make our buckles fast, we are going to the wedding feast at the King's castle."

When she heard this, Cinderella could not help crying, for she too would have liked to go to the dance, and she begged her stepmother to allow her. "What! You Cinderella!" said she, "in all your dust and dirt, you want to go to the festival! you that have no dress and no shoes! you want to dance!"

But as she persisted in asking, at last the step-mother said, "I have strewed a dishful of lentils in the ashes, and if you can pick them all up again in two hours you may go with us."

Then the maiden went to the back-door that led into the garden, and called out,

> "O gentle doves, O turtle-doves,
> And all the birds that be,
> The lentils that in ashes lie
> Come and pick up for me!
> The good must be put in the dish,
> The bad you may eat if you wish."

Then there came to the kitchen-window two white doves, and after them some turtle-doves, and at last a crowd of all the birds under heaven, chirping and fluttering, and they alighted among the ashes; and the doves nodded with their heads, and began to pick, peck, pick, peck, and then all the others began to pick, peck, pick, peck, and put all the good grains into the dish. Before an hour was over all was done, and they flew away.

Then the maiden brought the dish to her step-mother, feeling joyful, and thinking that now she should go to the feast; but the step-mother said, "No, Cinderella, you have no proper clothes, and you do not know how to dance, and you would be laughed at!" And when Cinderella cried for disappointment, she added, "If you can pick two dishes full of lentils out of the ashes, nice and clean, you shall go with us," thinking to herself, "for that is not possible." When she had strewed two dishes full of lentils among the ashes the maiden went through the back-door into the garden, and cried,

> "O gentle doves, O turtle-doves,
> And all the birds that be,
> The lentils that in ashes lie
> Come and pick up for me!
> The good must be put in the dish,
> The bad you may eat if you wish."

So there came to the kitchen-window two white doves, and then some turtle-doves, and at last a crowd of all the other birds under heaven, chirping and fluttering, and they alighted among the ashes, and the doves nodded with their heads and began to pick, peck, pick, peck, and then all the others began to pick, peck, pick, peck, and put all the good grains into the dish. And before half-an-hour was over it was all done, and they flew away. Then the maiden took the dishes to the step-mother, feeling joyful, and thinking that now she should go with them to the feast; but she said, "All this is of no good to you; you cannot come with us, for you have no proper clothes, and cannot dance; you would put us to shame." Then she turned her back on poor Cinderella and made haste to set out with her two proud daughters.

And as there was no one left in the house, Cinderella went to her mother's grave, under the hazel bush, and cried,

> "Little tree, little tree, shake over me,
> That silver and gold may come down and cover me."

Then the bird threw down a dress of gold and silver, and a pair of slippers embroidered with silk and silver. And in all haste she put on the dress and went to the festival. But her step-mother and sisters did not know her, and thought she must be a foreign Princess, she looked so beautiful in her golden dress. Of Cinderella they never thought at all, and supposed that she was sitting at home, and picking the lentils out of the ashes. The King's son came to meet her, and took her by the hand and danced with her, and he refused to stand up with any one else, so that he might not be obliged to let go her hand; and when any one came to claim it he answered, "She is my partner."

And when the evening came she wanted to go home, but the Prince said he would go with her to take care of her, for he wanted to see where the beautiful maiden lived. But she escaped him, and jumped up into the pigeon-house. Then the Prince waited until the father came, and told him the strange maiden had jumped into the pigeon-house. The father thought to himself, "It surely cannot be Cinderella," and called for axes and hatchets, and had the pigeon-house cut down, but there was no one in it. And when they entered the house there sat Cinderella in her dirty clothes among the cinders, and a little oil-lamp burnt dimly in the chimney; for Cinderella had been very quick, and had jumped out of the pigeon-house again, and had run to the hazel bush; and there she had taken off her beautiful dress and had laid it on the grave, and the bird had carried it away again, and then she had put on her little gray kirtle again, and had sat down in the kitchen among the cinders.

The next day, when the festival began anew, and the parents and step-sisters had gone to it, Cinderella went to the hazel bush and cried,

"Little tree, little tree, shake over me,
That silver and gold may come down and cover me."

Then the bird cast down a still more splendid dress than on the day before. And when she appeared in it among the guests every one was astonished at her beauty. The Prince had been waiting until she came, and he took her hand and danced with her alone. And when any one else came to invite her he said, "She is my partner."

And when the evening came she wanted to go home, and the Prince followed her, for he wanted to see to what house she belonged; but she broke away from him, and ran into the garden at the back of the house. There stood a fine large tree, bearing splendid pears; she leapt as lightly as a squirrel among the branches, and the Prince did not know what had become of her. So he waited until the father came, and then he told him that the strange maiden had rushed from him, and that he thought she had gone up into the pear tree. The father thought to himself, "It surely cannot be Cinderella," and called for an axe, and felled the tree, but there was no one in it. And when they went into the kitchen there sat Cinderella among the cinders, as usual, for she had got down the other side of the tree, and had taken back her beautiful clothes to the bird on the hazel bush, and had put on her old gray kirtle again.

On the third day, when the parents and the step-children had set off, Cinderella went again to her mother's grave, and said to the tree,

> "Little tree, little tree, shake over me,
> That silver and gold may come down and cover me."

Then the bird cast down a dress, the like of which had never been seen for splendor and brilliancy, and slippers that were of gold.

And when she appeared in this dress at the feast nobody knew what to say for wonderment. The Prince danced with her alone, and if any one else asked her he answered, "She is my partner."

And when it was evening Cinderella wanted to go home, and the Prince was about to go with her, when she ran past him so quickly that he could not follow her. But he had laid a plan, and had caused all the steps to be spread with pitch, so that as she rushed down them the left shoe of the maiden remained sticking in it. The Prince picked it up, and saw that it was of gold, and very small and slender. The next morning he went to the father and told him that none should be his bride save the one whose foot the golden shoe should fit.

Then the two sisters were very glad, because they had pretty feet. The eldest went to her room to try on the shoe, and her mother stood by. But she could not get her great toe into it, for the shoe was too small; then her mother handed her a knife, and said, "Cut the toe off, for when you are Queen you will never have to go on foot." So the girl cut her toe off, squeezed her foot into the shoe, concealed the pain, and went down to the Prince. Then he took her with him on his horse as his bride, and rode off. They had to pass by the grave, and there sat the two pigeons on the hazel bush, and cried,

"There they go, there they go!
There is blood on her shoe;
The shoe is too small—
Not the right bride at all!"

Then the Prince looked at her shoe, and saw the blood flowing. And he turned his horse round and took the false bride home again, saying she was not the right one, and that the other sister must try on the shoe. So she went into her room to do so, and got her toes comfortably in, but her heel was too large. Then her mother handed her the knife, saying, "Cut a piece off your heel; when you are Queen you will never have to go on foot."

So the girl cut a piece off her heel, and thrust her foot into the shoe, concealed the pain, and went down to the Prince, who took his bride before him on his horse and rode off. When they passed by the hazel bush the two pigeons sat there and cried,

"There they go, there they go!
There is blood on her shoe;
The shoe is too small—
Not the right bride at all!"

Then the Prince looked at her foot, and saw how the blood was flowing from the shoe, and staining the white stocking. And he turned his horse round and brought the false bride home again. "This is not the right one," said he, "have you no other daughter?"

"No," said the man, "only my dead wife left behind her a little stunted Cinderella; it is impossible that she can be the bride." But the King's son ordered her to be sent for, but the mother said, "Oh no! she is much too dirty, I could not let her be seen." But he would have her fetched, and so Cinderella had to appear.

First she washed her face and hands quite clean, and went in and curtseyed to the Prince, who held out to her the golden shoe. Then she sat down on a stool, drew her foot out of the heavy wooden shoe, and slipped it into the golden one, which fitted it perfectly. And when she stood up, and the Prince looked in her face, he knew again the beautiful maiden that had danced with him, and he cried, "This is the right bride!"

The step-mother and the two sisters were thunderstruck, and grew pale with anger; but he put Cinderella before him on his horse and rode off. And as they passed the hazel bush, the two white pigeons cried,

> "There they go, there they go!
> No blood on her shoe;
> The shoe's not too small,
> The right bride is she after all."

And when they had thus cried, they came flying after and perched on Cinderella's shoulders, one on the right, the other on the left, and so remained.

And when her wedding with the Prince was appointed to be held the false sisters came, hoping to curry favor, and to take part in the festivities. So as the bridal procession went to the church, the eldest walked on the right side and the younger on the left, and the pigeons picked out an eye of each of them. And as they returned the elder was on the left side and the younger on the right, and the pigeons picked out the other eye of each of them. And so they were condemned to go blind for the rest of their days because of their wickedness and falsehood.

The Glass Coffin

Let no one ever say that a poor tailor cannot do great things and win high honors; all that is needed is that he should go to the right smithy, and what is of most consequence, that he should have good luck. A civil, adroit tailor's apprentice once went out traveling, and came into a great forest, and, as he did not know the way, he lost himself. Night fell, and nothing was left for him to do, but to seek a bed in this painful solitude. He might certainly have found a good bed on the soft moss, but the fear of wild beasts let him have no rest there, and at last he was forced to make up his mind to spend the night in a tree. He sought out a high oak, climbed up to the top of it, and thanked God that he had his goose with him, for otherwise the wind which blew over the top of the tree would have carried him away.

After he had spent some hours in the darkness, not without fear and trembling, he saw at a very short distance the glimmer of a light, and as he thought that a human habitation might be there, where he would be better off than on the branches of a tree, he got carefully down and went towards the light. It guided him to a small hut that was woven together of reeds and rushes. He knocked boldly, the door opened, and by the light which came forth he saw a little hoary old man who wore a coat made of bits of colored stuff sewn together.

"Who are you, and what do you want?" asked the man in a grumbling voice. "I am a poor tailor," he answered, "whom night has surprised here in the wilderness, and I earnestly beg you to take me into your hut until morning." "Go your way," replied the old man in a surly voice, "I will have nothing to do with rascals. Seek shelter elsewhere." After these words he was about to slip into his hut again, but the tailor held him so tightly by the corner of his coat, and pleaded so piteously, that the old man, who was not so ill-natured as he wished to appear, was at last softened, and took him into the hut with him where he gave him something to eat, and then pointed out to him a very good bed in a corner.

The weary tailor needed no rocking; but slept sweetly till morning, but even then would not have thought of getting up, if he had not been aroused by a great noise. A violent sound of screaming and roaring forced its way through the thin walls of the hut. The tailor, full of unwonted courage, jumped up, put his clothes on in haste, and hurried out. Then close by the hut, he saw a great black bull and a beautiful stag, which were just preparing for a violent struggle. They rushed at each other with such extreme rage that the ground shook with their trampling, and the air resounded with their cries. For a long time it was uncertain which of the two would gain the victory; at length the stag thrust his horns into his adversary's body, whereupon the bull fell to the earth with a terrific roar, and was thoroughly despatched by a few strokes from the stag.

The tailor, who had watched the fight with astonishment, was still standing there motionless, when the stag in full career bounded up to him, and before he could escape, caught him up on his great horns. He had not much time to collect his thoughts, for it went in a swift race over stock and stone, mountain and valley, wood and meadow. He held with both hands to the tops of the horns, and resigned himself to his fate. It seemed to him, however, just as if he were flying away. At length the stag stopped in front of a wall of rock, and gently let the tailor down. The tailor, more dead than alive, required a longer time than that to come to himself. When he had in some degree recovered, the stag, which had remained standing by him, pushed its horns with such force against a door which was in the rock, that it sprang open. Flames of fire shot forth, after which followed a great smoke, which hid the stag from his sight.

The tailor did not know what to do, or whither to turn, in order to get out of this desert and back to human beings again. While he was standing thus undecided, a voice sounded out of the rock, which cried to him, "Enter without fear, no evil shall befall thee." He certainly hesitated, but driven by a mysterious force, he obeyed the voice and went through the iron-door into a large spacious hall, whose ceiling, walls and floor were made of shining polished square stones, on each of which were cut letters which were unknown to him. He looked at everything full of admiration, and was on the point of going out again, when he once more heard the voice which said to him, "Step on the stone which lies in the middle of the hall, and great good fortune awaits thee."

His courage had already grown so great that he obeyed the order. The stone began to give way under his feet, and sank slowly down into the depths. When it was once more firm, and the tailor looked round, he found himself in a hall which in size resembled the former. Here, however, there was more to look at and to admire. Hollow places were cut in the walls, in which stood vases of transparent glass which were filled with colored spirit or with a bluish vapor. On the floor of the hall two great glass chests stood opposite to each other, which at once excited his curiosity. When he went to one of them he saw inside it a handsome structure like a castle surrounded by farm-buildings, stables and barns, and a quantity of other good things. Everything was small, but exceedingly carefully and delicately made, and seemed to be cut out by a dexterous hand with the greatest exactitude.

He might not have turned away his eyes from the consideration of this rarity for some time, if the voice had not once more made itself heard. It ordered him to turn round and look at the glass chest which was standing opposite. How his admiration increased when he saw therein a maiden of the greatest beauty! She lay as if asleep, and was wrapped in her long fair hair as in a precious mantle. Her eyes were closely shut, but the brightness of her complexion and a ribbon which her breathing moved to and fro, left no doubt that she was alive.

The tailor was looking at the beauty with beating heart, when she suddenly opened her eyes, and started up at the sight of him in joyful terror. "Just Heaven!" cried she, "my deliverance is at hand! Quick, quick, help me out of my prison; if you push back the bolt of this glass coffin, then I shall be free." The tailor obeyed without delay, and she immediately raised up the glass lid, came out and hastened into the corner of the hall, where she covered herself with a large cloak. Then she seated herself on a stone, ordered the young man to come to her, and after she had imprinted a friendly kiss on his lips, she said, "My long-desired deliverer, kind Heaven has guided you to me, and put an end to my sorrows. On the self-same day when they end, shall your happiness begin. You are the husband chosen for me by Heaven, and you shall pass your life in unbroken joy, loved by me, and rich to overflowing in every earthly possession. Seat yourself and listen to the story of my life:

"I am the daughter of a rich count. My parents died when I was still in my tender youth, and recommended me in their last will to my elder brother, by whom I was brought up. We loved each other so tenderly, and were so alike in our way of thinking and our inclinations, that we both embraced the resolution never to marry, but to stay together to the end of our lives. In our house there was no lack of company; neighbors and friends visited us often, and we showed the greatest hospitality to every one. So it came to pass one evening that a stranger came riding to our castle, and, under pretext of not being able to get on to the next place, begged for shelter for the night. We granted his request with ready courtesy, and he entertained us in the most agreeable manner during supper by conversation intermingled with stories. My brother liked the stranger so much that he begged him to spend a couple of days with us, to which, after some hesitation, he consented. We did not rise from table until late in the night, the stranger was shown to a room, and I hastened, as I was tired, to lay my limbs in my soft bed.

"Hardly had I slept for a short time, when the sound of faint and delightful music awoke me. As I could not conceive from whence it came, I wanted to summon my waiting-maid who slept in the next room, but to my astonishment I found that speech was taken away from me by an unknown force. I felt as if a mountain were weighing down my breast, and was unable to make the very slightest sound. In the meantime, by the light of my night-lamp, I saw the stranger enter my room through two doors which were fast bolted. He came to me and said, that by magic arts which were at his command, he had caused the lovely music to sound in order to awaken me, and that he now forced his way through all fastenings with the intention of offering me his hand and heart. My repugnance to his magic arts was, however, so great that I vouchsafed him no answer. He remained for a time standing without moving, apparently with the idea of wait-ing for a favorable decision, but as I continued to keep silence, he angrily declared he would revenge himself and find means to punish my pride, and left the room. I passed the night in the greatest disqui-etude, and only fell asleep towards morning. When I awoke, I hurried to my brother, but did not find him in his room, and the attendants told me that he had ridden forth with the stranger to the chase by daybreak.

"I at once suspected nothing good. I dressed myself quickly, ordered my palfrey to be saddled, and accompanied only by one servant, rode full gallop to the forest. The servant fell with his horse, and could not follow me, for the horse had broken its foot. I pursued my way without halting, and in a few minutes I saw the stranger coming towards me with a beautiful stag which he led by a cord. I asked him where he had left my brother, and how he had come by this stag, out of whose great eyes I saw tears flowing. Instead of answering me, he began to laugh loudly. I fell into a great rage at this, pulled out a pistol and discharged it at the monster; but the ball rebounded from his breast and went into my horse's head. I fell to the ground, and the stranger muttered some words which deprived me of consciousness.

"When I came to my senses again I found myself in this underground cave in a glass coffin. The magician appeared once again, and said he had changed my brother into a stag, my castle with all that belonged to it, diminished in size by his arts, he had shut up in the other glass chest, and my people, who were all turned into smoke, he had confined in glass bottles. He told me that if I would now comply with his wish, it was an easy thing for him to put everything back in its former state, as he had nothing to do but open the vessels, and everything would return once more to its natural form. I answered him as little as I had done the first time. He vanished and left me in my prison, in which a deep sleep came on me. Among the visions which passed before my eyes, that was the most comforting in which a young man came and set me free, and when I opened my eyes today I saw you, and beheld my dream fulfilled. Help me to accomplish the other things which happened in those visions. The first is that we lift the glass chest in which my castle is enclosed, on to that broad stone."

As soon as the stone was laden, it began to rise up on high with the maiden and the young man, and mounted through the opening of the ceiling into the upper hall, from whence they then could easily reach the open air. Here the maiden opened the lid, and it was marvelous to behold how the castle, the houses, and the farm buildings which were enclosed, stretched themselves out and grew to their natural size with the greatest rapidity. After this, the maiden and the tailor returned to the cave beneath the earth, and had the vessels which were filled with smoke carried up by the stone. The maiden had scarcely opened the bottles when the blue smoke rushed out and changed itself into living men, in whom she recognized her servants and her people. Her joy was still more increased when her brother, who had killed the magician in the form of a bull, came out of the forest towards them in his human form. And on the self-same day the maiden, in accordance with her promise, gave her hand at the altar to the lucky tailor.

Rapunzel

There once lived a man and his wife who had long wished for a child, but in vain. Now there was at the back of their house a little window which overlooked a beautiful garden full of the finest vegetables and flowers; but there was a high wall all round it, and no one ventured into it, for it belonged to a witch of great might, and of whom all the world was afraid. One day when the wife was standing at the window, and looking into the garden, she saw a bed filled with the finest rampion; and it looked so fresh and green that she began to wish for some; and at length she longed for it greatly. This went on for days, and as she knew she could not get the rampion, she pined away, and grew pale and miserable.

Then the man was uneasy, and asked, "What is the matter, dear wife?" "Oh," answered she, "I shall die unless I can have some of that rampion to eat that grows in the garden at the back of our house." The man, who loved her very much, thought to himself, "Rather than lose my wife I will get some rampion, cost what it will."

So in the twilight he climbed over the wall into the witch's garden, plucked hastily a handful of rampion and brought it to his wife. She made a salad of it at once, and ate of it to her heart's content. But she liked it so much, and it tasted so good, that the next day she longed for it thrice as much as she had done before; if she was to have any rest the man must climb over the wall once more. So he went in the twilight again; and as he was climbing back, he saw, all at once, the witch standing before him, and was terribly frightened, as she cried, with angry eyes, "How dare you climb over into my garden like a thief, and steal my rampion! It shall be the worse for you!"

"Oh," answered he, "be merciful rather than just; I have only done it through necessity; for my wife saw your rampion out of the window, and became possessed with so great a longing that she would have died if she could not have had some to eat."

Then the witch said, "If it is all as you say, you may have as much rampion as you like, on one condition—the child that will come into the world must be given to me. It shall go well with the child, and I will care for it like a mother."

In his distress of mind the man promised everything; and when the time came when the child was born the witch appeared, and, giving the child the name of Rapunzel (which is the same as rampion), she took it away with her.

Rapunzel was the most beautiful child in the world. When she was twelve years old the witch shut her up in a tower in the midst of a wood, and it had neither steps nor door, only a small window above. When the witch wished to be let in, she would stand below and would cry, "Rapunzel, Rapunzel! Let down your hair!"

Rapunzel had beautiful long hair that shone like gold. When she heard the voice of the witch she would undo the fastening of the upper window, unbind the plaits of her hair, and let it down twenty ells below, and the witch would climb up by it.

After they had lived thus a few years it happened that as the King's son was riding through the wood, he came to the tower; and as he drew near he heard a voice singing so sweetly that he stood still and listened. It was Rapunzel in her loneliness trying to pass away the time with sweet songs. The King's son wished to go in to her, and sought to find a door in the tower, but there was none. So he rode home, but the song had entered into his heart, and every day he went into the wood and listened to it.

Once, as he was standing there under a tree, he saw the witch come up, and listened while she called out, "Oh Rapunzel, Rapunzel! Let down your hair."

Then he saw how Rapunzel let down her long tresses, and how the witch climbed up by them and went in to her, and he said to himself, "Since that is the ladder, I will climb it, and seek my fortune." And the next day, as soon as it began to grow dusk, he went to the tower and cried, "Oh Rapunzel, Rapunzel! Let down your hair." And she let down her hair, and the King's son climbed up by it.

Rapunzel was greatly terrified when she saw that a man had come in to her, for she had never seen one before; but the King's son began speaking so kindly to her, and told how her singing had entered into his heart, so that he could have no peace until he had seen her herself. Then Rapunzel forgot her terror, and when he asked her to take him for her husband, and she saw that he was young and beautiful, she thought to herself, "I certainly like him much better than old mother Gothel," and she put her hand into his hand, saying, "I would willingly go with you, but I do not know how I shall get out. When you come, bring each time a silken rope, and I will make a ladder, and when it is quite ready I will get down by it out of the tower, and you shall take me away on your horse."

They agreed that he should come to her every evening, as the old woman came in the day-time. So the witch knew nothing of all this until once Rapunzel said to her unwittingly, "Mother Gothel, how is it that you climb up here so slowly, and the King's son is with me in a moment?"

"O wicked child," cried the witch, "what is this I hear! I thought I had hidden you from all the world, and you have betrayed me!"

In her anger she seized Rapunzel by her beautiful hair, struck her several times with her left hand, and then grasping a pair of shears in her right—snip, snap—the beautiful locks lay on the ground. And she was so hard-hearted that she took Rapunzel and put her in a waste and desert place, where she lived in great woe and misery.

The same day on which she took Rapunzel away she went back to the tower in the evening and made fast the severed locks of hair to the window-hasp, and the King's son came and cried, "Rapunzel, Rapunzel! Let down your hair."

Then she let the hair down, and the King's son climbed up, but instead of his dearest Rapunzel he found the witch looking at him with wicked, glittering eyes.

"Aha!" cried she, mocking him, "you came for your darling, but the sweet bird sits no longer in the nest, and sings no more; the cat has got her, and will scratch out your eyes as well! Rapunzel is lost to you; you will see her no more."

The King's son was beside himself with grief, and in his agony he sprang from the tower; he escaped with life, but the thorns on which he fell put out his eyes. Then he wandered blind through the wood, eating nothing but roots and berries, and doing nothing but lament and weep for the loss of his dearest wife.

So he wandered several years in misery until at last he came to the desert place where Rapunzel lived with her twin-children that she had borne, a boy and a girl. At first he heard a voice that he thought he knew, and when he reached the place from which it seemed to come Rapunzel knew him, and fell on his neck and wept. And when her tears touched his eyes they became clear again, and he could see with them as well as ever.

Then he took her to his kingdom, where he was received with great joy, and there they lived long and happily.

The Sleeping Beauty

In times past there lived a King and Queen, who said to each other every day of their lives, "Would that we had a child!" and yet they had none. But it happened once that when the Queen was bathing, there came a frog out of the water, and he squatted on the ground, and said to her, "Thy wish shall be fulfilled; before a year has gone by, thou shalt bring a daughter into the world."

And as the frog foretold, so it happened; and the Queen bore a daughter so beautiful that the King could not contain himself for joy, and he ordained a great feast. Not only did he bid to it his relations, friends, and acquaintances, but also the wise women, that they might be kind and favorable to the child. There were thirteen of them in his kingdom, but as he had only provided twelve golden plates for them to eat from, one of them had to be left out.

However, the feast was celebrated with all splendor; and as it drew to an end, the wise women stood forward to present to the child their wonderful gifts: one bestowed virtue, one beauty, a third riches, and so on, whatever there is in the world to wish for. And when eleven of them had said their say, in came the uninvited thirteenth, burning to revenge herself, and without greeting or respect, she cried with a loud voice, "In the fifteenth year of her age the Princess shall prick herself with a spindle and shall fall down dead." And without speaking one more word she turned away and left the hall.

Every one was terrified at her saying, when the twelfth came forward, for she had not yet bestowed her gift, and though she could not do away with the evil prophecy, yet she could soften it, so she said, "The Princess shall not die, but fall into a deep sleep for a hundred years."

Now the King, being desirous of saving his child even from this misfortune, gave commandment that all the spindles in his kingdom should be burnt up.

The maiden grew up, adorned with all the gifts of the wise women; and she was so lovely, modest, sweet, and kind and clever, that no one who saw her could help loving her.

It happened one day, she being already fifteen years old, that the King and Queen rode abroad; and the maiden was left behind alone in the castle. She wandered about into all the nooks and corners, and into all the chambers and parlors, as the fancy took her, till at last she came to an old tower. She climbed the narrow winding stair which led to a little door, with a rusty key sticking out of the lock; she turned the key, and the door opened, and there in the little room sat an old woman with a spindle, diligently spinning her flax.

"Good day, mother," said the Princess, "what are you doing?" "I am spinning," answered the old woman, nodding her head. "What thing is that that twists round so briskly?" asked the maiden, and taking the spindle into her hand she began to spin; but no sooner had she touched it than the evil prophecy was fulfilled, and she pricked her finger with it. In that very moment she fell back upon the bed that stood there, and lay in a deep sleep, and this sleep fell upon the whole castle. The King and Queen, who had returned and were in the great hall, fell fast asleep, and with them the whole court. The horses in their stalls, the dogs in the yard, the pigeons on the roof, the flies on the wall, the very fire that flickered on the hearth, became still, and slept like the rest; and the meat on the spit ceased roasting, and the cook, who was going to pull the scullion's hair for some mistake he had made, let him go, and went to sleep. And the wind ceased, and not a leaf fell from the trees about the castle.

Then round about that place there grew a hedge of thorns thicker every year, until at last the whole castle was hidden from view, and nothing of it could be seen but the vane on the roof. And a rumor went abroad in all that country of the beautiful sleeping Rosamond, for so was the Princess called; and from time to time many Kings' sons came and tried to force their way through the hedge; but it was impossible for them to do so, for the thorns held fast together like strong hands, and the young men were caught by them, and not being able to get free, there died a lamentable death.

Many a long year afterwards there came a King's son into that country, and heard an old man tell how there should be a castle standing behind the hedge of thorns, and that there a beautiful enchanted Princess named Rosamond had slept for a hundred years, and with her the King and Queen, and the whole court. The old man had been told by his grandfather that many Kings' sons had sought to pass the thorn-hedge, but had been caught and pierced by the thorns, and had died a miserable death. Then said the young man, "Nevertheless, I

do not fear to try; I shall win through and see the lovely Rosamond."
The good old man tried to dissuade him, but he would not listen to
his words.

For now the hundred years were at an end, and the day had come
when Rosamond should be awakened. When the Prince drew near
the hedge of thorns, it was changed into a hedge of beautiful large
flowers, which parted and bent aside to let him pass, and then closed
behind him in a thick hedge. When he reached the castle-yard, he saw
the horses and brindled hunting-dogs lying asleep, and on the roof the
pigeons were sitting with their heads under their wings. And when
he came indoors, the flies on the wall were asleep, the cook in the
kitchen had his hand uplifted to strike the scullion, and the kitchen-
maid had the black fowl on her lap ready to pluck. Then he mounted
higher, and saw in the hall the whole court lying asleep, and above
them, on their thrones, slept the King and the Queen. And still he
went farther, and all was so quiet that he could hear his own breathing; and at last he came to the tower, and went up the winding stair,
and opened the door of the little room where Rosamond lay.

And when he saw her looking so lovely in her sleep, he could not
turn away his eyes; and presently he stooped and kissed her, and she
awaked, and opened her eyes, and looked very kindly on him. And
she rose, and they went forth together, the King and the Queen and
whole court waked up, and gazed on each other with great eyes of
wonderment. And the horses in the yard got up and shook themselves, the hounds sprang up and wagged their tails, the pigeons on
the roof drew their heads from under their wings, looked round, and
flew into the field, the flies on the wall crept on a little farther, the
kitchen fire leapt up and blazed, and cooked the meat, the joint on
the spit began to roast, the cook gave the scullion such a box on the
ear that he roared out, and the maid went on plucking the fowl.

Then the wedding of the Prince and Rosamond was held with all
splendor, and they lived very happily together until their lives' end.

Hansel and Gretel

Near a great forest there lived a poor woodcutter and his wife and his two children; the boy's name was Hansel and the girl's Gretel. They had very little to bite or to sup, and once, when there was great dearth in the land, the man could not even gain the daily bread.

As he lay in bed one night thinking of this, and turning and tossing, he sighed heavily, and said to his wife, "What will become of us? We cannot even feed our children; there is nothing left for ourselves."

"I will tell you what, husband," answered the wife; "we will take the children early in the morning into the forest, where it is thickest; we will make them a fire, and we will give each of them a piece of bread, then we will go to our work and leave them alone; they will never find the way home again, and we shall be quit of them."

"No, wife," said the man, "I cannot do that; I cannot find in my heart to take my children into the forest and to leave them there alone; the wild animals would soon come and devour them."

"O you fool," said she, "then we will all four starve; you had better get the coffins ready"—and she left him no peace until he consented.

"But I really pity the poor children," said the man.

The two children had not been able to sleep for hunger, and had heard what their step-mother had said to their father. Gretel wept bitterly, and said to Hansel, "It is all over with us." "Do be quiet, Gretel," said Hansel, "and do not fret. I will manage something."

And when the parents had gone to sleep he got up, put on his little coat, opened the back door, and slipped out. The moon was shining brightly, and the white flints that lay in front of the house glistened like pieces of silver. Hansel stooped and filled the little pocket of his coat as full as it would hold. Then he went back again, and said to Gretel, "Be easy, dear little sister, and go to sleep quietly; God will not forsake us," and laid himself down again in his bed.

When the day was breaking, and before the sun had risen, the wife came and awakened the two children, saying, "Get up, you lazy bones; we are going into the forest to cut wood."

Then she gave each of them a piece of bread, and said, "That is for dinner, and you must not eat it before then, for you will get no more."

Gretel carried the bread under her apron, for Hansel had his pockets full of the flints. Then they set off all together on their way to the forest. When they had gone a little way Hansel stood still and looked back towards the house, and this he did again and again, till his father said to him, "Hansel, what are you looking at? Take care not to forget your legs."

"O father," said Hansel, "I am looking at my little white kitten, who is sitting up on the roof to bid me good-bye."

"You young fool," said the woman, "that is not your kitten, but the sunshine on the chimney pot."

Of course Hansel had not been looking at his kitten, but had been taking every now and then a flint from his pocket and dropping it on the road.

When they reached the middle of the forest the father told the children to collect wood to make a fire to keep them warm; and Hansel and Gretel gathered brushwood enough for a little mountain; and it was set on fire, and when the flame was burning quite high the wife said, "Now lie down by the fire and rest yourselves, you children, and we will go and cut wood; and when we are ready we will come and fetch you."

So Hansel and Gretel sat by the fire, and at noon they each ate their pieces of bread. They thought their father was in the wood all the time, as they seemed to hear the strokes of the axe, but really it was only a dry branch hanging to a withered tree that the wind moved to and fro. So when they had stayed there a long time their eyelids closed with weariness, and they fell fast asleep.

When at last they woke it was night, and Gretel began to cry, and said, "How shall we ever get out of this wood?" But Hansel comforted her, saying, "Wait a little while longer, until the moon rises, and then we can easily find the way home."

And when the full moon got up Hansel took his little sister by the hand, and followed the way where the flint stones shone like silver, and showed them the road. They walked on the whole night through, and at the break of day they came to their father's house. They knocked at the door, and when the wife opened it and saw it was Hansel and Gretel she said, "You naughty children, why did you sleep so long in the wood? We thought you were never coming home again!" But the father was glad, for it had gone to his heart to leave them both in the woods alone.

Not very long after that there was again great scarcity in those parts, and the children heard their mother say at night in bed to their father, "Everything is finished up; we have only half a loaf, and after that the tale comes to an end. The children must be off; we will take them farther into the wood this time, so that they shall not be able to find the way back again; there is no other way to manage."

The man felt sad at heart, and he thought, "It would be better to share one's last morsel with one's children." But the wife would listen to nothing that he said, but scolded and reproached him. He who says A must say B too, and when a man has given in once he has to do it a second time.

But the children were not asleep, and had heard all the talk. When the parents had gone to sleep Hansel got up to go out and get more flint stones, as he did before, but the wife had locked the door, and Hansel could not get out; but he comforted his little sister, and said, "Don't cry, Gretel, and go to sleep quietly, and God will help us."

Early the next morning the wife came and pulled the children out of bed. She gave them each a little piece of bread—less than before; and on the way to the wood Hansel crumbled the bread in his pocket, and often stopped to throw a crumb on the ground.

"Hansel, what are you stopping behind and staring for?" said the father.

"I am looking at my little pigeon sitting on the roof, to say goodbye to me," answered Hansel.

"You fool," said the wife, "that is no pigeon, but the morning sun shining on the chimney pots."

Hansel went on as before, and strewed bread crumbs all along the road.

The woman led the children far into the wood, where they had never been before in all their lives. And again there was a large fire made, and the mother said, "Sit still there, you children, and when you are tired you can go to sleep; we are going into the forest to cut wood, and in the evening, when we are ready to go home we will come and fetch you."

So when noon came Gretel shared her bread with Hansel, who had strewed his along the road. Then they went to sleep, and the evening passed, and no one came for the poor children. When they awoke it was dark night, and Hansel comforted his little sister, and said, "Wait a little, Gretel, until the moon gets up, then we shall be able to see the way home by the crumbs of bread that I have scattered along it."

So when the moon rose they got up, but they could find no crumbs of bread, for the birds of the woods and of the fields had come and picked them up. Hansel thought they might find the way all the same, but they could not. They went on all that night, and the next day from the morning until the evening, but they could not find the way out of the wood, and they were very hungry, for they had nothing to eat but the few berries they could pick up. And when they were so tired that they could no longer drag themselves along, they lay down under a tree and fell asleep.

It was now the third morning since they had left their father's house. They were always trying to get back to it, but instead of that they only found themselves farther in the wood, and if help had not soon come they would have starved. About noon they saw a pretty snow-white bird sitting on a bough, and singing so sweetly that they stopped to listen. And when he had finished the bird spread his wings and flew before them, and they followed after him until they came to a little house, and the bird perched on the roof, and when they came nearer they saw that the house was built of bread, and roofed with cakes, and the window was of transparent sugar.

"We will have some of this," said Hansel, "and make a fine meal. I will eat a piece of the roof, Gretel, and you can have some of the window—that will taste sweet."

So Hansel reached up and broke off a bit of the roof, just to see how it tasted, and Gretel stood by the window and gnawed at it. Then they heard a thin voice call out from inside,

> "Nibble, nibble, like a mouse,
> Who is nibbling at my house?"

And the children answered,

> "Never mind,
> It is the wind."

And they went on eating, never disturbing themselves. Hansel, who found that the roof tasted very nice, took down a great piece of it, and Gretel pulled out a large round window-pane, and sat her down and began upon it. Then the door opened, and an aged woman came out, leaning upon a crutch. Hansel and Gretel felt very frightened, and let fall what they had in their hands. The old woman, however, nodded her head, and said, "Ah, my dear children, how come you here? You must come indoors and stay with me, you will be no trouble."

So she took them each by the hand, and led them into her little house. And there they found a good meal laid out, of milk and pancakes, with sugar, apples, and nuts. After that she showed them two little white beds, and Hansel and Gretel laid themselves down on them, and thought they were in heaven.

The old woman, although her behavior was so kind, was a wicked witch, who lay in wait for children, and had built the little house on purpose to entice them. When they were once inside she used to kill them, cook them, and eat them, and then it was a feastday with her. The witch's eyes were red, and she could not see very far, but she had a keen scent, like the beasts, and knew very well when human creatures were near. When she knew that Hansel and Gretel were coming, she gave a spiteful laugh, and said triumphantly, "I have them, and they shall not escape me!"

Early in the morning, before the children were awake, she got up to look at them, and as they lay sleeping so peacefully with round rosy cheeks, she said to herself, "What a fine feast I shall have!"

Then she grasped Hansel with her withered hand, and led him into a little stable, and shut him up behind a grating; and call and scream as he might, it was no good. Then she went back to Gretel and shook her, crying, "Get up, lazy bones; fetch water, and cook something nice for your brother; he is outside in the stable, and must be fattened up. And when he is fat enough I will eat him."

Gretel began to weep bitterly, but it was no use, she had to do what the wicked witch bade her.

And so the best kind of victuals was cooked for poor Hansel, while Gretel got nothing but crab-shells. Each morning the old woman visited the little stable, and cried, "Hansel, stretch out your finger, that I may tell if you will soon be fat enough."

Hansel, however, used to hold out a little bone, and the old woman, who had weak eyes, could not see what it was, and supposing it to be Hansel's finger, wondered very much that it was not getting fatter. When four weeks had passed and Hansel seemed to remain so thin, she lost patience and could wait no longer.

"Now then, Gretel," cried she to the little girl; "be quick and draw water; be Hansel fat or be he lean, tomorrow I must kill and cook him."

Oh what a grief for the poor little sister to have to fetch water, and how the tears flowed down over her cheeks! "Dear God, pray help us!" cried she; "if we had been devoured by wild beasts in the wood at least we should have died together."

"Spare me your lamentations," said the old woman; "they are of no avail."

Early next morning Gretel had to get up, make the fire, and fill the kettle. "First we will do the baking," said the old woman; "I have heated the oven already, and kneaded the dough."

She pushed poor Gretel towards the oven, out of which the flames were already shining. "Creep in," said the witch, "and see if it is properly hot, so that the bread may be baked."

And Gretel once in, she meant to shut the door upon her and let her be baked, and then she would have eaten her. But Gretel perceived her intention, and said, "I don't know how to do it; how shall I get in?"

"Stupid goose," said the old woman, "the opening is big enough, do you see? I could get in myself!" and she stooped down and put her head in the oven's mouth. Then Gretel gave her a push, so that she went in farther, and she shut the iron door upon her, and put up the bar. Oh how frightfully she howled! But Gretel ran away, and left the wicked witch to burn miserably. Gretel went straight to Hansel, opened the stable-door, and cried, "Hansel, we are free! the old witch is dead!"

Then out flew Hansel like a bird from its cage as soon as the door is opened. How rejoiced they both were! How they fell each on the other's neck and danced about, and kissed each other! And as they had nothing more to fear they went over all the old witch's house, and in every corner there stood chests of pearls and precious stones.

"This is something better than flint stones," said Hansel, as he filled his pockets; and Gretel, thinking she also would like to carry something home with her, filled her apron full.

"Now, away we go," said Hansel—"if we only can get out of the witch's wood."

When they had journeyed a few hours they came to a great piece of water. "We can never get across this," said Hansel, "I see no stepping-stones and no bridge." "And there is no boat either," said Gretel;

"but here comes a white duck; if I ask her she will help us over." So she cried,

> "Duck, duck, here we stand,
> Hansel and Gretel, on the land,
> Stepping-stones and bridge we lack,
> Carry us over on your nice white back."

And the duck came accordingly, and Hansel got upon her and told his sister to come too. "No," answered Gretel, "that would be too hard upon the duck; we can go separately, one after the other."

And that was how it was managed, and after that they went on happily, until they came to the wood, and the way grew more and more familiar, till at last they saw in the distance their father's house. Then they ran till they came up to it, rushed in at the door, and fell on their father's neck. The man had not had a quiet hour since he left his children in the wood; but the wife was dead. And when Gretel opened her apron the pearls and precious stones were scattered all over the room, and Hansel took one handful after another out of his pocket. Then was all care at an end, and they lived in great joy together.

> "Sing every one,
> My story is done.
> And look! round the house
> There runs a little mouse.
> He that can catch her before she scampers in
> May make himself a fur-cap out of her skin."

The Rabbit's Bride

There was once a woman who lived with her daughter in a beautiful cabbage-garden; and there came a rabbit and ate up all the cabbages. At last said the woman to her daughter, "Go into the garden, and drive out the rabbit."

"Shoo! shoo!" said the maiden; "don't eat up all our cabbages, little rabbit!" "Come, maiden," said the rabbit, "sit on my tail and go with me to my rabbit-hutch." But the maiden would not.

Another day, back came the rabbit, and ate away at the cabbages, until the woman said to her daughter, "Go into the garden, and drive away the rabbit."

"Shoo! shoo!" said the maiden; "don't eat up all our cabbages, little rabbit!" "Come, maiden," said the rabbit, "sit on my tail and go with me to my rabbit-hutch." But the maiden would not.

Again, a third time back came the rabbit, and ate away at the cabbages, until the woman said to her daughter, "Go into the garden, and drive away the rabbit."

"Shoo! shoo!" said the maiden; "don't eat up all our cabbages, little rabbit!" "Come, maiden," said the rabbit, "sit on my tail and go with me to my rabbit-hutch." And then the girl seated herself on the rabbit's tail, and the rabbit took her to his hutch.

"Now," said he, "set to work and cook some bran and cabbage; I am going to bid the wedding guests." And soon they were all collected. Would you like to know who they were? Well, I can only tell you what was told to me. All the hares came, and the crow who was to be the parson to marry them, and the fox for the clerk, and the altar was under the rainbow. But the maiden was sad, because she was so lonely.

"Get up! get up!" said the rabbit, "the wedding folk are all merry." But the bride wept and said nothing, and the rabbit went away, but very soon came back again. "Get up! get up!" said he, "the wedding folk are waiting." But the bride said nothing, and the rabbit went away.

Then she made a figure of straw, and dressed it in her own clothes, and gave it a red mouth, and set it to watch the kettle of bran, and then she went home to her mother. Back again came the rabbit, saying, "Get up! get up!" and he went up and hit the straw figure on the head, so that it tumbled down.

And the rabbit thought that he had killed his bride, and he went away and was very sad.

The Bremen Town Musicians

There was once an ass whose master had made him carry sacks to the mill for many a long year, but whose strength began at last to fail, so that each day as it came, found him less capable of work. Then his master began to think of turning him out, but the ass, guessing that something was in the wind that boded him no good, ran away, taking the road to Bremen; for there he thought he might get an engagement as town musician.

When he had gone a little way he found a hound lying by the side of the road panting, as if he had run a long way. "Now, Holdfast, what are you so out of breath about?" said the ass.

"Oh dear!" said the dog, "now I am old, I get weaker every day, and can do no good in the hunt, so, as my master was going to have me killed, I have made my escape; but now how am I to gain a living?"

"I will tell you what," said the ass, "I am going to Bremen to become town musician. You may as well go with me, and take up music too. I can play the lute, and you can beat the drum." And the dog consented, and they walked on together.

It was not long before they came to a cat sitting in the road, looking as dismal as three wet days. "Now then, what is the matter with you, old shaver?" said the ass.

"I should like to know who would be cheerful when his neck is in danger?" answered the cat. "Now that I am old my teeth are getting blunt, and I would rather sit by the oven and purr than run about after mice, and my mistress wanted to drown me, so I took myself off; but good advice is scarce, and I do not know what is to become of me."

"Go with us to Bremen," said the ass, "and become town musician. You understand serenading." The cat thought well of the idea, and went with them accordingly.

After that the three travelers passed by a yard, and a cock was perched on the gate crowing with all his might. "Your cries are enough to pierce bone and marrow," said the ass; "what is the matter?"

"I have foretold good weather for Lady-day, so that all the shirts may be washed and dried; and now on Sunday morning company is coming, and the mistress has told the cook that I must be made into soup, and this evening my neck is to be wrung, so that I am crowing with all my might while I can."

"You had much better go with us, Chanticleer," said the ass. "We are going to Bremen. At any rate that will be better than dying. You have a powerful voice, and when we are all performing together it will have a very good effect." So the cock consented, and they went on all four together.

But Bremen was too far off to be reached in one day, and towards evening they came to a wood, where they determined to pass the night. The ass and the dog lay down under a large tree; the cat got up among the branches; and the cock flew up to the top, as that was the safest place for him. Before he went to sleep he looked all round him to the four points of the compass, and perceived in the distance a little light shining, and he called out to his companions that there must be a house not far off, as he could see a light, so the ass said, "We had better get up and go there, for these are uncomfortable quarters." The dog began to fancy a few bones, not quite bare, would do him good. And they all set off in the direction of the light, and it grew larger and brighter, until at last it led them to a robber's house, all lighted up. The ass, being the biggest, went up to the window, and looked in.

"Well, what do you see?" asked the dog. "What do I see?" answered the ass; "here is a table set out with splendid eatables and drinkables, and robbers sitting at it and making themselves very comfortable." "That would just suit us," said the cock. "Yes, indeed, I wish we were there," said the ass.

Then they consulted together how it should be managed so as to get the robbers out of the house, and at last they hit on a plan. The ass was to place his fore-feet on the window-sill, the dog was to get on the ass's back, the cat on the top of the dog, and lastly, the cock was to fly up and perch on the cat's head. When that was done, at a given signal they all began to perform their music. The ass brayed, the dog barked, the cat mewed, and the cock crowed; then they burst through into the room, breaking all the panes of glass. The robbers fled at the dreadful sound; they thought it was some goblin, and fled to the wood in the utmost terror. Then the four companions sat down to table, made free with the remains of the meal, and feasted as if they had been hungry for a month. And when they had finished they put out the lights, and each sought out a sleeping-place to suit his nature and habits. The ass laid himself down outside on the dunghill, the dog behind the door, the cat on the hearth by the warm ashes, and the cock settled himself in the cockloft; and as they were all tired with their long journey they soon fell fast asleep.

When midnight drew near, and the robbers from afar saw that no light was burning, and that everything appeared quiet, their captain said to them that he thought that they had run away without reason, telling one of them to go and reconnoitre. So one of them went, and found everything quite quiet. He went into the kitchen to strike a light, and taking the glowing fiery eyes of the cat for burning coals, he held a match to them in order to kindle it. But the cat, not seeing the joke, flew into his face, spitting and scratching. Then he cried out in terror, and ran to get out at the back door, but the dog, who was lying there, ran at him and bit his leg; and as he was rushing through the yard by the dunghill the ass struck out and gave him a great kick with his hindfoot; and the cock, who had been wakened with the noise, and felt quite brisk, cried out, "Cock-a-doodle-doo!"

Then the robber got back as well as he could to his captain, and said, "Oh dear! in that house there is a gruesome witch, and I felt her breath and her long nails in my face; and by the door there stands a man who stabbed me in the leg with a knife; and in the yard there lies a black specter, who beat me with his wooden club; and above, upon the roof, there sits the justice, who cried, 'Bring that rogue here!' And so I ran away from the place as fast as I could."

From that time forward the robbers never ventured to that house, and the four Bremen town musicians found themselves so well off where they were, that there they stayed. And the person who last related this tale is still living, as you see.

The Wolf and the Seven Little Kids

There was once on a time an old goat who had seven little kids, and loved them with all the love of a mother for her children. One day she wanted to go into the forest and fetch some food. So she called all seven to her and said, "Dear children, I have to go into the forest; be on your guard against the wolf; if he comes in, he will devour you all—skin, hair, and all. The wretch often disguises himself, but you will know him at once by his rough voice and his black feet."

The kids said, "Dear mother, we will take good care of ourselves; you may go away without any anxiety." Then the old one bleated, and went on her way with an easy mind.

It was not long before some one knocked at the house-door and cried, "Open the door, dear children; your mother is here, and has brought something back with her for each of you."

But the little kids knew that it was the wolf, by the rough voice. "We will not open the door," cried they, "you are not our mother. She has a soft, pleasant voice, but your voice is rough; you are the wolf!" The wolf went away to a shopkeeper and bought himself a great lump of chalk, ate this and made his voice soft with it.

Then he came back, knocked at the door of the house, and cried, "Open the door, dear children, your mother is here and has brought something back with her for each of you."

But the wolf had laid his black paws against the window, and the children saw them and cried, "We will not open the door, our mother has not black feet like you: you are the wolf!" Then the wolf ran to a baker and said, "I have hurt my feet; rub some dough over them for me." And when the baker had rubbed his feet over, he ran to the miller and said, "Strew some white meal over my feet for me." The miller thought to himself, "The wolf wants to deceive some one," and refused; but the wolf said, "If you will not do it, I will devour you." Then the miller was afraid, and made his paws white for him.

Now the wretch went for the third time to the house-door, knocked at it and said, "Open the door for me, children, your dear little mother has come home, and has brought every one of you something back from the forest with her." The little kids cried, "First show us your paws that we may know if you are our dear little mother." Then he put his paws in through the window, and when the kids saw that they were white, they believed that all he said was true, and opened the door. But who should come in but the wolf!

They were terrified and wanted to hide themselves. One sprang under the table, the second into the bed, the third into the stove, the fourth into the kitchen, the fifth into the cupboard, the sixth under the washing-bowl, and the seventh into the clock-case. But the wolf found them all, and used no great ceremony; one after the other he swallowed them down his throat. The youngest in the clock-case was the only one he did not find.

When the wolf had satisfied his appetite he took himself off, laid himself down under a tree in the green meadow outside, and began to sleep.

Soon afterwards the old goat came home again from the forest. Ah! what a sight she saw there! The house-door stood wide open. The table, chairs, and benches were thrown down, the washing-bowl lay broken to pieces, and the quilts and pillows were pulled off the bed. She sought her children, but they were nowhere to be found. She called them one after another by name, but no one answered. At last, when she came to the youngest, a soft voice cried, "Dear mother, I am in the clock-case." She took the kid out, and it told her that the wolf had come and had eaten all the others. Then you may imagine how she wept over her poor children.

At length in her grief she went out, and the youngest kid ran with her. When they came to the meadow, there lay the wolf by the tree and snored so loud that the branches shook. She looked at him on every side and saw that something was moving and struggling in his gorged body. "Ah, heavens," said she, "is it possible that my poor children whom he has swallowed down for his supper, can be still alive?"

Then the kid had to run home and fetch scissors, and a needle and thread, and the goat cut open the monster's stomach, and hardly had she made one cut, than one little kid thrust its head out, and when she had cut farther, all six sprang out one after another, and were all still alive, and had suffered no injury whatever, for in his greediness the monster had swallowed them down whole. What rejoicing there was! Then they embraced their dear mother, and jumped like a tailor at his wedding.

The mother, however, said, "Now go and look for some big stones, and we will fill the wicked beast's stomach with them while he is still asleep." Then the seven kids dragged the stones thither with all speed, and put as many of them into his stomach as they could get in; and the mother sewed him up again in the greatest haste, so that he was not aware of anything and never once stirred.

When the wolf at length had had his sleep out, he got on his legs, and as the stones in his stomach made him very thirsty, he wanted to go to a well to drink. But when he began to walk and to move about, the stones in his stomach knocked against each other and rattled. Then cried he,

> "What rumbles and tumbles
> Against my poor bones?
> I thought 'twas six kids,
> But it's naught but big stones."

And when he got to the well and stooped over the water and was just about to drink, the heavy stones made him fall in and there was no help, but he had to drown miserably. When the seven kids saw that, they came running to the spot and cried aloud, "The wolf is dead! The wolf is dead!" and danced for joy round about the well with their mother.

Little Red Riding Hood

There was once a sweet little maid, much beloved by everybody, but most of all by her grandmother, who never knew how to make enough of her. Once she sent her a little riding hood of red velvet, and as it was very becoming to her, and she never wore anything else, people called her Little Red Riding Hood.

One day her mother said to her, "Come, Little Red Riding Hood, here are some cakes and a flask of wine for you to take to grandmother; she is weak and ill, and they will do her good. Make haste and start before it grows hot, and walk properly and nicely, and don't run, or you might fall and break the flask of wine, and there would be none left for grandmother. And when you go into her room, don't forget to say good morning, instead of staring about you." "I will be sure to take care," said Little Red Riding Hood to her mother, and gave her hand upon it.

Now the grandmother lived away in the wood, half an hour's walk from the village; and when Little Red Riding Hood had reached the wood, she met the wolf; but as she did not know what a bad sort of animal he was, she did not feel frightened.

"Good day, Little Red Riding Hood," said he. "Thank you kindly, wolf," answered she. "Where are you going so early, Little Red Riding Hood?" "To my grandmother's." "What are you carrying under your apron?" "Cakes and wine; we baked yesterday; and my grandmother is very weak and ill, so they will do her good, and strengthen her."

"Where does your grandmother live, Little Red Riding Hood?" "A quarter of an hour's walk from here; her house stands beneath the three oak trees, and you may know it by the hazel bushes," said Little Red Riding Hood.

The wolf thought to himself, "That tender young thing would be a delicious morsel, and would taste better than the old one; I must manage somehow to get both of them."

Then he walked by Little Red Riding Hood a little while, and said, "Little Red Riding Hood, just look at the pretty flowers that are growing all round you; and I don't think you are listening to the song of the birds; you are posting along just as if you were going to school, and it is so delightful out here in the wood."

Little Red Riding Hood glanced round her, and when she saw the sunbeams darting here and there through the trees, and lovely flowers everywhere, she thought to herself, "If I were to take a fresh nosegay to my grandmother she would be very pleased, and it is so early in the day that I shall reach her in plenty of time"; and so she ran about in the wood, looking for flowers. And as she picked one she saw a still prettier one a little farther off, and so she went farther and farther into the wood.

But the wolf went straight to the grandmother's house and knocked at the door. "Who is there?" cried the grandmother. "Little Red Riding Hood," he answered, "and I have brought you some cake and wine. Please open the door." "Lift the latch," cried the grandmother; "I am too feeble to get up."

So the wolf lifted the latch, and the door flew open, and he fell on the grandmother and ate her up without saying one word. Then he drew on her clothes, put on her cap, lay down in her bed, and drew the curtains.

Little Red Riding Hood was all this time running about among the flowers, and when she had gathered as many as she could hold, she remembered her grandmother, and set off to go to her. She was surprised to find the door standing open, and when she came inside she felt very strange, and thought to herself, "Oh dear, how uncomfortable I feel, and I was so glad this morning to go to my grandmother!"

And when she said, "Good morning," there was no answer. Then she went up to the bed and drew back the curtains; there lay the grandmother with her cap pulled over her eyes, so that she looked very odd.

"O grandmother, what large ears you have!" "The better to hear with."

"O grandmother, what great eyes you have!" "The better to see with."

"O grandmother, what large hands you have!" "The better to take hold of you with."

"But, grandmother, what a terrible large mouth you have!" "The better to devour you!" And no sooner had the wolf said it than he made one bound from the bed, and swallowed up poor Little Red Riding Hood.

Then the wolf, having satisfied his hunger, lay down again in the bed, went to sleep, and began to snore loudly. The huntsman heard him as he was passing by the house, and thought, "How the old woman snores—I had better see if there is anything the matter with her."

Then he went into the room, and walked up to the bed, and saw the wolf lying there. "At last I find you, you old sinner!" said he; "I have been looking for you a long time."

And he made up his mind that the wolf had swallowed the grandmother whole, and that she might yet be saved. So he did not fire, but took a pair of shears and began to slit up the wolf's body. When he made a few snips Little Red Riding Hood appeared, and after a few more snips she jumped out and cried, "Oh dear, how frightened I have been! It is so dark inside the wolf." And then out came the old grandmother, still living and breathing. But Little Red Riding Hood went and quickly fetched some large stones, with which she filled the wolf's body, so that when he waked up, and was going to rush away, the stones were so heavy that he sank down and fell dead.

They were all three very pleased. The huntsman took off the wolf's skin, and carried it home. The grandmother ate the cakes, and drank the wine, and held up her head again, and Little Red Riding Hood said to herself that she would never more stray about in the wood alone, but would mind what her mother told her.

It must also be related how a few days afterwards, when Little Red Riding Hood was again taking cakes to her grandmother, another wolf spoke to her, and wanted to tempt her to leave the path; but she was on her guard, and went straight on her way, and told her grandmother how that the wolf had met her, and wished her good day, but had looked so wicked about the eyes that she thought if it had not been on the high road he would have devoured her.

"Come," said the grandmother, "we will shut the door, so that he may not get in."

Soon after came the wolf knocking at the door, and calling out, "Open the door, grandmother, I am Little Red Riding Hood, bringing you cakes." But they remained still, and did not open the door. After that the wolf slunk by the house, and got at last upon the roof to wait until Little Red Riding Hood should return home in the evening; then he meant to spring down upon her, and devour her in the darkness. But the grandmother discovered his plot. Now there stood before the house a great stone trough, and the grandmother said to the child, "Little Red Riding Hood, I was boiling sausages yesterday, so take the bucket, and carry away the water they were boiled in, and pour it into the trough."

And Little Red Riding Hood did so until the great trough was quite full. When the smell of the sausages reached the nose of the wolf he snuffed it up, and looked round, and stretched out his neck so far that he lost his balance and began to slip, and he slipped down off the roof straight into the great trough, and was drowned. Then Little Red Riding Hood went cheerfully home, and came to no harm.

The Water of Life

A king was very ill, and no one believed that he would come out of it with his life. He had three sons who were much distressed about it, and went down into the palace-garden and wept. There they met an old man who inquired as to the cause of their grief. They told him that their father was so ill that he would most certainly die, for nothing seemed to cure him. Then the old man said, "I know of one more remedy, and that is the water of life; if he drinks of it he will become well again; but it is hard to find." The eldest said, "I will manage to find it," and went to the sick King, and begged to be allowed to go forth in search of the water of life, for that alone could save him. "No," said the King, "the danger of it is too great. I would rather die." But he begged so long that the King consented. The Prince thought in his heart, "If I bring the water, then I shall be best beloved of my father, and shall inherit the kingdom."

So he set out, and when he had ridden forth a little distance, a dwarf stood there in the road who called to him and said, "Whither away so fast?" "Silly shrimp," said the Prince, very haughtily, "it is nothing to you," and rode on. But the little dwarf had grown angry, and had wished an evil wish. Soon after this the Prince entered a ravine, and the further he rode the closer the mountains drew together, and at last the road became so narrow that he could not advance a step further; it was impossible either to turn his horse or to dismount from the saddle, and he was shut in there as if in prison. The sick King waited long for him, but he came not.

Then the second son said, "Father, let me go forth to seek the water," and thought to himself, "If my brother is dead, then the kingdom will fall to me." At first the King would not allow him to go either, but at last he yielded, so the Prince set out on the same road that his brother had taken, and he too met the dwarf, who stopped him to ask whither he was going in such haste. "Little shrimp," said the Prince, "that is nothing to you," and rode on without giving him another look. But the dwarf bewitched him, and he, like the other, got into a ravine, and could neither go forwards nor backwards. So fare haughty people.

As the second son also remained away, the youngest begged to be allowed to go forth to fetch the water, and at last the King was obliged to let him go. When he met the dwarf and the latter asked him whither he was going in such haste, he stopped, gave him an explanation, and said, "I am seeking the water of life, for my father is sick unto death." "Dost thou know, then, where that is to be found?" "No," said the Prince. Then said the dwarf: "As thou hast borne thyself politely and not haughtily like thy false brothers, I will give thee the information and tell thee how thou mayst obtain the water of life. It springs from a fountain in the court-yard of an enchanted castle, but thou wilt not be able to make thy way to it, if I do not give thee an iron wand and two small loaves of bread. Strike thrice with the wand on the iron door of the castle, and it will spring open. Inside lie two lions with gaping jaws, but if thou throwest a loaf to each of them, they will be quieted; then hasten to fetch some of the water of life before the clock strikes twelve, else the door will shut again, and thou wilt be imprisoned."

The Prince thanked him, took the wand and the bread, and set out on his way. When he arrived, everything was as the dwarf had said. The door sprang open at the third stroke of the wand, and when he had appeased the lions with the bread, he entered into the castle, and came in a large and splendid hall, wherein sat some enchanted Princes whose rings he drew off their fingers. A sword and a loaf of bread were lying there, which he carried away. After this, he entered a chamber in which was a beautiful maiden who rejoiced when she saw him, kissed him, and told him that he had delivered her, and should have the whole of her kingdom, and that if he would return in a year their wedding should be celebrated; likewise she told him where the spring of the water of life was, and that he was to hasten and draw some of it before the clock struck twelve. Then he went onwards, and at last entered a room where there was a beautiful newly-made bed, and as he was very weary, he felt inclined to rest a little. So he lay down and fell asleep.

When he awoke, it was striking a quarter to twelve. He sprang up in a fright, ran to the spring, drew some water in a cup which stood near, and hastened away. But just as he was passing through the iron door, the clock struck twelve, and the door fell to with such violence that it carried away a piece of his heel. He, however, rejoicing at having obtained the water of life, went homewards, and again passed the dwarf. When the latter saw the sword and the loaf, he said, "With these thou hast won great wealth; with the sword thou canst slay whole armies, and the bread will never come to an end."

But the Prince would not go home to his father without his brothers, and said, "Dear dwarf, canst thou not tell me where my two brothers are? They went out before I did in search of the water of life, and have not returned." "They are imprisoned between two mountains," said the dwarf. "I have condemned them to stay there, because they were so haughty." Then the Prince begged until the dwarf released them; he warned him, however, and said, "Beware of them, for they have bad hearts."

When his brothers came, he rejoiced, and told them how things had gone with him, that he had found the water of life, and had brought a cupful away with him, and had delivered a beautiful Princess, who was willing to wait a year for him, and then their wedding was to be celebrated, and he would obtain a great kingdom.

After that they rode on together, and chanced upon a land where war and famine reigned, and the King already thought he must perish, for the scarcity was so great. Then the Prince went to him and gave him the loaf, wherewith he fed and satisfied the whole of his kingdom, and then the Prince gave him the sword also, wherewith he slew the hosts of his enemies, and could now live in rest and peace. The Prince then took back his loaf and his sword, and the three brothers rode on.

After this they entered two more countries where war and famine reigned, and each time the Prince gave his loaf and his sword to the Kings, and had now delivered three kingdoms, and after that they went on board a ship and sailed over the sea. During the passage, the two eldest conversed apart and said, "The youngest has found the water of life and not we; for that our father will give him the kingdom—the kingdom which belongs to us, and he will rob us of all our fortune." They began to seek revenge, and plotted with each other to destroy him. They waited until once when they found him fast asleep, then they poured the water of life out of the cup, and took it for themselves, but into the cup they poured salt seawater. Now therefore, when they arrived at home, the youngest took his cup to the sick King in order that he might drink out of it, and be cured. But scarcely had he drunk a very little of the salt seawater than he became still worse than before. And as he was lamenting over this, the two eldest brothers came, and accused the youngest of having intended to poison him, and said that they had brought him the true water of life, and handed it to him. He had scarcely tasted it, when he felt his sickness departing, and became strong and healthy as in the days of his youth.

After that they both went to the youngest, mocked him, and said, "You certainly found the water of life, but you have had the pain, and we the gain. You should have been sharper, and should have kept your eyes open. We took it from you while you were asleep at sea, and when a year is over, one of us will go and fetch the beautiful Princess. But beware that you do not disclose aught of this to our father; indeed he does not trust you, and if you say a single word, you shall lose your life into the bargain, but if you keep silent, you shall have it as a gift."

The old King was angry with his youngest son, and thought he had plotted against his life. So he summoned the court together, and had sentence pronounced upon his son that he should be secretly shot. And once when the Prince was riding forth to the chase, suspecting no evil, the King's huntsman had to go with him, and when they were quite alone in the forest, the huntsman looked so sorrowful that the Prince said to him, "Dear huntsman, what ails you?" The huntsman said, "I cannot tell you, and yet I ought." Then the Prince said, "Say openly what it is, I will pardon you." "Alas!" said the huntsman, "I am to shoot you dead, the King has ordered me to do it." Then the Prince was shocked, and said, "Dear huntsman, let me live; there, I give you my royal garments; give me your common ones in their stead." The huntsman said, "I will willingly do that, indeed I should not have been able to shoot you." Then they exchanged clothes, and the huntsman returned home; the Prince, however, went further into the forest.

After a time three wagons of gold and precious stones came to the King for his youngest son, which were sent by the three Kings who had slain their enemies with the Prince's sword, and maintained their people with his bread, and who wished to show their gratitude for it. The old King then thought, "Can my son have been innocent?" and said to his people, "Would that he were still alive; how it grieves me that I have suffered him to be killed!" "He still lives," said the huntsman, "I could not find it in my heart to carry out your command," and told the King how it had happened. Then a great weight fell from the King's heart, and he had it proclaimed in every country that his son might return and be taken into favor again.

The Princess, however, had a road made up to her palace which was quite bright and golden, and told her people that whosoever came riding straight along it to her, would be the right wooer and was to be admitted, and whoever rode by the side of it, was not the right one, and was not to be admitted. As the time was now close at hand, the eldest son thought he would hasten to go to the King's daughter, and give himself out as her deliverer, and thus win her for his bride, and the kingdom to boot. Therefore he rode forth, and when he arrived in front of the palace, and saw the splendid golden road, he thought it would be a sin and a shame if he were to ride over that, and turned aside, and rode on the right side of it. When he came to the door, the servants told him that he was not the right man, and was to go away again.

Soon after this the second Prince set out, and when he came to the golden road, and his horse had put one foot on it, he thought it would be a sin and a shame to tread a piece of it off, and he turned aside and rode on the left side of it, and when he reached the door, the attendants told him he was not the right one, and was to go away again.

When at last the year had entirely expired, the third son likewise wished to ride out of the forest to his beloved, with her to forget his sorrows. So he set out and thought of her so incessantly, and wished to be with her so much, that he never noticed the golden road at all. So his horse rode onwards up the middle of it, and when he came to the door, it was opened and the Princess received him with joy, and said he was her deliverer, and lord of the kingdom, and their wedding was celebrated with great rejoicing.

When it was over she told him that his father invited him to come to him, and had forgiven him. So he rode thither, and told him everything; how his brothers had betrayed him, and how he had nevertheless kept silence. The old King wished to punish them, but they had put to sea, and never came back as long as they lived.

The Devil's Three Gold Hairs

Once there was a very poor woman who was delighted when her son was born with a caul enveloping his head. This was supposed to bring good fortune, and it was predicted that he would marry the King's daughter when he became nineteen. Soon after, a King came to the village, but no one knew that it was the King. When he asked for news, they told him that a few days before a child had been born in the village, with a caul, and it was prophesied that he would be very lucky. Indeed, it had been said that in his nineteenth year he would have the King's daughter for his wife.

The King, who had a wicked heart, was very angry when he heard this; but he went to the parents in a most friendly manner, and said to them kindly, "Good people, give up your child to me. I will take the greatest care of him."

At first they refused; but when the stranger offered them a large amount of gold, and then mentioned that if their child was born to be lucky everything must turn out for the best with him, they willingly at last gave him up.

The King placed the child in a box and rode away with it for a long distance, till he came to deep water, into which he threw the box containing the child, saying to himself as he rode away, "From this unwelcome suitor have I saved my daughter."

But the box did not sink; it swam like a boat on the water, and so high above it that not a drop got inside. It sailed on to a spot about two miles from the chief town of the King's dominions, where there were a mill and a weir, which stopped it, and on which it rested.

The miller's man, who happened to be standing near the bank, fortunately noticed it, and thinking it would most likely contain something valuable, drew it on shore with a hook; but when he opened it, there lay a beautiful baby, who was quite awake and lively.

He carried it in to the miller and his wife, and as they had no children they were quite delighted, and said Heaven had sent the little boy as a gift to them. They brought him up carefully, and he grew to manhood clever and virtuous.

It happened one day that the King was overtaken by a thunder-storm while passing near the mill, and stopped to ask for shelter. Noticing the youth, he asked the miller if that tall young man was his son.

"No," he replied; "he is a foundling. Nineteen years ago a box was seen sailing on the mill stream by one of our men, and when it was caught in the weir he drew it out of the water and found the child in it."

Then the King knew that this must be the child of fortune, and therefore the one which he had thrown into the water. He hid his vexation, however, and presently said kindly, "I want to send a letter to the Queen, my wife; if that young man will take it to her I will give him two gold-pieces for his trouble."

"We are at the King's service," replied the miller, and called to the young man to prepare for his errand. Then the King wrote a letter to the Queen, containing these words: "As soon as the boy who brings this letter arrives, let him be killed, and I shall expect to find him dead and buried when I come back."

The youth was soon on his way with this letter. He lost himself, however, in a large forest. But when darkness came on he saw in the distance a glimmering light, which he walked to, and found a small house. He entered and saw an old woman sitting by the fire, quite alone. She appeared frightened when she saw him, and said: "Where do you come from, and what do you want?"

"I am come from the mill," he replied, "and I am carrying a letter to the wife of the King, and, as I have lost my way, I should like very much to stay here during the night."

"You poor young man," she replied, "you are in a den of robbers, and when they come home they may kill you."

"They may come when they like," said the youth; "I am not afraid; but I am so tired that I cannot go a step further." Then he stretched himself on a bench and fell fast asleep.

Soon after the robbers came home, and asked angrily what that youth was lying there for.

"Ah," said the old woman, "he is an innocent child who has lost himself in the wood, and I took him in out of compassion. He is car-rying a letter to the Queen, which the King has sent."

Then the robbers went softly to the sleeping youth, took the letter from his pocket, and read in it that as soon as the bearer arrived at the palace he was to lose his life. Then pity arose in the hardhearted robbers, and their chief tore up the letter and wrote another, in which it was stated that as soon as the boy arrived he should be married to the King's daughter. Then they left him to lie and rest on the bench till the next morning, and when he awoke they gave him the letter and showed him the road he was to take.

As soon as he reached the palace and sent in the letter, the Queen read it, and she acted in exact accordance with what was written— ordered a grand marriage feast, and had the Princess married at once to the fortunate youth. He was very handsome and amiable, so that the King's daughter soon learned to love him very much, and was quite happy with him.

Not long after, when the King returned home to his castle, he found the prophecy respecting the child of fortune fulfilled, and that he was married to a King's daughter. "How has this happened?" said he. "I have in my letter given very different orders!"

Then the Queen gave him the letter, and said: "You may see for yourself what is stated there."

The King read the letter and saw very clearly that it was not the one he had written. He asked the youth what he had done with the letter he had entrusted to him, and where he had brought the other from. "I know not," he replied, "unless it was changed during the night while I slept in the forest."

Full of wrath, the King said, "You shall not get off so easily, for whoever marries my daughter must first bring me three golden hairs from the head of the demon of the Black Forest. If you bring them to me before long, then shall you keep my daughter as a wife, but not otherwise."

Then said the child of fortune, "I will fetch these golden hairs very quickly; I am not the least afraid of the demon." Thereupon he said farewell, and started on his travels. His way led him to a large city, and as he stood at the gate and asked admission, a watchman said to him, "What trade do you follow, and how much do you know?" "I know everything," he replied.

"Then you can do us a favor," answered the watchman, "if you can tell why our master's fountain, from which wine used to flow, is dried up, and never gives us even water now." "I will tell you when I come back," he said; "only wait till then."

He traveled on still further, and came by and by to another town, where the watchman also asked him what trade he followed, and what he knew. "I know everything," he answered.

"Then," said the watchman, "you can do us a favor, and tell us why a tree in our town, which once bore golden apples, now only produces leaves." "Wait till I return," he replied, "and I will tell you."

On he went again, and came to a broad river, over which he must pass in a ferryboat, and the ferryman asked him the same question about his trade and his knowledge. He gave the same reply, that he knew everything.

"Then," said the man, "you can do me a favor, and tell me how it is that I am obliged to go backward and forward in my ferryboat every day, without a change of any kind." "Wait till I come back," he replied, "then you shall know all about it."

As soon as he reached the other side of the water he found the entrance to the Black Forest, in which was the demon's cove. It was very dark and gloomy, and the demon was not at home; but his old mother was sitting in a large arm-chair, and she looked up and said, "What do you want? You don't look wicked enough to be one of us."

"I just want three golden hairs from the demon's head," he replied; "otherwise my wife will be taken away from me."

"That is asking a great deal," she replied; "for if the demon comes home and finds you here, he will have no mercy on you. However, if you will trust me, I will try to help you."

Then she turned him into an ant, and said: "Creep into the folds of my gown; there you will be safe."

"Yes," he replied, "that is all very good; but I have three things besides that I want to know. First, why a well, from which formerly wine used to flow, should be dry now, so that not even water can be got from it. Secondly, why a tree that once bore golden apples should now produce nothing but leaves. And, thirdly, why a ferryman is obliged to row forward and back every day, without ever leaving off."

"These are difficult questions," said the old woman; "but keep still and quiet, and when the demon comes in, pay great attention to what he says, while I pull the golden hairs out of his head."

Late in the evening the demon came home, and as soon as he entered he declared that the air was not clear. "I smell the flesh of man," he said, "and I am sure that there is some one here." So he peeped into all the corners, and searched everywhere, but could find nothing.

Then his old mother scolded him well, and said, "Just as I have been sweeping, and dusting, and putting everything in order, then you come home and give me all the work to do over again. You have always the smell of something in your nose. Do sit down and eat your supper."

The demon did as she told him, and when he had eaten and drunk enough, he complained of being tired. So his mother made him lie down so that she could place his head in her lap; and he was soon so comfortable that he fell fast asleep and snored.

Then the old woman lifted up a golden hair, twitched it out, and laid it by her side. "Oh!" screamed the demon, waking up; "what was that for?" "I have had a bad dream," answered she, "and it made me catch hold of your hair."

"What did you dream about?" asked the demon. "Oh, I dreamed of a well in a market-place from which wine once used to flow, but now it is dried up, and they can't even get water from it. Whose fault is that?" "Ah, they ought to know that there sits a toad under a stone in the well, and if he were dead wine would again flow."

Then the old woman combed his hair again, till he slept and snored so loud that the windows rattled, and she pulled out the second hair. "What are you about now?" asked the demon in a rage. "Oh, don't be angry," said the woman; "I have had another dream."

"What was this dream about?" he asked. "Why, I dreamed that in a certain country there grows a fruit tree which used to bear golden apples, but now it produces nothing but leaves. What is the cause of this?" "Why, don't they know," answered the demon, "that there is a mouse gnawing at the root? Were it dead the tree would again bear golden apples; and if it gnaws much longer the tree will wither and dry up. Bother your dreams; if you disturb me again, just as I am comfortably asleep, you will have a box on the ear."

Then the old woman spoke kindly to him, and smoothed and combed his hair again, till he slept and snored. Then she seized the third golden hair and pulled it out.

The demon, on this, sprang to his feet, roared out in a greater rage than ever, and would have done some mischief in the house, but she managed to appease him this time also, and said: "How can I help my bad dreams?" "And whatever did you dream?" he asked, with some curiosity. "Well, I dreamed about a ferryman, who complains that he is obliged to take people across the river, and is never free." "Oh, the stupid fellow!" replied the wizard, "he can very easily ask any person who wants to be ferried over to take the oar in his hand, and he will be free at once."

Then the demon laid his head down once more; and as the old mother had pulled out the three golden hairs, and got answers to all the three questions, she let the old fellow rest and sleep in peace till the morning dawned.

As soon as he had gone out next day, the old woman took the ant from the folds of her dress and restored the lucky youth to his former shape. "Here are the three golden hairs for which you wished," said she; "and did you hear all the answers to your three questions?" "Yes," he replied, "every word, and I will not forget them." "Well, then, I have helped you out of your difficulties, and now get home as fast as you can."

After thanking the old woman for her kindness, he turned his steps homeward, full of joy that everything had succeeded so well.

When he arrived at the ferry the man asked for the promised answer. "Ferry me over first," he replied, "and then I will tell you."

So when they reached the opposite shore he gave the ferryman the demon's advice, that the next person who came and wished to be ferried over should have the oar placed in his hand, and from that moment he would have to take the ferryman's place.

Then the youth journeyed on till he came to the town where the unfruitful tree grew, and where the watchman was waiting for his answer. To him the young man repeated what he had heard, and said, "Kill the mouse that is gnawing at the root; then will your tree again bear golden apples."

The watchman thanked him, and gave him in return for his information two asses laden with gold, which were led after him. He very soon arrived at the city which contained the dried-up fountain. The sentinel came forward to receive his answer. Said the youth, "Under a stone in the fountain sits a toad; it must be searched for and killed; then will wine again flow from it." To show how thankful he was for this advice, the sentinel also ordered two asses laden with gold to be sent after him.

At length the child of fortune reached home with his riches, and his wife was overjoyed at seeing him again, and hearing how well he had succeeded in his undertaking. He placed before the King the three golden hairs he had brought from the head of the black demon; and when the King saw these and the four asses laden with gold he was quite satisfied, and said, "Now that you have performed all the required conditions, I am quite ready to sanction your marriage with my daughter; but, my dear son-in-law, tell me how you obtained all this gold. It is indeed a very valuable treasure; where did you find it?"

"I crossed the river in a ferryboat, and on the opposite shore I found the gold lying in the sand."

"Can I find some if I go?" asked the King eagerly. "Yes, as much as you please," replied he. "There is a ferryman there who will row you over, and you can fill a sack in no time."

The greedy old King set out on his journey in all haste, and when he came near the river he beckoned to the ferryman to row him over the ferry.

The man told him to step in, and just as they reached the opposite shore he placed the rudder-oar in the King's hand, and sprang out of the boat; and so the King became a ferryman as a punishment for his sins.

I wonder if he still goes on ferrying people over the river! It is very likely, for no one has ever been persuaded to touch the oar since he took it.

Rumpelstiltskin

There was once a miller who was poor, but he had one beautiful daughter. It happened one day that he came to speak with the King, and, to give himself consequence, he told him that he had a daughter who could spin gold out of straw. The King said to the miller, "That is an art that pleases me well; if your daughter is as clever as you say, bring her to my castle tomorrow, that I may put her to the proof."

When the girl was brought to him, he led her into a room that was quite full of straw, and gave her a wheel and spindle, and said, "Now set to work, and if by the early morning you have not spun this straw to gold you shall die." And he shut the door himself, and left her there alone.

And so the poor miller's daughter was left there sitting, and could not think what to do for her life: she had no notion how to set to work to spin gold from straw, and her distress grew so great that she began to weep. Then all at once the door opened, and in came a little man, who said, "Good evening, miller's daughter; why are you crying?" "Oh!" answered the girl, "I have got to spin gold out of straw, and I don't understand the business."

Then the little man said, "What will you give me if I spin it for you?" "My necklace," said the girl.

The little man took the necklace, seated himself before the wheel, and whirr, whirr, whirr! three times round and the bobbin was full; then he took up another, and whirr, whirr, whirr! three times round, and that was full; and so he went on till the morning, when all the straw had been spun, and all the bobbins were full of gold. At sunrise came the King, and when he saw the gold he was astonished and very much rejoiced, for he was very avaricious. He had the miller's daughter taken into another room filled with straw, much bigger than the last, and told her that as she valued her life she must spin it all in one night.

The girl did not know what to do, so she began to cry, and then the door opened, and the little man appeared and said, "What will you give me if I spin all this straw into gold?" "The ring from my finger," answered the girl.

So the little man took the ring, and began again to send the wheel whirring round, and by the next morning all the straw was spun into glistening gold. The King was rejoiced beyond measure at the sight, but as he could never have enough of gold, he had the miller's daughter taken into a still larger room full of straw, and said, "This, too, must be spun in one night, and if you accomplish it you shall be my wife." For he thought, "Although she is but a miller's daughter, I am not likely to find any one richer in the whole world."

As soon as the girl was left alone, the little man appeared for the third time and said, "What will you give me if I spin the straw for you this time?" "I have nothing left to give," answered the girl. "Then you must promise me the first child you have after you are Queen," said the little man.

"But who knows whether that will happen?" thought the girl; but as she did not know what else to do in her necessity, she promised the little man what he desired, upon which he began to spin, until all the straw was gold. And when in the morning the King came and found all done according to his wish, he caused the wedding to be held at once, and the miller's pretty daughter became a Queen.

In a year's time she brought a fine child into the world, and thought no more of the little man; but one day he came suddenly into her room, and said, "Now give me what you promised me."

The Queen was terrified greatly, and offered the little man all the riches of the kingdom if he would only leave the child; but the little man said, "No, I would rather have something living than all the treasures of the world."

Then the Queen began to lament and to weep, so that the little man had pity upon her. "I will give you three days," said he, "and if at the end of that time you cannot tell my name, you must give up the child to me."

Then the Queen spent the whole night in thinking over all the names that she had ever heard, and sent a messenger through the land to ask far and wide for all the names that could be found. And when the little man came next day, beginning with Caspar, Melchior, Balthazar, she repeated all she knew, and went through the whole list, but after each the little man said, "That is not my name."

The second day the Queen sent to inquire of all the neighbors what the servants were called, and told the little man all the most unusual and singular names, saying, "Perhaps you are Roast-ribs, or Sheepshanks, or Spindleshanks?" But he answered nothing but "That is not my name."

The third day the messenger came back again, and said, "I have not been able to find one single new name; but as I passed through the woods I came to a high hill, and near it was a little house, and before the house burned a fire, and round the fire danced a comical little man, and he hopped on one leg and cried,

> 'Today do I bake, tomorrow I brew,
> The day after that the Queen's child comes in;
> And oh! I am glad that nobody knew
> That the name I am called is Rumpelstiltskin!'"

You cannot think how pleased the Queen was to hear that name, and soon afterwards, when the little man walked in and said, "Now, Mrs. Queen, what is my name?" she said at first, "Are you called Jack?" "No," answered he. "Are you called Harry?" she asked again. "No," answered he. And then she said, "Then perhaps your name is Rumpelstiltskin!"

"The devil told you that! the devil told you that!" cried the little man, and in his anger he stamped with his right foot so hard that it went into the ground above his knee; then he seized his left foot with both his hands in such a fury that he split in two, and there was an end of him.

The Golden Goose

There was a man who had three sons, the youngest of whom was called the Simpleton, and was despised, laughed at, and neglected, on every occasion. It happened one day that the eldest son wished to go into the forest to cut wood, and before he went his mother gave him a delicious pancake and a flask of wine, that he might not suffer from hunger or thirst. When he came into the forest a little old gray man met him, who wished him good day, and said, "Give me a bit of cake out of your pocket, and let me have a drink of your wine; I am so hungry and thirsty."

But the prudent youth answered, "Give you my cake and my wine? I haven't got any; be off with you." And leaving the little man standing there, he went off.

Then he began to fell a tree, but he had not been at it long before he made a wrong stroke, and the hatchet hit him in the arm, so that he was obliged to go home and get it bound up. That was what came of the little gray man.

Afterwards the second son went into the wood, and the mother gave to him, as to the eldest, a pancake and a flask of wine. The little old gray man met him also, and begged for a little bit of cake and a drink of wine. But the second son spoke out plainly, saying, "What I give you I lose myself, so be off with you." And leaving the little man standing there, he went off.

The punishment followed. As he was chopping away at the tree, he hit himself in the leg so severely that he had to be carried home.

Then said the Simpleton, "Father, let me go for once into the forest to cut wood"; and the father answered, "Your brothers have hurt themselves by so doing; give it up, you understand nothing about it."

But the Simpleton went on begging so long, that the father said at last, "Well, be off with you; you will only learn by experience."

The mother gave him a cake (it was only made with water, and baked in the ashes), and with it a flask of sour beer. When he came into the forest the little old gray man met him, and greeted him, saying, "Give me a bit of your cake, and a drink from your flask; I am so hungry and thirsty."

And the Simpleton answered, "I have only a flour and water cake and sour beer; but if that is good enough for you, let us sit down together and eat." Then they sat down, and as the Simpleton took out his flour and water cake it became a rich pancake, and his sour beer became good wine. Then they ate and drank, and afterwards the little man said, "As you have such a kind heart, and share what you have so willingly, I will bestow good luck upon you. Yonder stands an old tree; cut it down, and at its roots you will find something," and thereupon the little man took his departure.

The Simpleton went there, and hewed away at the tree, and when it fell he saw, sitting among the roots, a goose with feathers of pure gold. He lifted it out and took it with him to an inn where he intended to stay the night.

The landlord had three daughters who, when they saw the goose, were curious to know what wonderful kind of bird it was, and ended by longing for one of its golden feathers. The eldest thought, "I will wait for a good opportunity, and then I will pull out one of its feathers for myself"; and so, when the Simpleton was gone out, she seized the goose by its wing—but there her finger and hand had to stay, held fast. Soon after came the second sister with the same idea of plucking out one of the golden feathers for herself; but scarcely had she touched her sister than she also was obliged to stay, held fast. Lastly came the third with the same intentions; but the others screamed out, "Stay away! for heaven's sake stay away!" But she did not see why she should stay away, and thought, "If they do so, why should not I?" and went towards them. But when she reached her sisters there she stopped, hanging on with them. And so they had to stay, all night.

The next morning the Simpleton took the goose under his arm and went away, unmindful of the three girls that hung on to it. The three had to run after him, left and right, wherever his legs carried him. In the midst of the fields they met the parson, who, when he saw the procession, said, "Shame on you, girls, running after a young fellow through the fields like this," and forthwith he seized hold of the youngest by the hand to drag her away, but hardly had he touched her when he too was obliged to run after them himself.

Not long after the sexton came that way, and seeing the respected parson following at the heels of the three girls, he called out, "Ho, your reverence, whither away so quickly? You forget that we have another christening today"; and he seized hold of him by his gown; but no sooner had he touched him than he was obliged to follow on too. As the five tramped on, one after another, two peasants with their hoes came up from the fields, and the parson cried out to them, and begged them to come and set him and the sexton free, but no sooner had they touched the sexton than they had to follow on too; and now there were seven following the Simpleton and the goose.

By and by they came to a town where a King reigned, who had an only daughter who was so serious that no one could make her laugh; therefore the King had given out that whoever should make her laugh should have her in marriage. The Simpleton, when he heard this, went with his goose and his hangers-on into the presence of the King's daughter, and as soon as she saw the seven people following always one after the other, she burst out laughing, and seemed as if she could never stop. And so the Simpleton earned a right to her as his bride; but the King did not like him for a son-in-law and made all kinds of objections, and said he must first bring a man who could drink up a whole cellar of wine.

The Simpleton thought that the little gray man would be able to help him, and went out into the forest, and there, on the very spot where he felled the tree, he saw a man sitting with a very sad countenance. The Simpleton asked him what was the matter, and he answered, "I have a great thirst, which I cannot quench: cold water does not agree with me; I have indeed drunk up a whole cask of wine, but what good is a drop like that?"

Then said the Simpleton, "I can help you; only come with me, and you shall have enough."

He took him straight to the King's cellar, and the man sat himself down before the big vats, and drank, and drank, and before a day was over he had drunk up the whole cellar-full. The Simpleton again asked for his bride, but the King was annoyed that a wretched fellow, called the Simpleton by everybody, should carry off his daughter, and so he made new conditions. He was to produce a man who could eat up a mountain of bread. The Simpleton did not hesitate long, but ran quickly off to the forest, and there in the same place sat a man who had fastened a strap round his body, making a very piteous face, and saying, "I have eaten a whole bakehouse full of rolls, but what is the use of that when one is so hungry as I am? My stomach feels quite empty, and I am obliged to strap myself together, that I may not die of hunger."

The Simpleton was quite glad of this, and said, "Get up quickly, and come along with me, and you shall have enough to eat."

He led him straight to the King's courtyard, where all the meal in the kingdom had been collected and baked into a mountain of bread. The man out of the forest settled himself down before it and hastened to eat, and in one day the whole mountain had disappeared.

Then the Simpleton asked for his bride the third time. The King, however, found one more excuse, and said he must have a ship that should be able to sail on land or on water. "So soon," said he, "as you come sailing along with it, you shall have my daughter for your wife."

The Simpleton went straight to the forest, and there sat the little old gray man with whom he had shared his cake, and he said, "I have eaten for you, and I have drunk for you, I will also give you the ship; and all because you were kind to me at the first."

Then he gave him the ship that could sail on land and on water, and when the King saw it he knew he could no longer withhold his daughter. The marriage took place immediately, and at the death of the King the Simpleton possessed the kingdom, and lived long and happily with his wife.

The Three Feathers

There was once a King who had three sons. Two of them were considered wise and prudent; but the youngest, who said very little, appeared to others so silly that they gave him the name of Simple. When the King became old and weak, and began to think that his end was near, he knew not to which of his sons to leave his kingdom.

So he sent for them, and said, "I have made a determination that whichever of you brings me the finest carpet shall be King after my death."

They immediately prepared to start on their expedition, and that there might be no dispute between them, they took three feathers. As they left the castle each blew a feather into air, and said, "We will travel in whatever direction these feathers take." One flew to the east, and the other to the west; but the third soon fell on the earth and remained there. Then the two eldest brothers turned one to the right, and the other to the left, and they laughed at Simple because where his feather fell he was obliged to remain.

Simple sat down after his brothers were gone, feeling very sad; but presently, looking round, he noticed near where his feather lay a kind of trap-door. He rose quickly, went toward it, and lifted it up. To his surprise he saw a flight of steps, down which he descended, and reached another door; hearing voices within he knocked hastily. The voices were singing,

> "Little frogs, crooked legs,
> Where do you hide?
> Go and see quickly
> Who is outside."

At this the door opened of itself, and the youth saw a large fat frog seated with a number of little frogs round her.

On seeing him the large frog asked what he wanted. "I have a great wish for the finest and most beautiful carpet that can be got," he replied. Then the old frog called again to her little ones,

"Little frogs, crooked legs,
Run here and there;
Bring me the large bag
That hangs over there."

The young frogs fetched the bag, and when it was opened the old frog took from it a carpet so fine and so beautifully worked that nothing on earth could equal it. This she gave to the young man, who thanked her and went away up the steps.

Meanwhile, his elder brothers, quite believing that their foolish brother would not be able to get any carpet at all, said one to another, "We need not take the trouble to go further and seek for anything very wonderful; ours is sure to be the best." And as the first person they met was a shepherd, wearing a shepherd's plaid, they bought the large plaid cloth and carried it home to the King.

At the same time the younger brother returned with his beautiful carpet, and when the King saw it he was astonished, and said, "If justice is done, then the kingdom belongs to my youngest son."

But the two elder brothers gave the King no peace; they said it was impossible for Simple to become King, for his understanding failed in everything, and they begged their father to make another condition.

At last he said, "Whoever finds the most beautiful ring and brings it to me shall have the kingdom."

Away went the brothers a second time, and blew three feathers into the air to direct their ways. The feathers of the elder two flew east and west, but that of the youngest fell, as before, near the trap-door and there rested. He at once descended the steps, and told the great frog that he wanted a most beautiful ring. She sent for her large bag and drew from it a ring which sparkled with precious stones, and was so beautiful that no goldsmith on earth could make one like it.

The elder brothers had again laughed at Simple when his feather fell so soon to the ground, and forgetting his former success with the carpet, scorned the idea that he could ever find a gold ring. So they gave themselves no trouble, but merely took a plated ring from the harness of a carriage horse, and brought it to their father.

But when the King saw Simple's splendid ring he said at once, "The kingdom belongs to my youngest son."

His brothers, however, were not yet inclined to submit to the decision; they begged their father to make a third condition, and at last he promised to give the kingdom to the son who brought home the most beautiful woman to be his wife.

They all were again guided by blowing the feathers, and the two elder took the roads pointed out to them. But Simple, without hesitation, went at once to the frog, and said, "This time I am to take home the most beautiful woman."

"Hey-day!" said the frog. "I have not one by me at present, but you shall have one soon." So she gave him a carrot which had been hollowed out, and to which six mice were harnessed.

Simple took it quite sorrowfully, and said, "What am I to do with this?" "Seat one of my little frogs in it," she said.

The youth, on this, caught one up at a venture, and seated it in the carrot. No sooner had he done so than it became a most beautiful young lady; the carrot was turned into a gilded coach; and the mice were changed to prancing horses.

He kissed the maiden, seated himself in the carriage with her, drove away to the castle, and led her to the King.

Meanwhile his brothers had proved more silly than he; not forgetting the beautiful carpet and the ring, they still thought it was impossible for Simple to find a beautiful woman also. They therefore took no more trouble than before, and merely chose the handsomest peasant maidens they could find to bring to their father.

When the King saw the beautiful maiden his youngest son had brought he said, "The kingdom must now belong to my youngest son after my death."

But the elder brothers deafened the King's ears with their cries, "We cannot consent to let our stupid brother be King. Give us one more trial. Let a ring be hung in the hall, and let each woman spring through it." For they thought the peasant maidens would easily manage to do this, because they were strong, and that the delicate lady would, no doubt, kill herself. To this trial the old King consented.

The peasant maidens jumped first; but they were so heavy and awkward that they fell, and one broke her arm and the other her leg. But the beautiful lady whom Simple had brought home sprang as lightly as a deer through the ring, and thus put an end to all opposition.

The youngest brother married the beautiful maiden, and after his father's death ruled the kingdom for many years with wisdom and equity.

Snow-white and Rose-red

There was once a poor widow who lived in a lonely cottage. In front of the cottage was a garden wherein stood two rose trees, one of which bore white and the other red roses. She had two children who were like the two rose trees, and one was called Snow-white, and the other Rose-red. They were as good and happy, as busy and cheerful as ever two children in the world were, only Snow-white was more quiet and gentle than Rose-red. Rose-red liked better to run about in the meadows and fields seeking flowers and catching butterflies; but Snow-white sat at home with her mother, and helped her with her house-work, or read to her when there was nothing to do.

The two children were so fond of each other that they always held each other by the hand when they went out together, and when Snow-white said, "We will not leave each other," Rose-red answered, "Never so long as we live," and their mother would add, "What one has she must share with the other."

They often ran about the forest alone and gathered red berries, and no beasts did them any harm, but came close to them trustfully. The little hare would eat a cabbage-leaf out of their hands, the roe grazed by their side, the stag leapt merrily by them, and the birds sat still upon the boughs, and sang whatever they knew.

No mishap overtook them; if they had stayed too late in the forest, and night came on, they laid themselves down near one another upon the moss, and slept until morning came, and their mother knew this and had no distress on their account.

Once when they had spent the night in the wood and the dawn had roused them, they saw a beautiful child in a shining white dress sitting near their bed. He got up and looked quite kindly at them, but said nothing and went away into the forest. And when they looked round they found that they had been sleeping quite close to a precipice, and would certainly have fallen into it in the darkness if they had gone only a few paces further. And their mother told them that it must have been the angel who watches over good children.

Snow-white and Rose-red kept their mother's little cottage so neat that it was a pleasure to look inside it. In the summer Rose-red took care of the house, and every morning laid a wreath of flowers by her mother's bed before she awoke, in which was a rose from each tree. In the winter Snow-white lit the fire and hung the kettle on the hob. The kettle was of copper and shone like gold, so brightly was it polished. In the evening, when the snowflakes fell, the mother said, "Go, Snow-white, and bolt the door," and then they sat round the hearth, and the mother took her spectacles and read aloud out of a large book, and the two girls listened as they sat and spun. And close by them lay a lamb upon the floor, and behind them upon a perch sat a white dove with its head hidden beneath its wings.

One evening, as they were thus sitting comfortably together, some one knocked at the door as if he wished to be let in. The mother said, "Quick, Rose-red, open the door, it must be a traveler who is seeking shelter." Rose-red went and pushed back the bolt, thinking that it was a poor man, but it was not; it was a bear that stretched his broad, black head within the door.

Rose-red screamed and sprang back, the lamb bleated, the dove fluttered, and Snow-white hid herself behind her mother's bed. But the bear began to speak and said, "Do not be afraid, I will do you no harm! I am half-frozen, and only want to warm myself a little beside you."

"Poor bear," said the mother, "lie down by the fire, only take care that you do not burn your coat." Then she cried, "Snow-white, Rose-red, come out, the bear will do you no harm, he means well." So they both came out, and by-and-by the lamb and dove came nearer, and were not afraid of him. The bear said, "Here, children, knock the snow out of my coat a little"; so they brought the broom and swept the bear's hide clean; and he stretched himself by the fire and growled contentedly and comfortably. It was not long before they grew quite at home, and played tricks with their clumsy guest. They tugged his hair with their hands, put their feet upon his back and rolled him about, or they took a hazel-switch and beat him, and when he growled they laughed. But the bear took it all in good part, only when they were too rough he called out, "Leave me alive, children,

> 'Snowy-white, Rosy-red,
> Will you beat your lover dead?'"

When it was bed-time, and the others went to bed, the mother said to the bear, "You can lie there by the hearth, and then you will be safe from the cold and the bad weather." As soon as day dawned the two children let him out, and he trotted across the snow into the forest.

Henceforth the bear came every evening at the same time, laid himself down by the hearth, and let the children amuse themselves with him as much as they liked; and they got so used to him that the doors were never fastened until their black friend had arrived.

When spring had come and all outside was green, the bear said one morning to Snow-white, "Now I must go away, and cannot come back for the whole summer." "Where are you going, then, dear bear?" asked Snow-white. "I must go into the forest and guard my treasures from the wicked dwarfs. In the winter, when the earth is frozen hard, they are obliged to stay below and cannot work their way through; but now, when the sun has thawed and warmed the earth, they break through it, and come out to pry and steal; and what once gets into their hands, and in their caves, does not easily see daylight again."

Snow-white was quite sorry for his going away, and as she unbolted the door for him, and the bear was hurrying out, he caught against the bolt and a piece of his hairy coat was torn off, and it seemed to Snow-white as if she had seen gold shining through it, but she was not sure about it. The bear ran away quickly, and was soon out of sight behind the trees.

A short time afterwards the mother sent her children into the forest to get fire-wood. There they found a big tree which lay felled on the ground, and close by the trunk something was jumping backwards and forwards in the grass, but they could not make out what it was. When they came nearer they saw a dwarf with an old withered face and a snow-white beard a yard long. The end of the beard was caught in a crevice of the tree, and the little fellow was jumping backwards and forwards like a dog tied to a rope, and did not know what to do.

He glared at the girls with his fiery red eyes and cried, "Why do you stand there? Can you not come here and help me?" "What are you about there, little man?" asked Rose-red. "You stupid, prying goose!" answered the dwarf; "I was going to split the tree to get a little wood for cooking. The little bit of food that one of us wants gets burnt up directly with thick logs; we do not swallow so much as you coarse, greedy folk. I had just driven the wedge safely in, and everything was going as I wished; but the wretched wood was too smooth and suddenly sprang asunder, and the tree closed so quickly that I could not pull out my beautiful white beard; so now it is tight in and I cannot get away, and the silly, sleek, milk-faced things laugh! Ugh! how odious you are!"

The children tried very hard, but they could not pull the beard out, it was caught too fast. "I will run and fetch some one," said Rose-red. "You senseless goose!" snarled the dwarf; "why should you fetch some one? You are already two too many for me; can you not think of something better?" "Don't be impatient," said Snow-white, "I will help you," and she pulled her scissors out of her pocket, and cut off the end of the beard.

As soon as the dwarf felt himself free he laid hold of a bag which lay amongst the roots of the tree, and which was full of gold, and lifted it up, grumbling to himself, "Uncouth people, to cut off a piece of my fine beard. Bad luck to you!" and then he swung the bag upon his back, and went off without even once looking at the children.

Some time after that Snow-white and Rose-red went to catch a dish of fish. As they came near the brook they saw something like a large grasshopper jumping towards the water, as if it were going to leap in. They ran to it and found it was the dwarf. "Where are you going?" said Rose-red; "you surely don't want to go into the water?" "I am not such a fool!" cried the dwarf; "don't you see that the accursed fish wants to pull me in?" The little man had been sitting there fishing, and unluckily the wind had twisted his beard with the fishing-line; just then a big fish bit, and the feeble creature had not strength to pull it out; the fish kept the upper hand and pulled the dwarf towards him. He held on to all the reeds and rushes, but it was of little good, he was forced to follow the movements of the fish, and was in urgent danger of being dragged into the water.

The girls came just in time; they held him fast and tried to free his beard from the line, but all in vain, beard and line were entangled fast together. Nothing was left but to bring out the scissors and cut the beard, whereby a small part of it was lost. When the dwarf saw that he screamed out, "Is that civil, you toadstool, to disfigure one's face? Was it not enough to clip off the end of my beard? Now you have cut off the best part of it. I cannot let myself be seen by my people. I wish you had been made to run the soles off your shoes!" Then he took out a sack of pearls which lay in the rushes, and without saying a word more he dragged it away and disappeared behind a stone.

It happened that soon afterwards the mother sent the two children to the town to buy needles and thread, and laces and ribbons. The road led them across a heath upon which huge pieces of rock lay strewn here and there. Now they noticed a large bird hovering in the air, flying slowly round and round above them; it sank lower and lower, and at last settled near a rock not far off. Directly afterwards they heard a loud, piteous cry. They ran up and saw with horror that the eagle had seized their old acquaintance the dwarf, and was going to carry him off.

The children, full of pity, at once took tight hold of the little man, and pulled against the eagle so long that at last he let his booty go. As soon as the dwarf had recovered from his first fright he cried with his shrill voice, "Could you not have done it more carefully! You dragged at my brown coat so that it is all torn and full of holes, you helpless clumsy creatures!" Then he took up a sack full of precious stones, and slipped away again under the rock into his hole. The girls, who by this time were used to his thanklessness, went on their way and did their business in the town.

As they crossed the heath again on their way home they surprised the dwarf, who had emptied out his bag of precious stones in a clean spot, and had not thought that any one would come there so late. The evening sun shone upon the brilliant stones; they glittered and sparkled with all colors so beautifully that the children stood still and looked at them. "Why do you stand gaping there?" cried the dwarf, and his ashen-gray face became copper-red with rage. He was going on with his bad words when a loud growling was heard, and a black bear came trotting towards them out of the forest. The dwarf sprang up in a fright, but he could not get to his cave, for the bear was already close. Then in the dread of his heart he cried, "Dear Mr. Bear, spare me, I will give you all my treasures; look, the beautiful jewels lying there! Grant me my life; what do you want with such a slender little fellow as I? you would not feel me between your teeth. Come, take these two wicked girls, they are tender morsels for you, fat as young quails; for mercy's sake eat them!" The bear took no heed of his words, but gave the wicked creature a single blow with his paw, and he did not move again.

The girls had run away, but the bear called to them, "Snow-white and Rose-red, do not be afraid; wait, I will come with you." Then they knew his voice and waited, and when he came up to them suddenly his bearskin fell off, and he stood there a handsome man, clothed all in gold. "I am a King's son," he said, "and I was bewitched by that wicked dwarf, who had stolen my treasures; I have had to run about the forest as a savage bear until I was freed by his death. Now he has got his well-deserved punishment."

Snow-white was married to him, and Rose-red to his brother, and they divided between them the great treasure which the dwarf had gathered together in his cave. The old mother lived peacefully and happily with her children for many years. She took the two rose trees with her, and they stood before her window, and every year bore the most beautiful roses, white and red.

The Poor Miller's Boy and the Cat

There once lived an old miller who had neither wife nor child, and three apprentices served under him. As they had been with him several years, one day he said to them, "I am old, and want to sit in the chimney-corner; go out, and whichsoever of you brings me the best horse home, to him will I give the mill, and in return for it he shall take care of me till my death." The third of the boys was, however, the drudge, who was looked on as foolish by the others; they begrudged the mill to him, and afterwards he would not have it. Then all three went out together, and when they came to the village, the two said to stupid Hans, "Thou mayst just as well stay here; as long as thou livest thou wilt never get a horse."

Hans, however, went with them, and when it was night they came to a cave in which they lay down to sleep. The two sharp ones waited until Hans had fallen asleep, then they got up, and went away leaving him where he was. And they thought they had done a very clever thing, but it was certain to turn out ill for them. When the sun arose, and Hans woke up, he was lying in a deep cavern. He looked around on every side and exclaimed, "Oh, heavens, where am I?" Then he got up and clambered out of the cave, went into the forest, and thought, "Here I am quite alone and deserted, how shall I obtain a horse now?"

While he was thus walking full of thought, he met a small tabby-cat which said quite kindly, "Hans, where are you going?" "Alas, you cannot help me." "I well know your desire," said the cat. "You wish to have a beautiful horse. Come with me, and be my faithful servant for seven years long, and then I will give you one more beautiful than any you have ever seen in your whole life." "Well, this is a wonderful cat!" thought Hans, "but I am determined to see if she is telling the truth."

So she took him with her into her enchanted castle, where there were nothing but cats who were her servants. They leapt nimbly upstairs and downstairs, and were merry and happy. In the evening when they sat down to dinner, three of them had to make music. One played the bassoon, the other the fiddle, and the third put the trumpet to his lips, and blew out his cheeks as much as he possibly could. When they had dined, the table was carried away, and the cat said, "Now, Hans, come and dance with me." "No," said he, "I won't dance with a pussy-cat. I have never done that yet." "Then take him to bed," said she to the cats. So one of them lighted him to his bed-room, one pulled his shoes off, one his stockings, and at last one of them blew out the candle.

Next morning they returned and helped him out of bed, one put his stockings on for him, one tied his garters, one brought his shoes, one washed him, and one dried his face with her tail. "That feels very soft!" said Hans. He, however, had to serve the cat, and chop some wood every day, and to do that he had an axe of silver, and the wedge and saw were of silver and the mallet of copper. So he chopped the wood small; stayed there in the house and had good meat and drink, but never saw any one but the tabby-cat and her servants.

Once she said to him, "Go and mow my meadow, and dry the grass," and gave him a scythe of silver, and a whetstone of gold, but bade him deliver them up again carefully. So Hans went thither, and did what he was bidden, and when he had finished the work, he carried the scythe, whetstone, and hay to the house, and asked if it was not yet time for her to give him his reward. "No," said the cat, "you must first do something more for me of the same kind. There is timber of silver, carpenter's axe, square, and everything that is needful, all of silver; with these build me a small house." Then Hans built the small house, and said that he had now done everything, and still he had no horse. Nevertheless, the seven years had gone by with him as if they were six months.

The cat asked him if he would like to see her horses? "Yes," said Hans. Then she opened the door of the small house, and when she had opened it, there stood twelve horses—such horses, so bright and shining, that his heart rejoiced at the sight of them. She gave him something to eat and to drink, and said, "Go home, I will not give you your horse away with you; but in three days' time I will follow you and bring it." So Hans set out, and she showed him the way to the mill. She had, however, never once given him a new coat, and he had been obliged to keep on his dirty old smock-frock, which he had brought with him, and which during the seven years had everywhere become too small for him.

When he reached home, the two other apprentices were there again as well, and each of them certainly had brought a horse with him, but one of them was a blind one, and the other lame. They asked Hans where his horse was. "It will follow me in three days' time." Then they laughed and said, "Indeed, stupid Hans, where wilt thou get a horse? It will be a fine one!" Hans went into the parlor, but the miller said he should not sit down to table, for he was so ragged and torn, that they would all be ashamed of him if any one came in. So they gave him a mouthful of food outside, and at night, when they went to rest, the two others would not let him have a bed, and at last he was forced to creep into the goose-house, and lie down on a little hard straw. In the morning when he awoke, the three days had passed, and a coach came with six horses and they shone so bright that it was delightful to see them! And a servant brought a seventh as well, which was for the poor miller's boy.

A magnificent Princess alighted from the coach and went into the mill, and this princess was the little tabby-cat whom poor Hans had served for seven years. She asked the miller where the miller's boy and drudge was? Then the miller said, "We cannot have him here in the mill, for he is so ragged; he is lying in the goose-house." Then the King's daughter said that they were to bring him immediately. So they brought him out, and he had to hold his little smock-frock together to cover himself. The servants unpacked splendid garments, and washed him and dressed him, and when that was done, no King could have looked more handsome. Then the maiden desired to see the horses which the other apprentices had brought home with them, and one of them was blind and the other lame.

So she ordered the servant to bring the seventh horse, and when the miller saw it, he said that such a horse as that had never yet entered his yard. "And that is for the third miller's-boy," said she. "Then he must have the mill," said the miller, but the King's daughter said that the horse was there, and that he was to keep his mill as well, and took her faithful Hans and set him in the coach, and drove away with him.

They first drove to the little house which he had built with the silver tools, and behold it was a great castle, and everything inside it was of silver and gold; and then she married him, and he was rich, so rich that he had enough for all the rest of his life. After this, let no one ever say that any one who is silly can never become a person of importance.

The Old Woman in the Wood

A poor servant-girl was once traveling with the family she served through a great forest, and when they were in the midst of it, robbers came out of the thicket, and murdered all they found. All perished together except the girl, who had jumped out of the carriage in a fright, and hidden herself behind a tree. When the robbers had gone away with their booty, she came out and beheld the great disaster. Then she began to weep bitterly, and said, "What can a poor girl like me do now? I do not know how to get out of the forest, no human being lives in it, so I must certainly starve." She walked about and looked for a road, but could find none. When it was evening she seated herself under a tree, gave herself into God's keeping, and resolved to sit waiting there and not go away, let what might happen.

When, however, she had sat there for a while, a white dove came flying to her with a little golden key in its mouth. It put the little key in her hand, and said, "Do you see that great tree, therein is a little lock, it opens with the tiny key; inside the tree you will find food enough, and suffer no more hunger." Then she went to the tree and opened it, and found milk in a little dish, and white bread to break into it, so that she could eat her fill. When she was satisfied, she said, "It is now the time when the hens at home go to roost; I am so tired I could go to bed too." Then the dove flew to her again, and brought another golden key in its bill, and said, "Open that tree there, and you will find a bed." So she opened it, and found a beautiful white bed, and she prayed God to protect her during the night, and lay down and slept. In the morning the dove came for the third time, and again brought a little key, and said, "Open that tree there, and you will find clothes." And when she opened it, she found garments beset with gold and with jewels, more splendid than those of any King's daughter. So she lived there for some time, and the dove came every day and provided her with all she needed, and it was a quiet good life.

Once, however, the dove came and said, "Will you do something for my sake?" "With all my heart," said the girl. Then said the little dove, "I will guide you to a small house; enter it, and inside it, an old woman will be sitting by the fire and will say, 'Good-day.' But on your life give her no answer, let her do what she will, but pass by her on the right side; further on, there is a door, open it, and you will enter into a room where a quantity of rings of all kinds are lying, among which are some magnificent ones with shining stones. Leave them, however, where they are, and seek out a plain one, which must likewise be among them, and bring it here to me as quickly as you can."

The girl went to the little house, and came to the door. There sat an old woman who stared when she saw her, and said, "Good-day, my child." The girl gave her no answer, and opened the door. "Whither away," cried the old woman, and seized her by the gown, and wanted to hold her fast, saying, "That is my house; no one can go in there if I choose not to allow it." But the girl was silent, got away from her, and went straight into the room.

On the table lay an enormous quantity of rings, which gleamed and glittered before her eyes. She turned them over and looked for the plain one, but could not find it. While she was seeking, she saw the old woman and how she was stealing away, and wanting to get off with a bird-cage which she had in her hand. So she went after her and took the cage out of her hand, and when she raised it up and looked into it, a bird was inside which had the plain ring in its bill. Then she took the ring, and ran quite joyously home with it, and thought the little white dove would come and get the ring, but it did not.

Then she leant against a tree and determined to wait for the dove, and, as she thus stood, it seemed just as if the tree was soft and pliant, and was letting its branches down. And suddenly the branches twined around her, and were two arms, and when she looked round, the tree was a handsome man, who embraced and kissed her heartily, and said, "You have delivered me from the power of the old woman, who is a wicked witch. She had changed me into a tree, and every day for two hours I was a white dove, and so long as she possessed the ring I could not regain my human form." Then his servants and his horses, who had likewise been changed into trees, were freed from the enchantment also, and stood beside him. And he led them forth to his kingdom, for he was a King's son, and they married, and lived happily.

The Juniper Tree

A long, long time ago, perhaps as much as two thousand years, there was a rich man, and he had a beautiful and pious wife, and they loved each other very much, and they had no children, though they wished greatly for some, and the wife prayed for one day and night. Now, in the courtyard in front of their house stood a juniper tree; and one day in winter the wife was standing beneath it, and paring an apple, and as she pared it she cut her finger, and the blood fell upon the snow.

"Ah," said the woman, sighing deeply, and looking down at the blood, "if only I could have a child as red as blood, and as white as snow!"

And as she said these words, her heart suddenly grew light, and she felt sure she should have her wish. So she went back to the house, and when a month had passed the snow was gone; in two months everything was green; in three months the flowers sprang out of the earth; in four months the trees were in full leaf, and the branches were thickly entwined; the little birds began to sing, so that the woods echoed, and the blossoms fell from the trees; when the fifth month had passed the wife stood under the juniper tree, and it smelt so sweet that her heart leaped within her, and she fell on her knees for joy; and when the sixth month had gone, the fruit was thick and fine, and she remained still; and the seventh month she gathered the berries and ate them eagerly, and was sick and sorrowful; and when the eighth month had passed she called to her husband, and said, weeping, "If I die, bury me under the juniper tree."

Then she was comforted and happy until the ninth month had passed, and then she bore a child as white as snow and as red as blood, and when she saw it her joy was so great that she died.

Her husband buried her under the juniper tree, and he wept sore; time passed, and he became less sad; and after he had grieved a little more he left off, and then he took another wife.

His second wife bore him a daughter, and his first wife's child was a son, as red as blood and as white as snow. Whenever the wife looked at her daughter she felt great love for her, but whenever she looked at the little boy, evil thoughts came into her heart, of how she could get all her husband's money for her daughter, and how the boy stood in the way; and so she took great hatred to him, and drove him from one corner to another, and gave him a buffet here and cuff there, so that the poor child was always in disgrace; when he came back after school hours there was no peace for him.

Once, when the wife went into the room upstairs, her little daughter followed her, and said, "Mother, give me an apple."

"Yes, my child," said the mother, and gave her a fine apple out of the chest, and the chest had a great heavy lid with a strong iron lock.

"Mother," said the little girl, "shall not my brother have one too?"

That was what the mother expected; and she said, "Yes, when he comes back from school."

And when she saw from the window that he was coming, an evil thought crossed her mind, and she snatched the apple, and took it from her little daughter, saying, "You shall not have it before your brother."

Then she threw the apple into the chest, and shut the lid. Then the little boy came in at the door, and she said to him in a kind tone, but with evil looks, "My son, will you have an apple?"

"Mother," said the boy, "how terrible you look! Yes, give me an apple!"

Then she spoke as kindly as before, holding up the cover of the chest, "Come here and take out one for yourself."

And as the boy was stooping over the open chest, crash went the lid down, so that his head flew off among the red apples. But then the woman felt great terror, and wondered how she could escape the blame. And she went to the chest of drawers in her bedroom and took a white handkerchief out of the nearest drawer, and fitting the head to the neck, she bound them with a handkerchief, so that nothing should be seen, and set him on a chair before the door with the apple in his hand.

Then came little Marjory into the kitchen to her mother, who was standing before the fire stirring a pot of hot water.

"Mother," said Marjory, "my brother is sitting before the door and he has an apple in his hand, and looks very pale; I asked him to give me the apple, but he did not answer me; it seems very strange." "Go again to him," said the mother, "and if he will not answer you, give him a box on the ear."

So Marjory went again and said, "Brother, give me the apple."

But as he took no notice, she gave him a box on the ear, and his head fell off, at which she was greatly terrified, and began to cry and scream, and ran to her mother, and said, "Oh mother! I have knocked my brother's head off!" and cried and screamed, and would not cease.

"Oh Marjory!" said her mother, "what have you done? But keep quiet, that no one may see there is anything the matter; it can't be helped now; we will put him out of the way safely."

When the father came home and sat down to table, he said, "Where is my son?" But the mother was filling a great dish full of black broth, and Marjory was crying bitterly, for she could not refrain. Then the father said again, "Where is my son?" "Oh," said the mother, "he is gone into the country to his great-uncle's to stay for a little while." "What should he go for?" said the father, "and without bidding me good-bye, too!" "Oh, he wanted to go so much, and he asked me to let him stay there six weeks; he will be well taken care of." "Dear me," said the father, "I am quite sad about it; it was not right of him to go without bidding me good-bye."

With that he began to eat, saying, "Marjory, what are you crying for? Your brother will come back some time."

After a while he said, "Well, wife, the food is very good; give me some more."

And the more he ate the more he wanted, until he had eaten it all up, and he threw the bones under the table. Then Marjory went to her chest of drawers, and took one of her best handkerchiefs from the bottom drawer, and picked up all the bones from under the table and tied them up in her handkerchief, and went out at the door crying bitterly. She laid them in the green grass under the juniper tree, and immediately her heart grew light again, and she wept no more.

Then the juniper tree began to wave to and fro, and the boughs drew together and then parted, just like a clapping of hands for joy; then a cloud rose from the tree, and in the midst of the cloud there burned a fire, and out of the fire a beautiful bird arose, and, singing most sweetly, soared high into the air; and when he had flown away, the juniper tree remained as it was before, but the handkerchief full of bones was gone. Marjory felt quite glad and light-hearted, just as if her brother were still alive. So she went back merrily into the house and had her dinner.

The bird, when it flew away, perched on the roof of a goldsmith's house, and began to sing,

> "It was my mother who murdered me;
> It was my father who ate of me;
> It was my sister Marjory
> Who all my bones in pieces found;
> Them in a handkerchief she bound,
> And laid them under the juniper tree.
> Kywitt, kywitt, kywitt, I cry,
> Oh what a beautiful bird am I!"

The goldsmith was sitting in his shop making a golden chain, and when he heard the bird, who was sitting on his roof and singing, he started up to go and look, and as he passed over his threshold he lost one of his slippers; and he went into the middle of the street with a slipper on one foot and only a sock on the other; with his apron on, and the gold chain in one hand and the pincers in the other; and so he stood in the sunshine looking up at the bird.

"Bird," said he, "how beautifully you sing; do sing that piece over again." "No," said the bird, "I do not sing for nothing twice; if you will give me that gold chain I will sing again." "Very well," said the goldsmith, "here is the gold chain; now do as you said."

Down came the bird and took the gold chain in his right claw, perched in front of the goldsmith, and sang,

> "It was my mother who murdered me;
> It was my father who ate of me;
> It was my sister Marjory
> Who all my bones in pieces found;
> Them in a handkerchief she bound,
> And laid them under the juniper tree.
> Kywitt, kywitt, kywitt, I cry,
> Oh what a beautiful bird am I!"

Then the bird flew to a shoemaker's, and perched on his roof, and sang,

> "It was my mother who murdered me;
> It was my father who ate of me;
> It was my sister Marjory
> Who all my bones in pieces found;
> Them in a handkerchief she bound,
> And laid them under the juniper tree.
> Kywitt, kywitt, kywitt, I cry,
> Oh what a beautiful bird am I!"

When the shoemaker heard, he ran out of his door in his shirt sleeves and looked up at the roof of his house, holding his hand to shade his eyes from the sun. "Bird," said he, "how beautifully you sing!" Then he called in at his door, "Wife, come out directly; here is a bird singing beautifully. Just listen."

Then he called his daughter, all his children, and acquaintance, both young men and maidens, and they came up the street and gazed on the bird, and saw how beautiful it was with red and green feathers, and round its throat was as it were gold, and its eyes twinkled in its head like stars.

"Bird," said the shoemaker, "do sing that piece over again." "No," said the bird, "I may not sing for nothing twice; you must give me something." "Wife," said the man, "go into the shop; on the top shelf stands a pair of red shoes; bring them here." So the wife went and brought the shoes. "Now bird," said the man, "sing us that piece again."

And the bird came down and took the shoes in his left claw, and flew up again to the roof, and sang,

> "It was my mother who murdered me;
> It was my father who ate of me;
> It was my sister Marjory
> Who all my bones in pieces found;
> Them in a handkerchief she bound,
> And laid them under the juniper tree.
> Kywitt, kywitt, kywitt, I cry,
> Oh what a beautiful bird am I!"

And when he had finished he flew away, with the chain in his right claw and the shoes in his left claw, and he flew till he reached a mill, and the mill went "clip-clap, clip-clap, clip-clap." And in the mill sat twenty miller's-men hewing a millstone—"hick-hack, hick-hack, hick-hack," while the mill was going "clip-clap, clip-clap, clip-clap." And the bird perched on a linden tree that stood in front of the mill, and sang,

> "It was my mother who murdered me";

Here one of the men looked up.

> "It was my father who ate of me";

Then two more looked up and listened.

> "It was my sister Marjory"

Here four more looked up.

> "Who all my bones in pieces found;
> Them in a handkerchief she bound,"

Now there were only eight left hewing.

> "And laid them under the juniper tree."

Now only five.

> "Kywitt, kywitt, kywitt, I cry,"

Now only one.

> "Oh what a beautiful bird am I!"

At length the last one left off, and he only heard the end.

"Bird," said he, "how beautifully you sing; let me hear it all. Sing that again!" "No," said the bird, "I may not sing it twice for nothing; if you will give me the millstone I will sing it again." "Indeed," said the man, "if it belonged to me alone you should have it." "All right," said the others, "if he sings again he shall have it."

Then the bird came down, and all the twenty millers heaved up the stone with poles—"yo! heave-ho! yo! heave-ho!" and the bird stuck his

head through the hole in the middle, and with the millstone round
his neck he flew up to the tree and sang,

> "It was my mother who murdered me;
> It was my father who ate of me;
> It was my sister Marjory
> Who all my bones in pieces found;
> Them in a handkerchief she bound,
> And laid them under the juniper tree.
> Kywitt, kywitt, kywitt, I cry,
> Oh what a beautiful bird am I!"

And when he had finished, he spread his wings, having in the right
claw the chain, and in the left claw the shoes, and round his neck the
millstone, and he flew away to his father's house.

In the parlor sat the father, the mother, and Marjory at the table;
the father said, "How light-hearted and cheerful I feel." "Nay," said the
mother, "I feel very low, just as if a great storm were coming."

But Marjory sat weeping; and the bird came flying, and perched
on the roof.

"Oh," said the father, "I feel so joyful, and the sun is shining so
bright; it is as if I were going to meet with an old friend." "Nay," said
the wife, "I am terrified, my teeth chatter, and there is fire in my
veins," and she tore open her dress to get air; and Marjory sat in a
corner and wept, with her plate before her, until it was quite full of
tears. Then the bird perched on the juniper tree, and sang,

> "It was my mother who murdered me";

And the mother stopped her ears and hid her eyes, and would neither see nor hear; nevertheless, the noise of a fearful storm was in her
ears, and in her eyes a quivering and burning as of lightning.

> "It was my father who ate of me";

"Oh, mother!" said the father, "there is a beautiful bird singing
so finely, and the sun shines, and everything smells as sweet as cin-
namon."

> "It was my sister Marjory"

Marjory hid her face in her lap and wept, and the father said, "I must go out to see the bird." "Oh do not go!" said the wife, "I feel as if the house were on fire."

But the man went out and looked at the bird.

> "Who all my bones in pieces found;
> Them in a handkerchief she bound,
> And laid them under the juniper tree.
> Kywitt, kywitt, kywitt, I cry,
> Oh what a beautiful bird am I!"

With that the bird let fall the gold chain upon his father's neck, and it fitted him exactly. So he went indoors and said, "Look what a beautiful chain the bird has given me!"

Then his wife was so terrified that she fell down on the floor, and her cap came off. Then the bird began again to sing,

> "It was my mother who murdered me";

"Oh," groaned the mother, "that I were a thousand fathoms under ground, so as not to be obliged to hear it."

> "It was my father who ate of me";

Then the woman lay as if she were dead.

> "It was my sister Marjory"

"Oh," said Marjory, "I will go out, too, and see if the bird will give me anything." And so she went.

> "Who all my bones in pieces found;
> Them in a handkerchief she bound,"

Then he threw the shoes down to her.

> "And laid them under the juniper tree.
> Kywitt, kywitt, kywitt, I cry,
> Oh what a beautiful bird am I!"

And poor Marjory all at once felt happy and joyful, and put on her red shoes, and danced and jumped for joy. "Oh dear," said she, "I felt so sad before I went outside, and now my heart is so light! He is a charming bird to have given me a pair of red shoes."

But the mother's hair stood on end, and looked like flame, and she said, "Even if the world is coming to an end, I must go out for a little relief."

Just as she came outside the door, crash went the millstone on her head, and crushed her flat. The father and daughter rushed out, and saw smoke and flames of fire rise up; but when that had gone by, there stood the little brother; and he took his father and Marjory by the hand, and they felt very happy and content, and went indoors, and sat at the table, and had their dinner.

The Three Little Men in the Wood

There was once a man, whose wife was dead, and a woman, whose husband was dead; the man had a daughter, and so had the woman. The girls were well acquainted with each other, and used to play together in the woman's house. One day the woman said to the man's daughter,

"Listen to me, tell your father that I will marry him, and then you shall have milk to wash in every morning and wine to drink, and my daughter shall have water to wash in and water to drink."

The girl went home and told her father what the woman had said. The man said, "What shall I do! Marriage is a joy, and also a torment."

At last, as he could come to no conclusion, he took off his boot, and said to his daughter, "Take this boot, it has a hole in the sole; go up with it into the loft, hang it on the big nail and pour water in it. If it holds water, I will once more take to me a wife; if it lets out the water, so will I not."

The girl did as she was told, but the water held the hole together, and the boot was full up to the top. So she went and told her father how it was. And he went up to see with his own eyes, and as there was no mistake about it, he went to the widow and courted her, and then they had the wedding.

The next morning, when the two girls awoke, there stood by the bedside of the man's daughter milk to wash in and wine to drink, and by the bedside of the woman's daughter there stood water to wash in and water to drink.

On the second morning there stood water to wash in and water to drink for both of them alike. On the third morning there stood water to wash in and water to drink for the man's daughter, and milk to wash in and wine to drink for the woman's daughter; and so it remained ever after. The woman hated her step-daughter, and never knew how to treat her badly enough from one day to another. And she was jealous because her step-daughter was pleasant and pretty, and her real daughter was ugly and hateful.

Once in winter, when it was freezing hard, and snow lay deep on hill and valley, the woman made a frock out of paper, called her step-daughter, and said, "Here, put on this frock, go out into the wood and fetch me a basket of strawberries; I have a great wish for some."

"Oh dear," said the girl, "there are no strawberries to be found in winter; the ground is frozen, and the snow covers everything. And why should I go in the paper frock? It is so cold out of doors that one's breath is frozen; the wind will blow through it, and the thorns will tear it off my back!"

"How dare you contradict me!" cried the step-mother, "be off, and don't let me see you again till you bring me a basket of strawberries." Then she gave her a little piece of hard bread, and said, "That will do for you to eat during the day," and she thought to herself, "She is sure to be frozen or starved to death out of doors, and I shall never set eyes on her again."

So the girl went obediently, put on the paper frock, and started out with the basket. The snow was lying everywhere, far and wide, and there was not a blade of green to be seen. When she entered the wood she saw a little house with three little men peeping out of it. She wished them good-day, and knocked modestly at the door. They called her in, and she came into the room and sat down by the side of the oven to warm herself and eat her breakfast.

The little men said, "Give us some of it." "Willingly," answered she, breaking her little piece of bread in two, and giving them half. They then said, "What are you doing here in the wood this winter time in your little thin frock?" "Oh," answered she, "I have to get a basket of strawberries, and I must not go home without them."

When she had eaten her bread they gave her a broom, and told her to go and sweep the snow away from the back door. When she had gone outside to do it the little men talked among themselves about what they should do for her, as she was so good and pretty, and had shared her bread with them. Then the first one said, "She shall grow prettier every day." The second said, "Each time she speaks a piece of gold shall fall from her mouth." The third said, "A king shall come and take her for his wife."

In the meanwhile the girl was doing as the little men had told her, and had cleared the snow from the back of the little house, and what do you suppose she found?—fine ripe strawberries, showing dark red against the snow! Then she joyfully filled her little basket full, thanked the little men, shook hands with them all, and ran home in haste to bring her step-mother the thing she longed for. As she went in and said, "Good evening," a piece of gold fell from her mouth at once. Then she related all that had happened to her in the wood, and at each word that she spoke gold pieces fell out of her mouth, so that soon they were scattered all over the room.

"Just look at her pride and conceit!" cried the step-sister, "throwing money about in this way!" but in her heart she was jealous because of it, and wanted to go too into the wood to fetch strawberries. But the mother said, "No, my dear little daughter, it is too cold, you will be frozen to death."

But she left her no peace, so at last the mother gave in, got her a splendid fur coat to put on, and gave her bread and butter and cakes to eat on the way.

The girl went into the wood and walked straight up to the little house. The three little men peeped out again, but she gave them no greeting, and without looking round or taking any notice of them she came stumping into the room, sat herself down by the oven, and began to eat her bread and butter and cakes.

"Give us some of that," cried the little men, but she answered, "I've not enough for myself; how can I give away any?"

Now when she had done with her eating, they said, "Here is a broom, go and sweep all clean by the back door." "Oh, go and do it yourselves," answered she; "I am not your housemaid."

But when she saw that they were not going to give her anything, she went out to the door. Then the three little men said among themselves, "What shall we do to her, because she is so unpleasant, and has such a wicked jealous heart, grudging everybody everything?" The first said, "She shall grow uglier every day." The second said, "Each time she speaks a toad shall jump out of her mouth at every word." The third said, "She shall die a miserable death."

The girl was looking outside for strawberries, but as she found none, she went sulkily home. And directly she opened her mouth to tell her mother what had happened to her in the wood a toad sprang out of her mouth at each word, so that every one who came near her was quite disgusted.

The step-mother became more and more set against the man's daughter, whose beauty increased day by day, and her only thought was how to do her some injury. So at last she took a kettle, set it on the fire, and scalded some yarn in it. When it was ready she hung it over the poor girl's shoulder, and gave her an axe, and she was to go to the frozen river and break a hole in the ice, and there to rinse the yarn. She obeyed, and went and hewed a hole in the ice, and as she was about it there came by a splendid coach, in which the King sat. The coach stood still, and the King said, "My child, who art thou, and what art thou doing there?" She answered, "I am a poor girl, and am rinsing yarn."

Then the King felt pity for her, and as he saw that she was very beautiful, he said, "Will you go with me?" "Oh yes, with all my heart," answered she; and she felt very glad to be out of the way of her mother and sister.

So she stepped into the coach and went off with the King; and when they reached his castle the wedding was celebrated with great splendor, as the little men in the wood had foretold.

At the end of a year the young Queen had a son; and as the stepmother had heard of her great good fortune she came with her daughter to the castle, as if merely to pay the King and Queen a visit. One day, when the King had gone out, and when nobody was about, the bad woman took the Queen by the head, and her daughter took her by the heels, and dragged her out of bed, and threw her out of the window into a stream that flowed beneath it. Then the old woman put her ugly daughter in the bed, and covered her up to her chin. When the King came back, and wanted to talk to his wife a little, the old woman cried, "Stop, stop! she is sleeping nicely; she must be kept quiet today."

The King dreamt of nothing wrong, and came again the next morning; and as he spoke to his wife, and she answered him, there jumped each time out of her mouth a toad instead of the piece of gold as heretofore. Then he asked why that should be, and the old woman said it was because of her great weakness, and that it would pass away.

But in the night, the boy who slept in the kitchen saw how something in the likeness of a duck swam up the gutter, and said,

> "My King, what mak'st thou?
> Sleepest thou, or wak'st thou?"

But there was no answer. Then it said,

"What cheer my two guests keep they?"

So the kitchen-boy answered,

"In bed all soundly sleep they."

It asked again,

"And my little baby, how does *he*?"

And he answered,

"He sleeps in his cradle quietly."

Then the duck took the shape of the Queen, and went to the child, and gave him to drink, smoothed his little bed, covered him up again, and then, in the likeness of a duck, swam back down the gutter. In this way she came two nights, and on the third she said to the kitchen-boy, "Go and tell the King to brandish his sword three times over me on the threshold!"

Then the kitchen-boy ran and told the King, and he came with his sword and brandished it three times over the duck, and at the third time his wife stood before him living, and hearty, and sound, as she had been before.

The King was greatly rejoiced, but he hid the Queen in a chamber until the Sunday came when the child was to be baptized. And after the baptism he said, "What does that person deserve who drags another out of bed and throws him in the water?" And the old woman answered, "No better than to be put into a cask with iron nails in it, and to be rolled in it down the hill into the water."

Then said the King, "You have spoken your own sentence"; and he ordered a cask to be fetched, and the old woman and her daughter were put into it, and the top hammered down, and the cask was rolled down the hill into the river.

Brother and Sister

A brother took his sister's hand and said to her, "Since our mother died we have had no good days; our step-mother beats us every day, and if we go near her she kicks us away; we have nothing to eat but hard crusts of bread left over; the dog under the table fares better; he gets a good piece every now and then. If our mother only knew, how she would pity us! Come, let us go together out into the wide world!"

So they went, and journeyed the whole day through fields and meadows and stony places, and if it rained the sister said, "The skies and we are weeping together."

In the evening they came to a great wood, and they were so weary with hunger and their long journey, that they climbed up into a high tree and fell asleep.

The next morning, when they awoke, the sun was high in heaven, and shone brightly through the leaves. Then said the brother, "Sister, I am thirsty; if I only knew where to find a brook, that I might go and drink! I almost think that I hear one rushing." So the brother got down and led his sister by the hand, and they went to seek the brook. But their wicked step-mother was a witch, and had known quite well that the two children had run away, and had sneaked after them, as only witches can, and had laid a spell on all the brooks in the forest. So when they found a little stream flowing smoothly over its pebbles, the brother was going to drink of it; but the sister heard how it said in its rushing,

> "He a tiger will be who drinks of me,
> Who drinks of me a tiger will be!"

Then the sister cried, "Pray, dear brother, do not drink, or you will become a wild beast, and will tear me in pieces."

So the brother refrained from drinking, though his thirst was great, and he said he would wait till he came to the next brook. When they came to a second brook the sister heard it say,

"He a wolf will be who drinks of me,
Who drinks of me a wolf will be!"

Then the sister cried, "Pray, dear brother, do not drink, or you will be turned into a wolf, and will eat me up!"

So the brother refrained from drinking, and said, "I will wait until we come to the next brook, and then I must drink, whatever you say; my thirst is so great."

And when they came to the third brook the sister heard how in its rushing it said,

"He a fawn will be who drinks of me,
Who drinks of me a fawn will be!"

Then the sister said, "O my brother, I pray drink not, or you will be turned into a fawn, and run away far from me."

But he had already kneeled by the side of the brook and stooped and drunk of the water, and as the first drops passed his lips he became a fawn. And the sister wept over her poor lost brother, and the fawn wept also, and stayed sadly beside her. At last the maiden said, "Be comforted, dear fawn, indeed I will never leave you."

Then she untied her golden girdle and bound it round the fawn's neck, and went and gathered rushes to make a soft cord, which she fastened to him; and then she led him on, and they went deeper into the forest. And when they had gone a long long way, they came at last to a little house, and the maiden looked inside, and as it was empty she thought, "We might as well live here."

And she fetched leaves and moss to make a soft bed for the fawn, and every morning she went out and gathered roots and berries and nuts for herself, and fresh grass for the fawn, who ate out of her hand with joy, frolicking round her. At night, when the sister was tired, and had said her prayers, she laid her head on the fawn's back, which served her for a pillow, and softly fell asleep. And if only the brother could have got back his own shape again, it would have been a charming life. So they lived a long while in the wilderness alone.

Now it happened that the King of that country held a great hunt in the forest. The blowing of the horns, the barking of the dogs, and the lusty shouts of the huntsmen sounded through the wood, and the fawn heard them and was eager to be among them.

"Oh," said he to his sister, "do let me go to the hunt; I cannot stay behind any longer," and begged so long that at last she consented.

"But mind," said she to him, "come back to me at night. I must lock my door against the wild hunters, so, in order that I may know you, you must knock and say, 'Little sister, let me in,' and unless I hear that I shall not unlock the door."

Then the fawn sprang out, and felt glad and merry in the open air. The King and his huntsmen saw the beautiful animal, and began at once to pursue him, but they could not come within reach of him, for when they thought they were certain of him he sprang away over the bushes and disappeared. As soon as it was dark he went back to the little house, knocked at the door, and said, "Little sister, let me in."

Then the door was opened to him, and he went in, and rested the whole night long on his soft bed. The next morning the hunt began anew, and when the fawn heard the hunting-horns and the tally-ho of the huntsmen he could rest no longer, and said, "Little sister, let me out, I must go." The sister opened the door and said, "Now, mind you must come back at night and say the same words."

When the King and his hunters saw the fawn with the golden collar again, they chased him closely, but he was too nimble and swift for them. This lasted the whole day, and at last the hunters surrounded him, and one of them wounded his foot a little, so that he was obliged to limp and to go slowly. Then a hunter slipped after him to the little house, and heard how he called out, "Little sister, let me in," and saw the door open and shut again after him directly. The hunter noticed all this carefully, went to the King, and told him all he had seen and heard. Then said the King, "Tomorrow we will hunt again."

But the sister was very terrified when she saw that her fawn was wounded. She washed his foot, laid cooling leaves round it, and said, "Lie down on your bed, dear fawn, and rest, that you may be soon well." The wound was very slight, so that the fawn felt nothing of it the next morning. And when he heard the noise of the hunting outside, he said, "I cannot stay in, I must go after them; I shall not be taken easily again!" The sister began to weep, and said, "I know you will be killed, and I left alone here in the forest, and forsaken of everybody. I cannot let you go!"

"Then I shall die here with longing," answered the fawn; "when I hear the sound of the horn I feel as if I should leap out of my skin."

Then the sister, seeing there was no help for it, unlocked the door with a heavy heart, and the fawn bounded away into the forest, well and merry. When the King saw him, he said to his hunters, "Now, follow him up all day long till the night comes, and see that you do him no hurt."

So as soon as the sun had gone down, the King said to the huntsmen: "Now, come and show me the little house in the wood." And when he got to the door he knocked at it, and cried, "Little sister, let me in!" Then the door opened, and the King went in, and there stood a maiden more beautiful than any he had seen before.

The maiden shrieked out when she saw, instead of the fawn, a man standing there with a gold crown on his head. But the King looked kindly on her, took her by the hand, and said, "Will you go with me to my castle, and be my dear wife?" "Oh yes," answered the maiden, "but the fawn must come too. I could not leave him." And the King said, "He shall remain with you as long as you live, and shall lack nothing." Then the fawn came bounding in, and the sister tied the cord of rushes to him, and led him by her own hand out of the little house.

The King put the beautiful maiden on his horse, and carried her to his castle, where the wedding was held with great pomp; so she became lady Queen, and they lived together happily for a long while; the fawn was well tended and cherished, and he gamboled about the castle garden.

Now the wicked step-mother, whose fault it was that the children were driven out into the world, never dreamed but that the sister had been eaten up by wild beasts in the forest, and that the brother, in the likeness of a fawn, had been slain by the hunters. But when she heard that they were so happy, and that things had gone so well with them, jealousy and envy arose in her heart, and left her no peace, and her chief thought was how to bring misfortune upon them.

Her own daughter, who was as ugly as sin, and had only one eye, complained to her, and said, "I never had the chance of being a Queen." "Never mind," said the old woman, to satisfy her; "when the time comes, I shall be at hand."

After a while the Queen brought a beautiful baby boy into the world, and that day the King was out hunting. The old witch took the shape of the bed-chamber woman, and went into the room where the Queen lay, and said to her, "Come, the bath is ready; it will give you refreshment and new strength. Quick, or it will be cold."

Her daughter was within call, so they carried the sick Queen into the bath-room, and left her there. And in the bath-room they had made a great fire, so as to suffocate the beautiful young Queen.

When that was managed, the old woman took her daughter, put a cap on her, and laid her in the bed in the Queen's place, gave her also the Queen's form and countenance, only she could not restore the lost eye. So, in order that the King might not remark it, she had to lie on the side where there was no eye.

In the evening, when the King came home and heard that a little son was born to him, he rejoiced with all his heart, and was going at once to his dear wife's bedside to see how she did. Then the old woman cried hastily, "For your life, do not draw back the curtains, to let in the light upon her; she must be kept quiet." So the King went away, and never knew that a false Queen was lying in the bed.

Now, when it was midnight, and every one was asleep, the nurse, who was sitting by the cradle in the nursery and watching there alone, saw the door open, and the true Queen come in. She took the child out of the cradle, laid it in her bosom, and fed it. Then she shook out its little pillow, put the child back again, and covered it with the coverlet. She did not forget the fawn either; she went to him where he lay in the corner, and stroked his back tenderly. Then she went in perfect silence out at the door, and the nurse next morning asked the watchmen if any one had entered the castle during the night, but they said they had seen no one. And the Queen came many nights, and never said a word; the nurse saw her always, but she did not dare speak of it to any one.

After some time had gone by in this manner, the Queen seemed to find voice, and said one night,

> "My child my fawn twice more I come to see,
> Twice more I come and then the end must be."

The nurse said nothing, but as soon as the Queen had disappeared she went to the King and told him all. The King said, "Ah, heaven! what do I hear! I will myself watch by the child tomorrow night."

So at evening he went into the nursery, and at midnight the Queen appeared, and said,

> "My child my fawn once more I come to see,
> Once more I come, and then the end must be."

And she tended the child, as she was accustomed to do, before she vanished. The King dared not speak to her, but he watched again the following night, and heard her say,

> "My child my fawn this once I come to see,
> This once I come, and now the end must be."

Then the King could contain himself no longer, but rushed towards her, saying, "You are no other than my dear wife!" Then she answered, "Yes, I am your dear wife," and in that moment, by the grace of heaven, her life returned to her, and she was once more well and strong. Then she told the King the snare that the wicked witch and her daughter had laid for her.

The King had them both brought to judgment, and sentence was passed upon them. The daughter was sent away into the woods, where she was devoured by the wild beasts, and the witch was burned, and ended miserably. As soon as her body was in ashes the spell was removed from the fawn, and he took human shape again. Then the sister and brother lived happily together until the end.

The Two Brothers

There were once two brothers; one was rich, the other poor. The rich brother was a goldsmith, and had a wicked heart. The poor brother supported himself by making brooms, and was good and honest. He had two children, twin brothers, who resembled each other as closely as one drop of water resembles another. The two boys went sometimes to the house of their rich uncle to get the pieces that were left from the table, for they were often very hungry.

It happened one day that while their father was in the wood, gathering rushes for his brooms, he saw a bird whose plumage shone like gold—he had never seen in his life any bird like it. He picked up a stone and threw it at the bird, hoping to be lucky enough to secure it; but the stone only knocked off a golden feather, and the bird flew away.

The man took the feather and brought it to his brother, who, when he saw it, exclaimed, "That is real gold!" and gave him a great deal of money for it. Another day, as the man climbed up a beech tree, hoping to find the golden bird's nest, the same bird flew over his head, and on searching further he found a nest, and in it lay two golden eggs. He took the eggs home and showed them to his brother, who said again, "They are real gold," and gave him what they were worth. At last the goldsmith said, "You may as well get me the bird, if you can."

So the poor brother went again to the wood, and after a time, seeing the bird perched on a tree, he knocked it down with a stone and brought it to his brother, who gave him a large heap of money for it. "Now," thought he, "I can support myself for the future," and went home to his house full of joy.

The goldsmith, however, who was clever and cunning, knew well the real value of the bird. So he called his wife, and said, "Roast the gold bird for me, and be careful that no one comes in, as I wish to eat it quite alone."

The bird was, indeed, not a common bird; it had a wonderful power even when dead. For any person who ate the heart and liver would every morning find under his pillow a piece of gold. The goldsmith's wife prepared the bird, stuck it on the spit, and left it to roast.

Now, it happened that while it was roasting, and the mistress absent from the kitchen about other household work, the two children of the broom-binder came in and stood for a few moments watching the spit as it turned round. Presently two little pieces fell from the bird into the dripping-pan underneath. One of them said, "I think we may have those two little pieces; no one will ever miss them, and I am so hungry." So the children each took a piece and ate it up.

In a few moments the goldsmith's wife came in and saw that they had been eating something, and said, "What have you been eating?" "Only two little pieces that fell from the bird," they replied.

"Oh!" exclaimed the wife in a great fright, "they must have been the heart and liver of the bird!" and then, that her husband might not miss them, for she was afraid of his anger, she quickly killed a chicken, took out the heart and liver, and laid them on the golden bird.

As soon as it was ready she carried it in to the goldsmith, who ate it all up, without leaving her a morsel. The next morning, however, when he felt under his pillow, expecting to find the gold-pieces, nothing was there.

The two children, however, who knew nothing of the good fortune which had befallen them, never thought of searching under their pillow. But the next morning, as they got out of bed, something fell on the ground and tinkled, and when they stooped to pick it up, there were two pieces of gold. They carried them at once to their father, who wondered very much, and said, "What can this mean?"

As, however, there were two more pieces the next morning, and again each day, the father went to his brother and told him of the wonderful circumstances. The goldsmith, as he listened, knew well that these gold-pieces must be the result of the children having eaten the heart and liver of the golden bird, and therefore that he had been deceived. He determined to be revenged, and though hard-hearted and jealous, he managed to conceal the real truth from his brother, and said to him, "Your children are in league with the Evil One; do not touch the gold, and on no account allow your children to remain in your house any longer, for the Evil One has power over them, and could bring ruin upon you through them."

The father feared this power, and therefore, sad as it was to him, he led the twins out into the forest and left them there with a heavy heart.

When they found themselves alone the two children ran here and there in the wood to try and discover the way home, but they wandered back always to the same place. At last they met a hunter, who said to them, "Whose children are you?"

"We are a poor broom-binder's children," they replied, "and our father will not keep us any longer in the house because every morning there is a piece of gold found under our pillows."

"Ah," exclaimed the hunter, "that is not bad! Well, if you are honest, and have told me the truth, I will take you home and be a father to you." In fact, the children pleased the good man, and as he had no children of his own, he gladly took them home with him.

While they were with him he taught them to hunt in the forest, and the gold-pieces which they found every morning under their pillows they gave to him; so for the future he had nothing to fear about poverty.

As soon as the twins were grown up their foster-father took them one day into the wood, and said, "Today you are going to make your first trial at shooting, for I want you to be free if you like, and to be hunters for yourselves."

Then they went with him to a suitable point, and waited a long time, but no game appeared. Presently the hunter saw flying over his head a flock of wild geese, in the form of a triangle, so he said, "Aim quickly at each corner and fire." They did so, and their first proof-shot was successful.

Soon after another flock appeared in the form of a figure 2. "Now," he exclaimed, "shoot again at each corner and bring them down!" This proof-shot was also successful, and the hunter directly said, "Now I pronounce you free; you are quite accomplished sportsmen."

Then the two brothers went away into the wood together, to hold counsel with each other, and at last came to an agreement about what they wished to do.

In the evening, when they sat down to supper, one of them said to their foster-father, "We will not remain to supper, or eat one bit, till you have granted us our request." "And what is your request?" he asked. "You have taught us to hunt, and to earn our living," they replied, "and we want to go out in the world and seek our fortune. Will you give us permission to do so?"

The good old man replied joyfully, "You speak like brave hunters; what you desire is my own wish. Go when you will, you will be sure to succeed." Then they ate and drank together joyfully.

When the appointed day came the hunter presented each of them with a new rifle and a dog, and allowed them to take as much as they would from his store of the gold-pieces. He accompanied them for some distance on the way, and before saying farewell he gave them each a white penknife, and said, "If at any time you should get separated from each other, the knife must be placed crossways in a tree, one side of the blade turning east, the other west, pointing out the road which each should take. If one should die the blade will rust on one side; but as long as he lives it will remain bright."

After saying this he wished the brothers farewell, and they started on their way.

After traveling for some time they came to an immense forest, so large that it was impossible to cross it in one day. They stayed there all night, and ate what they had in their game-bags; but for two days they walked on through the forest without finding themselves any nearer the end.

By this time they had nothing left to eat, so one said to the other, "We must shoot something, for this hunger is not to be endured." So he loaded his gun, and looked about him. Presently an old hare came running by; but as he raised his rifle the hare cried,

> "Dearest hunters, let me live;
> I will to you my young ones give."

Then she sprang up into the bushes, and brought out two young ones, and laid them before the hunters. The little animals were so full of tricks and played about so prettily that the hunters had not the heart to kill them; they kept them, therefore, alive, and the little animals soon learned to follow them about like dogs.

By and by a fox appeared, and they were about to shoot him, but he cried also,

> "Dearest hunters, let me live,
> And I will you my young ones give."

Then he brought out two little foxes, but the hunters could not kill them, so they gave them to the hares as companions, and the little creatures followed the hunters wherever they went.

Not long after a wolf stepped before them out of the thicket, and one of the brothers instantly leveled his gun at him, but the wolf cried out,

> "Dear, kind hunters, let me live;
> I will to you my young ones give."

The hunters took the young wolves and treated them as they had done the other animals, and they followed them also.

Presently a bear came by, and they quite intended to kill him, but he also cried out,

> "Dear, kind hunters, let me live,
> And I will you my young ones give."

The two young bears were placed with the others, of whom there were already eight.

At last who should come by but a lion, shaking his mane. The hunters were not at all alarmed; they only pointed their guns at him. But the lion cried out in the same manner,

> "Dear, kind hunters, let me live,
> And I will you two young ones give."

So he fetched two of his cubs, and the hunters placed them with the rest. They had now two lions, two bears, two wolves, two foxes, and two hares, who traveled with them and served them. Yet, after all, their hunger was not appeased.

So one of them said to the fox, "Here, you little sneak, who are so clever and sly, go find us something to eat."

Then the fox answered, "Not far from here lies a town where we have many times fetched away chickens. I will show you the way."

So the fox showed them the way to the village, where they bought some provisions for themselves and food for the animals, and went on further.

The fox, however, knew quite well the best spots in that part of the country, and where to find the hen-houses; and he could, above all, direct the hunters which road to take.

After traveling for a time in this way they could find no suitable place for them all to remain together, so one said to the other, "The only thing for us to do is to separate"; and to this the other agreed. Then they divided the animals so that each had one lion, one bear, one wolf, one fox, and one hare. When the time came to say farewell they promised to live in brotherly love till death, stuck the knives that their foster-father had given them in a tree, and then one turned to the east, and the other to the west.

The youngest, whose steps we will follow first, soon arrived at a large town, in which the houses were all covered with black crape. He went to an inn, and asked the landlord if he could give shelter to his animals. The landlord pointed out a stable for them, and their master led them in and shut the door.

But in the wall of the stable was a hole, and the hare slipped through easily and fetched a cabbage for herself. The fox followed, and came back with a hen; and as soon as he had eaten it he went for the cock also. The wolf, the bear, and the lion, however, were too large to get through the hole. Then the landlord had a cow killed and brought in for them, or they would have starved.

The hunter was just going out to see if his animals were being cared for when he asked the landlord why the houses were so hung with mourning crape. "Because," he replied, "tomorrow morning our King's daughter will die." "Is she seriously ill, then?" asked the hunter. "No," he answered; "she is in excellent health; still, she must die." "What is the cause of this?" said the young man.

Then the landlord explained. "Outside the town," he said, "is a high mountain in which dwells a dragon, who every year demands a young maiden to be given up to him, otherwise he will destroy the whole country. He has already devoured all the young maidens in the town, and there are none remaining but the King's daughter. Not even for her is any favor shown, and tomorrow she must be delivered up to him."

"Why do you not kill the dragon?" exclaimed the young hunter.

"Ah!" replied the landlord, "many young knights have sought to do so, and lost their lives in the attempt. The King has even promised his daughter in marriage to whoever will destroy the dragon, and also that he shall be heir to his throne."

The hunter made no reply to this; but the next morning he rose early, and taking his animals with him climbed up the dragon's mountain.

There stood near the top a little church, and on the altar inside were three full goblets, bearing this inscription: "Whoever drinks of these goblets will be the strongest man upon earth, and will discover the sword which lies buried before the threshold of this door."

The hunter did not drink; he first went out and sought for the sword in the ground, but he could not find the place. Then he returned and drank up the contents of the goblets. How strong it made him feel! And how quickly he found the sword, which, heavy as it was, he could wield easily!

Meanwhile the hour came when the young maiden was to be given up to the dragon, and she came out accompanied by the King, the marshal, and the courtiers.

They saw from the distance the hunter on the mountain, and the Princess, thinking it was the dragon waiting for her, would not go on. At last she remembered that to save the town from being lost, she must make this painful sacrifice, and therefore wished her father farewell. The King and the court returned home full of great sorrow. The King's marshal, however, was to remain, and see from a distance all that took place.

When the King's daughter reached the top of the mountain, she found, instead of the dragon, a handsome young hunter, who spoke to her comforting words, and, telling her he had come to rescue her, led her into the church, and locked her in.

Before long, with a rushing noise and a roar, the seven-headed dragon made his appearance. As soon as he caught sight of the hunter he wondered to himself, and said at last, "What business have you here on this mountain?" "My business is a combat with you!" replied the hunter.

"Many knights and nobles have tried that, and lost their lives," replied the dragon; "with you I shall make short work!"

And he breathed out fire as he spoke from his seven throats.

The flames set fire to the dry grass, and the hunter would have been stifled with heat and smoke had not his faithful animals run forward and stamped out the fire. Then in a rage the dragon drew near, but the hunter was too quick for him; swinging his sword on high, it whizzed through the air and, falling on the dragon, cut off three of his heads.

Then was the monster furious; he raised himself on his hind legs, spat fiery flames on the hunter, and tried to overthrow him. But the young man again swung his sword, and as the dragon approached, he with one blow cut off three more of his heads. The monster, mad with rage, sank on the ground, still trying to get at the hunter; but the young man, exerting his remaining strength, had no difficulty in cutting off his seventh head, and his tail; and then, finding he could resist no more, he called to his animals to come and tear the dragon in pieces.

As soon as the combat was ended the hunter unlocked the church door, and found the King's daughter lying on the ground; for during the combat all sense and life had left her, from fear and terror.

He raised her up, and as she came to herself and opened her eyes he showed her the dragon torn in pieces, and told her that she was released from all danger.

Oh, how joyful she felt when she saw and heard what he had done! She said, "Now you will be my dear husband, for my father has himself promised me in marriage to whoever should kill the dragon."

Then she took off her coral necklace of five strings, and divided it among the animals as a reward; the lion's share being in addition the gold clasp. Her pocket handkerchief, which bore her name, she presented to the hunter, who went out, and cut the seven tongues out of the dragon's heads, which he wrapped up carefully in the handkerchief.

After all the fighting, and the fire and smoke, the hunter felt so faint and tired that he said to the maiden, "I think a little rest would do us both good after all the fight and the struggles with the dragon that I have had, and your terror and alarm. Shall we sleep for a little while before I take you home safely to your father's house?" "Yes," she replied, "I can sleep peacefully now."

So she laid herself down, and as soon as she slept he said to the lion, "You must lie near and watch that no one comes to harm us." Then he threw himself on the ground, quite worn out, and was soon fast asleep.

The lion laid himself down at a little distance to watch; but he was also tired and overcome with the combat, so he called to the bear, and said, "Lie down near me; I must have a little rest, and if any one comes, wake me up."

Then the bear lay down; but he was also very tired, so he cried to the wolf, "Just lie down by me; I must have a little sleep, and if anything happens, wake me up."

The wolf complied; but as he was also tired, he called to the fox, and said, "Lie down near me; I must have a little sleep, and if anything comes, wake me up."

Then the fox came and laid himself down by the wolf; but he too was tired, and called out to the hare, "Lie down near me; I must sleep a little, and, whatever comes, wake me up."

The hare seated herself near the fox; but the poor little hare was very tired, and although she had no one to ask to watch and call her, she also went fast asleep. And now the King's daughter, the hunter, the bear, the lion, the wolf, the fox, and the hare were all in a deep sleep, while danger was at hand.

The marshal, from the distance, had tried to see what was going on, and being surprised that the dragon had not yet flown away with the King's daughter, and that all was quiet on the mountain, took courage, and ventured to climb up to the top. There he saw the mangled and headless body of the dragon, and at a little distance the King's daughter, the hunter, and all the animals sunk in a deep sleep. He knew in a moment that the stranger hunter had killed the dragon, and, being wicked and envious, he drew his sword and cut off the hunter's head. Then he seized the sleeping maiden by the arm, and carried her away from the mountain.

She woke and screamed; but the marshal said, "You are in my power, and therefore you shall say that I have killed the dragon!" "I cannot say so," she replied, "for I saw the hunter kill him, and the animals tear him in pieces."

Then he drew his sword, and threatened to kill her if she did not obey him; so that to save her life she was forced to promise to say all he wished.

Thereupon he took her to the King, who knew not how to contain himself for joy at finding his dear child still alive, and that she had been saved from the monster's power.

Then the marshal said, "I have killed the dragon and freed the King's daughter, therefore I demand her for my wife, according to the King's promise."

"Is this all true?" asked the King of his daughter.

"Ah, yes," she replied, "I suppose it is true; but I shall refuse to allow the marriage to take place for one year and a day. For," thought she, "in that time I may hear something of my dear hunter."

All this while on the dragon's mountain the animals lay sleeping near their dead master. At last a large bumble-bee settled on the hare's nose, but she only whisked it off with her paw, and slept again. The bee came a second time, but the hare again shook him off, and slept as soundly as before. Then came the bumble-bee a third time, and stung the hare in the nose; thereupon she woke. As soon as she was quite aroused she woke the fox; the fox, the wolf; the wolf, the bear; and the bear, the lion.

But when the lion roused himself, and saw that the maiden was gone and his master dead, he gave a terrible roar, and cried, "Whose doing is this? Bear, why did you not wake me?" Then said the bear to the wolf, "Wolf, why did you not wake me?" "Fox," cried the wolf, "why did you not wake me?" "Hare," said the fox, "and why did you not wake me?"

The poor hare had no one to ask why he did not wake her, and she knew she must bear all the blame. Indeed, they were all ready to tear her to pieces, but she cried, "Don't destroy my life! I will restore our master. I know a mountain on which grows a root that will cure every wound and every disease if it is placed in the person's mouth; but the mountain on which it grows lies two hundred miles from here."

"Then," said the lion, "we will give you twenty-four hours, but not longer, to find this root and bring it to us."

Away sprang the hare very fast, and in twenty-four hours she returned with the root. As soon as they saw her the lion quickly placed the head of the hunter on the neck; and the hare, when she had joined the wounded parts together, put the root into the mouth, and in a few moments the heart began to beat, and life came back to the hunter.

On awaking he was terribly alarmed to find that the maiden had disappeared. "She must have gone away while I slept," he said, "and is lost to me forever!"

These sad thoughts so occupied him that he did not notice anything wrong about his head, but in truth the lion had placed it on in such a hurry that the face was turned the wrong way. He first noticed it when they brought him something to eat, and then he found that his face looked backward. He was so astonished that he could not imagine what had happened, and asked his animals the cause. Then the lion confessed that they had all slept in consequence of being so tired, and that when they at last awoke they found the Princess gone, and himself lying dead, with his head cut off. The lion told him also that the hare had fetched the healing root, but in their haste they had placed the head on the wrong way. This mistake, they said, could be easily rectified. So they took the hunter's head off again, turned it round, placed it on properly, and the hare stuck the parts together with the wonderful root. After this the hunter went away again to travel about the world, feeling very sorrowful, and he left his animals to be taken care of by the people of the town.

It so happened that at the end of a year he came back again to the same town where he had freed the King's daughter and killed the dragon. This time, instead of black crape the houses were hung with scarlet cloth. "What does it mean?" he said to the landlord. "Last year when I came your houses were all hung with black crape, and now it is scarlet cloth."

"Oh," replied the landlord, "last year we were expecting our King's daughter to be given up to the dragon, but the marshal fought with him and killed him, and tomorrow his marriage with the King's daughter will take place; that is the cause of our town being so gay and bright—it is joy now instead of sorrow."

The next day, when the marriage was to be celebrated, the hunter said, "Landlord, do you believe that I shall eat bread from the King's table here with any one who will join me?"

"I will lay a hundred gold-pieces," replied the landlord, "that you will do nothing of the kind."

The hunter took the bet, and taking out his purse placed the gold-pieces aside for payment if he should lose.

Then he called the hare, and said to her, "Go quickly to the castle, dear Springer, and bring me some of the bread which the King eats."

Now, the hare was such an insignificant little thing that no one ever thought of ordering a conveyance for her, so she was obliged to go on foot. "Oh," thought she, "when I am running through the streets, suppose the cruel hound should see me." Just as she got near the castle she looked behind her, and there truly was a hound ready to seize her. But she gave a start forward, and before the sentinel was aware rushed into the sentry-box. The dog followed, and wanted to bring her out, but the soldier stood in the doorway and would not let him pass, and when the dog tried to get in he struck him with his staff, and sent him away howling.

As soon as the hare saw that the coast was clear she rushed out of the sentry-box and ran to the castle, and finding the door of the room where the Princess was sitting open, she darted in and hid under her chair. Presently the Princess felt something scratching her foot, and thinking it was the dog, she said, "Be quiet, Sultan; go away!" The hare scratched again at her foot, but she still thought it was the dog, and cried, "Will you go away, Sultan?" But the hare did not allow herself to be sent away, so she scratched the foot a third time. Then the Princess looked down and recognized the hare by her necklace. She took the creature at once in her arms, carried her to her own room, and said, "Dear little hare, what do you want?"

The hare replied instantly, "My master, who killed the dragon, is here, and he has sent me to ask for some of the bread that the King eats."

Then was the King's daughter full of joy; she sent for the cook, and ordered him to bring her some of the bread which was made for the King. When he brought it the hare cried, "The cook must go with me, or that cruel hound may do me some harm." So the cook carried the bread, and went with the hare to the door of the inn.

As soon as he was gone she stood on her hind legs, took the bread in her fore-paws, and brought it to her master.

"There!" cried the hunter; "here is the bread, landlord, and the hundred gold-pieces are mine."

The landlord was much surprised, but when the hunter declared he would also have some of the roast meat from the King's table, he said: "The bread may be here, but I'll warrant you will get nothing more."

The hunter called the fox, and said to him, "My fox, go and fetch me some of the roast meat such as the King eats."

The red fox knew a better trick than the hare: he went across the fields, and slipped in without being seen by the hound. Then he placed himself under the chair of the King's daughter, and touched her foot. She looked down immediately, and recognizing him by his necklace, took him into her room. "What do you want, dear fox?" she asked.

"My master, who killed the dragon, is here," he replied, "and has sent me to ask for some of the roast meat that is cooked for the King."

The cook was sent for again, and the Princess desired him to carry some meat for the fox to the door of the inn. On arriving, the fox took the dish from the cook, and after whisking away the flies that had settled on it, with his tail, brought it to his master.

"See, landlord," cried the hunter, "here are bread and meat such as the King eats, and now I will have vegetables." So he called the wolf, and said, "Dear wolf, go and fetch me vegetables such as the King eats."

Away went the wolf straight to the castle, for he had no fear of anything, and as soon as he entered the room he went behind the Princess and pulled her dress, so that she was obliged to look round. She recognized the wolf immediately by the necklace, took him into her chamber, and said, "Dear wolf, what do you want?" He replied, "My master, who killed the dragon, is here, and has sent me to ask for some vegetables such as the King eats."

The cook was sent for again, and told to take some vegetables also to the inn door; and as soon as they arrived the wolf took the dish from him and carried it to his master.

"Look here, landlord," cried the hunter, "I have now bread, meat, and vegetables; but I will also have some sweetmeats from the King's table." He called the bear, and said, "Dear bear, I know you are fond of sweets. Now go and fetch me some sweetmeats such as the King eats."

The bear trotted off to the castle, and every one ran away when they saw him coming. But when he reached the castle gates, the sentinel held his gun before him and would not let him pass in. But the bear rose on his hind legs, boxed his ears right and left with his forepaws, and leaving him tumbled all of a heap in his sentry-box, went into the castle. Seeing the King's daughter entering he followed her and gave a slight growl. She looked behind her and, recognizing the bear, called him into her chamber, and said, "Dear bear, what do you want?"

"My master, who killed the dragon, is here," he replied, "and he has sent me to ask for some sweetmeats like those which the King eats."

The Princess sent for the confectioner, and desired him to bake some sweetmeats and take them with the bear to the door of the inn. As soon as they arrived the bear first licked up the sugar drips which had dropped on his fur, then stood upright, took the dish, and carried it to his master.

"See now, landlord," cried the hunter, "I have bread, and meat, and vegetables, and sweetmeats, and I mean to have wine also, such as the King drinks." So he called the lion to him, and said, "Dear lion, you drink till you are quite tipsy sometimes. Now go and fetch me some wine such as the King drinks."

As the lion trotted through the streets all the people ran away from him. The sentinel, when he saw him coming, tried to stop the way; but the lion gave a little roar, and made him run for his life. Then the lion entered the castle, passed through the King's apartment, and knocked at the door of the Princess's room with his tail. The Princess, when she opened it and saw the lion, was at first rather frightened; but presently she observed on his neck the gold necklace clasp, and knew it was the hunter's lion. She called him into her chamber, and said, "Dear lion, what do you want?"

"My master, who killed the dragon," he replied, "is here, and he has sent me to ask for some wine, such as the King drinks."

Then she sent for the King's cup-bearer, and told him to give the lion some of the King's wine.

"I will go with him," said the lion, "and see that he draws the right sort." So the lion went with the cup-bearer to the wine-cellar, and when he saw him about to draw some of the ordinary wine which the King's vassals drank, the lion cried, "Stop! I will taste the wine first." So he drew himself a pint, and swallowed it down at a gulp. "No," he said, "that is not the right sort."

The cup-bearer saw he was found out; however, he went over to another cask that was kept for the King's marshal. "Stop!" cried the lion again, "I will taste the wine first." So he drew another pint and drank it off. "Ah!" he said, "that is better, but still not the right wine."

Then the cup-bearer was angry, and said, "What can a stupid beast like you understand about wine?"

But the lion, with a lash of his tail, knocked him down, and before the man could move himself found his way stealthily into a little private cellar, in which were casks of wine never tasted by any but the King. The lion drew half a pint, and when he had tasted it, he said to himself, "That is wine of the right sort." So he called the cup-bearer and made him draw six flagons full.

As they came up from the cellar into the open air the lion's head swam a little, and he was almost tipsy; but as the cup-bearer was obliged to carry the wine for him to the door of the inn, it did not much matter. When they arrived, the lion took the handle of the basket in his mouth, and carried the wine to his master.

"Now, Master landlord," said the hunter, "I have bread, meat, vegetables, sweetmeats, and wine, such as the King has, so I will sit down and with my faithful animals enjoy a good meal"; and, indeed, he felt very happy, for he knew now that the King's daughter still loved him.

After they had finished, the hunter said to the landlord, "Now that I have eaten and drunk of the same provisions as the King, I will go to the King's castle and marry his daughter."

"Well," said the landlord, "how that is to be managed I cannot tell, when she has already a bridegroom to whom she will today be married."

The hunter, without a word, took out the pocket handkerchief which the King's daughter had given him on the dragon's mountain, and opening it, showed the landlord the seven tongues of the monster, which he had cut out and wrapped in the handkerchief. "That which I have so carefully preserved will help me," said the hunter.

The landlord looked at the handkerchief and said, "I may believe all the rest, but I would bet my house and farm-yard that you will never marry the King's daughter."

"Very well," said the hunter, "I accept your bet, and if I lose, there are my hundred gold-pieces"; and he laid them on the table.

That same day, when the King and his daughter were seated at table, the King said, "What did all those wild animals want who came to you today, going in and out of my castle?" "I cannot tell you yet," she replied; "but if you will send into the town for the master of these animals, then I will do so."

The King sent, on hearing this, a servant at once to the inn with an invitation to the stranger who owned the animals, and the servant arrived just as the hunter had finished his bet with the landlord.

"See, landlord!" he cried, "the King has sent me an invitation by his servant; but I cannot accept it yet." He turned to the man who waited, and said, "Tell my lord the King that I cannot obey his commands to visit him unless he sends me suitable clothes for a royal palace, and a carriage with six horses, and servants to wait upon me."

The servant returned with the message, and when the King heard it he said to his daughter, "What shall I do?"

"I would send for him as he requests," she replied.

So they sent royal robes, and a carriage and six horses with servants, and when the hunter saw them coming he said to the landlord, "See! they have sent for me as I wished."

He dressed himself in the kingly clothes, took the handkerchief containing the dragon's tongues, and drove away to the castle.

As soon as he arrived the King said to his daughter, "How shall I receive him?" "I should go and meet him," she replied.

So the King went to meet him, and led him into the royal apartment, and all his animals followed. The King pointed him to a seat by his daughter. The marshal sat on her other side as bridegroom, but the visitor knew it not.

Just at this moment the dragon's seven heads were brought into the room to show to the company, and the King said: "These heads belonged to the dragon who was for so many years the terror of this town. The marshal slew the dragon, and saved my daughter's life; therefore I have given her to him in marriage, according to my promise."

At this the hunter rose, and advancing, opened the seven throats of the dragon, and said, "Where are the tongues?"

The marshal turned white with fear, and knew not what to do. At last he said in his terror, "Dragons have no tongues."

"Liars get nothing for their pains," said the hunter; "the dragon's tongues shall prove who was his conqueror!"

He unfolded the handkerchief as he spoke. There lay the seven tongues. He took them up and placed each in the mouth of the dragon's head to which it belonged, and it fitted exactly. Then he took up the pocket handkerchief which was marked with the name of the King's daughter, showed it to the maiden, and asked her if she had not given it to him. "Yes," she replied; "I gave it to you on the day you killed the dragon."

He called his animals to him, took from each the necklace, and from the lion the one with the golden clasp, and asked to whom they belonged.

"They are mine," she replied; "they are a part of my coral necklace which had five strings of beads, which I divided among the animals because they aided you in killing the dragon, and afterward tore him in pieces. I cannot tell how the marshal could have carried me away from you," she continued, "for you told me to lie down and sleep after the fatigue and fright I had endured."

"I slept myself," he replied, "for I was quite worn out with my combat, and as I lay sleeping the marshal came and cut off my head."

"I begin to understand now," said the King; "the marshal carried away my daughter, supposing you were dead, and made us believe that he had killed the dragon, till you arrived with the tongues, the handkerchief, and the necklace. But what restored you to life?" asked the King.

Then the hunter related how one of his animals had healed him and restored him to life through the application of a wonderful root, and how he had been wandering about for a whole year, and had only returned to the town that very day, and heard from the landlord of the marshal's deceit.

Then said the King to his daughter, "Is it true that this man killed the dragon?"

"Yes," she answered, "quite true, and I can venture now to expose the wickedness of the marshal; for he carried me away that day against my wish, and forced me with threats to keep silent. I did not know he had tried to kill the real slayer of the dragon, but I hoped he would come back, and on that account I begged to have the marriage put off for a year and a day."

The King, after this, ordered twelve judges to be summoned to try the marshal, and the sentence passed upon him was that he should be torn to pieces by wild oxen. As soon as the marshal was punished the King gave his daughter to the hunter, and appointed him to the high position of stadtholder over the whole kingdom.

The marriage caused great joy, and the hunter, who was now a Prince, sent for his father and foster-father, and overloaded them with treasures.

Neither did he forget the landlord, but sent for him to come to the castle, and said, "See, landlord, I have married the King's daughter, and your house and farm-yard belong to me." "That is quite true," replied the landlord.

"Ah," said the Prince, "but I do not mean to keep them; they are still yours, and I make you a present of the hundred gold-pieces also."

For a time the young Prince and his wife lived most happily together. He still, however, went out hunting, which was his great delight, and his faithful animals remained with him. They lived, however, in a wood close by, from which he could call them at any time; yet the wood was not safe, for he once went in and did not get out again very easily.

Whenever the Prince had a wish to go hunting, he gave the King no rest till he allowed him to do so. On one occasion, while riding with a large number of attendants in the wood, he saw at a distance a snow-white deer, and he said to his people, "Stay here till I come back; I must have that beautiful creature, and so many will frighten her."

Then he rode away through the wood, and only his animals followed him. The attendants drew rein, and waited till evening, but as he did not come they rode home and told the young Princess that her husband had gone into an enchanted forest to hunt a white deer, and had not returned.

This made her very anxious, more especially when the morrow came and he did not return; indeed, he could not, for he kept riding after the beautiful wild animal, but without being able to overtake it. At times, when he fancied she was within reach of his gun, the next moment she was leaping away at a great distance, and at last she vanished altogether.

Not till then did he notice how far he had penetrated into the forest. He raised his horn and blew, but there was no answer, for his attendants could not hear it; and then as night came on he saw plainly that he should not be able to find his way home till the next day, so he alighted from his horse, lit a fire by a tree, and determined to make himself as comfortable as he could for the night.

As he sat under the tree by the fire, with his animals lying near him, he heard, as he thought, a human voice. He looked round, but could see nothing. Presently there was a groan over his head; he looked up and saw an old woman sitting on a branch, who kept grumbling, "Oh, oh, how cold I am! I am freezing!" "If you are cold, come down and warm yourself," he said. "No, no," she replied; "your animals will bite me." "Indeed they will do no such thing. Come down, old mother," he said kindly; "none of them shall hurt you."

He did not know that she was a wicked witch, so when she said, "I will throw you down a little switch from the tree, and if you just touch them on the back with it they cannot hurt me," he did as she told him, and as soon as they were touched by the wand the animals were all turned to stone. Then she jumped down, and touching the Prince on the back with the switch, he also was instantly turned into stone. Thereupon she laughed maliciously, and dragged him and his animals into a grave where several similar stones lay.

When the Princess found that her husband did not return, her anxiety and care increased painfully, and she became at last very unhappy.

Now, it so happened that just at this time the twin brother of the Prince, who since their separation had been wandering in the East, arrived in the country of which his brother's father-in-law was King. He had tried to obtain a situation, but could not succeed, and only his animals were left to him.

One day, as he was wandering from one place to another, it occurred to his mind that he might as well go and look at the knife which they had stuck in the trunk of a tree at the time of their separation. When he came to it there was his brother's side of the knife half-rusted, and the other half still bright.

In great alarm he thought, "My brother must have fallen into some terrible trouble. I will go and find him. I may be able to rescue him, as the half of the knife is still bright."

He set out with his animals on a journey, and while traveling west came to the town in which his brother's wife, the King's daughter, lived. As soon as he reached the gate of the town the watchman advanced toward him and asked if he should go and announce his arrival to the Princess, who had for two days been in great trouble

about him, fearing that he had been detained in the forest by enchantment.

The watchman had not the least idea that the young man was any
other than the Prince himself, especially as he had the wild animals
running behind him. The twin brother saw this, and he said to himself, "Perhaps it will be best for me to allow myself to be taken for my
brother; I shall be able more easily to save him." So he followed the
sentinel to the castle, where he was received with great joy.

The young Princess had no idea that this was not her husband, and
asked him why he had remained away so long.

He replied, "I rode a long distance into the wood, and could not
find my way out again." At night he was taken to the royal bed, but he
laid a two-edged sword between him and the young Princess; she did
not know what that could mean, but did not venture to ask.

In a few days he discovered all about his brother that he wished to
know, and was determined to go and seek for him in the enchanted
wood. So he said, "I must go to the hunt just once more."

The King and the young Princess said all they could to dissuade
him, but to no purpose, and at length he left the castle with a large
company of attendants.

When he reached the wood all happened as it had done with his
brother. He saw the beautiful white deer, and told his attendants to
wait while he went after it, followed only by his animals; but neither
could he overtake it; and the white deer led him far down into the
forest, where he found he must remain all night.

After he had lighted a fire he heard, as his brother had done, the
old woman in the tree, crying out that she was freezing with cold, and
he said to her, "If you are cold, old mother, come down and warm
yourself!" "No," she cried, "your animals will bite me!" "No, indeed
they will not," he said. "I can't trust them!" she cried; "here, I will
throw you a little switch, and if you gently strike them across the back,
then they will not be able to hurt me."

When the hunter heard that he began to mistrust the old woman,
and said, "No; I will not strike my animals; you come down, or I will
fetch you." "Do as you like," she said; "you can't hurt me." "If you don't
come down," he replied, "I will shoot you." "Shoot away," she said;
"your bullet can do me no harm."

He pointed his gun and shot at her; but the witch was proof against
a leaden bullet. She gave a shrill laugh, and cried, "It is no use trying
to hit me."

The hunter knew, however, what to do; he cut off three silver buttons from his coat, and loaded his gun with them. Against these she knew all her arts were vain; so as he drew the trigger she fell suddenly to the ground with a scream. Then he placed his foot upon her, and said, "Old witch, if you do not at once confess where my brother is, I will take you up and throw you into the fire."

She was in a great fright, begged for pardon, and said, "He is lying with his animals, turned to stone, in a grave."

Then he forced her to go with him, and said, "You old cat, if you don't instantly restore my brother to life, and all the creatures that are with him, over you go into the fire."

She was obliged to take a switch and strike the stones, and immediately the brother, his animals, and many others—traders, mechanics, and shepherds—stood before him, alive and in their own forms.

Thankful for having gained their freedom and their lives, they all hastened home; but the twin brothers, when they saw each other again, were full of joy, and embraced and kissed each other with great affection. They seized the old witch, bound her, and placed her on the fire, and as soon as she was burned the forest became suddenly clear and light, and the King's castle appeared at a very little distance.

After this the twin brothers walked away together toward the castle, and on the road related to each other the events that had happened to them since they parted. At last the youngest told his brother of his marriage to the King's daughter, and that the King had made him lord over the whole land.

"I know all about it," replied the other; "for when I came to the town, they all took me for you and treated me with kingly state; even the young Princess mistook me for her husband, and made me sit by her side."

But as he spoke his brother became so fierce with jealousy and anger that he drew his sword and cut off his brother's head. Then as he saw him lie dead at his feet his anger was quelled in a moment, and he repented bitterly, crying, "Oh, my brother is dead, and it is I who have killed him!" and kneeling by his side he mourned with loud cries and tears.

In a moment the hare appeared and begged to be allowed to fetch the life-giving root, which she knew would cure him. She was not away long, and when she returned, the head was replaced and fastened with the healing power of the plant, and the brother restored to life, while not even a sign of the wound remained to be noticed.

The brothers now walked on most lovingly together, and the one who had married the King's daughter said, "I see that you have kingly clothes, as I have; your animals are the same as mine. Let us enter the castle at two opposite doors, and approach the old King from two sides together."

So they separated; and as the King sat with his daughter in the royal apartment a sentinel approached him from two distant entrances at the same time, and informed him that the Prince, with his animals, had arrived. "That is impossible!" cried the King; "one of you must be wrong; for the gates at which you watch are quite a quarter of a mile apart."

But while the King spoke the two young men entered at opposite ends of the room, and both came forward and stood before the King.

With a bewildered look the King turned to his daughter, and said, "Which is your husband? For they are both so exactly alike I cannot tell."

She was herself very much frightened, and could not speak; at last she thought of the necklace that she had given to the animals, and looking earnestly among them she saw the glitter of the golden clasp on the lion's neck. "See," she cried in a happy voice, "he whom that lion follows is my husband!"

The Prince laughed, and said, "Yes; you are right; and this is my twin brother."

So they sat down happily together and told the King and the young Princess all their adventures.

When the King's daughter and her husband were alone she said to him, "Why have you for the last several nights always laid a two-edged sword in our bed? I thought you had a wish to kill me."

Then the Prince knew how true and honorable his twin brother had been.

Ferdinand the Faithful and Ferdinand the Unfaithful

Once upon a time there lived a man and a woman who, so long as they were rich, had no children; but when they were poor they had a little boy. They could, however, find no godfather for him, so the man said he would just go to another place to see if he could get one there. As he went, a poor man met him, who asked him where he was going. He said he was going to see if he could get a godfather; that he was poor, so no one would stand as godfather for him. "Oh," said the poor man, "thou art poor, and I am poor; I will be godfather for thee, but I am so ill-off I can give the child nothing. Go home and tell the nurse that she is to come to the church with the child."

When they all got to the church together, the beggar was already there, and he gave the child the name of Ferdinand the Faithful.

When he was going out of the church, the beggar said, "Now go home, I can give thee nothing, and thou likewise ought to give me nothing." But he gave a key to the nurse, and told her when she got home she was to give it to the father, who was to take care of it until the child was fourteen years old, and then he was to go on the heath where there was a castle, which the key would fit, and that all which was therein should belong to him.

Now when the child was seven years old and had grown very big, he once went to play with some other boys, and each of them boasted that he had got more from his godfather than the other; but the child could say nothing, and was vexed, and went home and said to his father, "Did I get nothing at all, then, from my godfather?" "Oh, yes," said the father, "thou hadst a key—if there is a castle standing on the heath, just go to it and open it." Then the boy went thither, but no castle was to be seen, or heard of.

After seven years more, when he was fourteen years old, he again went thither, and there stood the castle. When he had opened it, there was nothing within but a horse—a white one. Then the boy was so full of joy because he had a horse, that he mounted on it and galloped back to his father. "Now I have a white horse, and I will travel," said he. So he set out, and as he was on his way, a pen was lying on the road. At first he thought he would pick it up, but then again he thought to himself, "Thou shouldst leave it lying there; thou wilt easily find a pen where thou art going, if thou hast need of one." As he was thus riding away, a voice called after him, "Ferdinand the Faithful, take it with thee." He looked around, but saw no one; then he went back again and picked it up.

When he had ridden a little way farther, he passed by a lake, and a fish was lying on the bank, gasping and panting for breath, so he said, "Wait, my dear fish, I will help thee to get into the water," and he took hold of it by the tail, and threw it into the lake. Then the fish put its head out of the water and said, "As thou hast helped me out of the mud, I will give thee a flute; when thou art in any need, play on it, and then I will help thee, and if ever thou lettest anything fall in the water, just play and I will reach it out to thee."

Then he rode away, and there came to him a man who asked him where he was going. "Oh, to the next place." Then the man asked what his name was. "Ferdinand the Faithful." "So! then we have almost the same name, I am called Ferdinand the Unfaithful." And they both set out to the inn in the nearest place.

Now it was unfortunate that Ferdinand the Unfaithful knew everything that the other had ever thought and everything he was about to do; he knew it by means of all kinds of wicked arts.

There was, however, in the inn an honest girl, who had a bright face and behaved very prettily. She fell in love with Ferdinand the Faithful because he was a handsome man, and she asked him whither he was going. "Oh, I am just traveling round about," said he. Then she said he ought to stay there, for the King of that country wanted an attendant or an outrider, and he ought to enter his service. He answered he could not very well go to any one like that and offer himself. Then said the maiden, "Oh, but I will soon do that for thee." And so she went straight to the King, and told him that she knew of an excellent servant for him. He was well pleased with that, and had Ferdinand the Faithful brought to him, and wanted to make him his servant. He, however, liked better to be an outrider, for where his horse was, there he also wanted to be, so the King made him an outrider. When Ferdinand the Unfaithful learnt that, he said to the girl, "What! Dost thou help him and not me?" "Oh," said the girl, "I will help thee too." She thought, "I must keep friends with that man, for he is not to be trusted." She went to the King, and offered him as a servant, and the King was willing.

Now when the King met his lords in the morning, he always lamented and said, "Oh, if I had but my love with me." Ferdinand the Unfaithful was, however, always hostile to Ferdinand the Faithful. So once, when the King was complaining thus, he said, "Thou hast the outrider, send him away to get her, and if he does not do it, his head must be struck off." Then the King sent for Ferdinand the Faithful, and told him that there was, in this place or in that place, a girl he loved, and that he was to bring her to him, and if he did not do it he should die.

Ferdinand the Faithful went into the stable to his white horse, and complained and lamented, "Oh, what an unhappy man I am!" Then some one behind him cried, "Ferdinand the Faithful, why weepest thou?" He looked round but saw no one, and went on lamenting; "Oh, my dear little white horse, now must I leave thee; now must I die." Then some one cried once more, "Ferdinand the Faithful, why weepest thou?" Then for the first time he was aware that it was his little white horse who was putting that question. "Dost thou speak, my little white horse; canst thou do that?" And again, he said, "I am to go to this place and to that, and am to bring the bride; canst thou tell me how I am to set about it?" Then answered the little white horse, "Go thou to the King, and say if he will give thee what thou must have, thou wilt get her for him. If he will give thee a ship full of meat, and a ship full of bread, it will succeed. Great giants dwell on the lake, and if thou takest no meat with thee for them, they will tear thee to pieces, and there are the large birds which would pick the eyes out of thy head if thou hadst no bread for them."

Then the King made all the butchers in the land kill, and all the bakers bake, that the ships might be filled. When they were full, the little white horse said to Ferdinand the Faithful, "Now mount me, and go with me into the ship and then when the giants come, say,

'Peace, peace, my dear little giants,
I have had thought of ye,
Something I have brought for ye.'

"When the birds come, thou shalt again say,

'Peace, peace, my dear little birds,
I have had thought of ye,
Something I have brought for ye.'

"They will do nothing to thee, and when thou comest to the castle,
the giants will help thee. Then go up to the castle, and take a couple
of giants with thee. There the Princess lies sleeping; thou must, however, not awaken her, but the giants must lift her up, and carry her
in her bed to the ship." And now everything took place as the little
white horse had said, and Ferdinand the Faithful gave the giants and
the birds what he had brought with him for them, and that made the
giants willing, and they carried the Princess in her bed to the King.
And when she came to the King, she said she could not live, she must
have her writings, they had been left in her castle. Then by the instigation of Ferdinand the Unfaithful, Ferdinand the Faithful was called,
and the King told him he must fetch the writings from the castle, or
he should die.

Then he went once more into the stable, and bemoaned himself
and said, "Oh, my dear little white horse, now I am to go away again,
how am I to do it?" Then the little white horse said he was just to load
the ships full again. So it happened again as it had happened before,
and the giants and the birds were satisfied, and made gentle by the
meat. When they came to the castle, the white horse told Ferdinand
the Faithful that he must go in, and that on the table in the Princess's
bed-room lay the writings. And Ferdinand the Faithful went in, and
fetched them. When they were on the lake, he let his pen fall into the
water. Then said the white horse, "Now I cannot help thee at all." But
he remembered his flute, and began to play on it, and the fish came
with the pen in its mouth, and gave it to him. So he took the writings
to the castle, where the wedding was celebrated.

The Queen, however, did not love the King because he had no
nose, but she would have much liked to love Ferdinand the Faithful.
Once, therefore, when all the lords of the court were together, the
Queen said she could do feats of magic, that she could cut off any
one's head and put it on again, and that one of them ought just to try
it. But none of them would be the first, so Ferdinand the Faithful,
again at the instigation of Ferdinand the Unfaithful, undertook it
and she hewed off his head, and put it on again for him, and it healed
together directly, so that it looked as if he had a red thread round his
throat.

Then the King said to her, "My child, and where hast thou learnt that?" "Yes," she said, "I understand the art; shall I just try it on thee also?" "Oh, yes," said he. But she cut off his head, and did not put it on again; but pretended that she could not get it on, and that it would not keep fixed. Then the King was buried, but she married Ferdinand the Faithful.

He, however, always rode on his white horse, and once when he was seated on it, it told him that he was to go on to the heath which he knew, and gallop three times round it. And when he had done that, the white horse stood up on its hind legs, and was changed into a King's son.

Snow White

It was the middle of winter, and the snow-flakes were falling like feathers from the sky, and a Queen sat at her window working, and her embroidery-frame was of ebony. And as she worked, gazing at times out on the snow, she pricked her finger, and there fell from it three drops of blood on the snow. And when she saw how bright and red it looked, she said to herself, "Oh that I had a child as white as snow, as red as blood, and as black as the wood of the embroidery frame!"

Not very long after she had a daughter, with a skin as white as snow, lips as red as blood, and hair as black as ebony, and she was named Snow White. And when she was born the Queen died.

After a year had gone by the King took another wife, a beautiful woman, but proud and overbearing, and she could not bear to be surpassed in beauty by any one. She had a magic looking-glass, and she used to stand before it, and look in it, and say,

"Looking-glass upon the wall,
Who is fairest of us all?"

And the looking-glass would answer,

"You are fairest of them all."

And she was contented, for she knew that the looking-glass spoke the truth.

Now, Snow White was growing prettier and prettier, and when she was seven years old she was as beautiful as day, far more so than the Queen herself. So one day when the Queen went to her mirror and said,

"Looking-glass upon the wall,
Who is fairest of us all?"

it answered,

"Queen, you are full fair, 'tis true,
But Snow White fairer is than you."

This gave the Queen a great shock, and she became yellow and green with envy, and from that hour her heart turned against Snow White, and she hated her. And envy and pride like ill weeds grew in her heart higher every day, until she had no peace day or night. At last she sent for a huntsman, and said, "Take the child out into the woods, so that I may set eyes on her no more. You must put her to death, and bring me her heart for a token."

The huntsman consented, and led her away; but when he drew his cutlass to pierce Snow White's innocent heart, she began to weep, and to say, "Oh, dear huntsman, do not take my life; I will go away into the wild wood, and never come home again."

And as she was so lovely the huntsman had pity on her, and said, "Away with you then, poor child"; for he thought the wild animals would be sure to devour her, and it was as if a stone had been rolled away from his heart when he did not put her to death. Just at that moment a young wild boar came running by, so he caught and killed it, and taking out its heart, he brought it to the Queen for a token. And it was salted and cooked, and the wicked woman ate it up, thinking that there was an end of Snow White.

Now, when the poor child found herself quite alone in the wild woods, she felt full of terror, even of the very leaves on the trees, and she did not know what to do for fright. Then she began to run over the sharp stones and through the thorn bushes, and the wild beasts after her, but they did her no harm. She ran as long as her feet would carry her; and when the evening drew near she came to a little house, and she went inside to rest. Everything there was very small, but as pretty and clean as possible. There stood the little table ready laid, and covered with a white cloth, and seven little plates, and seven knives and forks, and drinking-cups. By the wall stood seven little beds, side by side, covered with clean white quilts. Snow White, being very hungry and thirsty, ate from each plate a little porridge and bread, and drank out of each little cup a drop of wine, so as not to finish up one portion alone. After that she felt so tired that she lay down on one of the beds, but it did not seem to suit her; one was too long, another too short, but at last the seventh was quite right; and so she lay down upon it, committed herself to Heaven, and fell asleep.

When it was quite dark, the masters of the house came home. They were seven dwarfs, whose occupation was to dig underground among the mountains. When they had lighted their seven candles, and it was quite light in the little house, they saw that some one must have been in, as everything was not in the same order in which they left it.

The first said, "Who has been sitting in my little chair?"

The second said, "Who has been eating from my little plate?"

The third said, "Who has been taking my little loaf?"

The fourth said, "Who has been tasting my porridge?"

The fifth said, "Who has been using my little fork?"

The sixth said, "Who has been cutting with my little knife?"

The seventh said, "Who has been drinking from my little cup?"

Then the first one, looking round, saw a hollow in his bed, and cried, "Who has been lying on my bed?" And the others came running, and cried, "Some one has been on our beds too!"

But when the seventh looked at his bed, he saw little Snow White lying there asleep. Then he told the others, who came running up, crying out in their astonishment, and holding up their seven little candles to throw a light upon Snow White.

"O goodness! O gracious!" cried they, "what beautiful child is this?" and were so full of joy to see her that they did not wake her, but let her sleep on. And the seventh dwarf slept with his comrades, an hour at a time with each, until the night had passed.

When it was morning, and Snow White awoke and saw the seven dwarfs, she was very frightened; but they seemed quite friendly, and asked her what her name was, and she told them; and then they asked how she came to be in their house. And she related to them how her step-mother had wished her to be put to death, and how the huntsman had spared her life, and how she had run the whole day long, until at last she had found their little house.

Then the dwarfs said, "If you will keep our house for us, and cook, and wash, and make the beds, and sew and knit, and keep everything tidy and clean, you may stay with us, and you shall lack nothing."

"With all my heart," said Snow White; and so she stayed, and kept the house in good order. In the morning the dwarfs went to the mountain to dig for gold; in the evening they came home, and their supper had to be ready for them. All the day long the maiden was left alone, and the good little dwarfs warned her, saying, "Beware of your step-mother, she will soon know you are here. Let no one into the house."

Now the Queen, having eaten Snow White's heart, as she supposed, felt quite sure that now she was the first and fairest, and so she came to her mirror, and said,

> "Looking-glass upon the wall,
> Who is fairest of us all?"

And the glass answered,

> "Queen, thou art of beauty rare,
> But Snow White living in the glen
> With the seven little men
> Is a thousand times more fair."

Then she was very angry, for the glass always spoke the truth, and she knew that the huntsman must have deceived her, and that Snow White must still be living. And she thought and thought how she could manage to make an end of her, for as long as she was not the fairest in the land, envy left her no rest. At last she thought of a plan; she painted her face and dressed herself like an old peddler woman, so that no one would have known her. In this disguise she went across the seven mountains, until she came to the house of the seven little dwarfs, and she knocked at the door and cried, "Fine wares to sell! fine wares to sell!"

Snow White peeped out of the window and cried, "Good-day, good woman, what have you to sell?"

"Good wares, fine wares," answered she, "laces of all colors"; and she held up a piece that was woven of variegated silk.

"I need not be afraid of letting in this good woman," thought Snow White, and she unbarred the door and bought the pretty lace.

"What a figure you are, child!" said the old woman, "come and let me lace you properly for once."

Snow White, suspecting nothing, stood up before her, and let her lace her with the new lace; but the old woman laced so quickly and tightly that it took Snow White's breath away, and she fell down as dead.

"Now you have done with being the fairest," said the old woman as she hastened away.

Not long after that, towards evening, the seven dwarfs came home, and were terrified to see their dear Snow White lying on the ground, without life or motion; they raised her up, and when they saw how tightly she was laced they cut the lace in two; then she began to draw breath, and little by little she returned to life. When the dwarfs heard what had happened they said, "The old peddler woman was no other than the wicked Queen; you must beware of letting any one in when we are not here!"

And when the wicked woman got home she went to her glass and said,

> "Looking-glass against the wall,
>   Who is fairest of us all?"

And it answered as before,

> "Queen, thou art of beauty rare,
>   But Snow White living in the glen
>   With the seven little men
>   Is a thousand times more fair."

When she heard that she was so struck with surprise that all the blood left her heart, for she knew that Snow White must still be living.

"But now," said she, "I will think of something that will be her ruin." And by witchcraft she made a poisoned comb. Then she dressed herself up to look like another different sort of old woman. So she went across the seven mountains and came to the house of the seven dwarfs, and knocked at the door and cried, "Good wares to sell! good wares to sell!"

Snow White looked out and said, "Go away, I must not let anybody in."

"But you are not forbidden to look," said the old woman, taking out the poisoned comb and holding it up. It pleased the poor child so much that she was tempted to open the door; and when the bargain was made the old woman said, "Now, for once, your hair shall be properly combed."

Poor Snow White, thinking no harm, let the old woman do as she would, but no sooner was the comb put in her hair than the poison began to work, and the poor girl fell down senseless.

"Now, you paragon of beauty," said the wicked woman, "this is the end of you," and went off. By good luck it was now near evening, and the seven little dwarfs came home. When they saw Snow White lying on the ground as dead, they thought directly that it was the step-mother's doing, and looked about, found the poisoned comb, and no sooner had they drawn it out of her hair than Snow White came to herself, and related all that had passed. Then they warned her once more to be on her guard, and never again to let any one in at the door.

And the Queen went home and stood before the looking-glass and said,

> "Looking-glass against the wall,
> Who is fairest of us all?"

And the looking-glass answered as before,

> "Queen, thou art of beauty rare,
> But Snow White living in the glen
> With the seven little men
> Is a thousand times more fair."

When she heard the looking-glass speak thus she trembled and shook with anger. "Snow White shall die," cried she, "though it should cost me my own life!"

And then she went to a secret lonely chamber, where no one was likely to come, and there she made a poisonous apple. It was beautiful to look upon, being white with red cheeks, so that any one who should see it must long for it, but whoever ate even a little bit of it must die. When the apple was ready she painted her face and clothed herself like a peasant woman, and went across the seven mountains to where the seven dwarfs lived. And when she knocked at the door Snow White put her head out of the window and said, "I dare not let anybody in; the seven dwarfs told me not to."

"All right," answered the woman; "I can easily get rid of my apples elsewhere. There, I will give you one."

"No," answered Snow White, "I dare not take anything."

"Are you afraid of poison?" said the woman, "look here, I will cut the apple in two pieces; you shall have the red side, I will have the white one."

For the apple was so cunningly made, that all the poison was in the rosy half of it. Snow White longed for the beautiful apple, and as she saw the peasant woman eating a piece of it she could no longer refrain, but stretched out her hand and took the poisoned half. But no sooner had she taken a morsel of it into her mouth than she fell to the earth as dead. And the Queen, casting on her a terrible glance, laughed aloud and cried, "As white as snow, as red as blood, as black as ebony! This time the dwarfs will not be able to bring you to life again."

And when she went home and asked the looking-glass,

> "Looking-glass against the wall,
> Who is fairest of us all?"

at last it answered, "You are the fairest now of all."

Then her envious heart had peace, as much as an envious heart can have.

The dwarfs, when they came home in the evening, found Snow White lying on the ground, and there came no breath out of her mouth, and she was dead. They lifted her up, sought if anything poisonous was to be found, cut her laces, combed her hair, washed her with water and wine, but all was of no avail, the poor child was dead, and remained dead. Then they laid her on a bier, and sat all seven of them round it, and wept and lamented three whole days. And then they would have buried her, but that she looked still as if she were living, with her beautiful blooming cheeks.

So they said, "We cannot hide her away in the black ground." And they had made a coffin of clear glass, so as to be looked into from all sides, and they laid her in it, and wrote in golden letters upon it her name, and that she was a King's daughter. Then they set the coffin out upon the mountain, and one of them always remained by it to watch. And the birds came too, and mourned for Snow White, first an owl, then a raven, and lastly, a dove.

Now, for a long while Snow White lay in the coffin and never changed, but looked as if she were asleep, for she was still as white as snow, as red as blood, and her hair was as black as ebony.

It happened, however, that one day a King's son rode through the wood and up to the dwarfs' house, which was near it. He saw on the mountain the coffin, and beautiful Snow White within it, and he read what was written in golden letters upon it. Then he said to the dwarfs, "Let me have the coffin, and I will give you whatever you like to ask for it."

But the dwarfs told him that they could not part with it for all the gold in the world. But he said, "I beseech you to give it me, for I cannot live without looking upon Snow White; if you consent I will bring you to great honor, and care for you as if you were my brethren."

When he so spoke the good little dwarfs had pity upon him and gave him the coffin, and the King's son called his servants and bid them carry it away on their shoulders. Now it happened that as they were going along they stumbled over a bush, and with the shaking the bit of poisoned apple flew out of her throat. It was not long before she opened her eyes, threw up the cover of the coffin, and sat up, alive and well.

"Oh dear! where am I?" cried she. The King's son answered, full of joy, "You are near me," and, relating all that had happened, he said, "I would rather have you than anything in the world; come with me to my father's castle and you shall be my bride."

And Snow White was kind, and went with him, and their wedding was held with pomp and great splendor.

But Snow White's wicked step-mother was also bidden to the feast, and when she had dressed herself in beautiful clothes she went to her looking-glass and said,

> "Looking-glass upon the wall,
> Who is fairest of us all?"

The looking-glass answered,

> "O Queen, although you are of beauty rare,
> The young bride is a thousand times more fair."

Then she railed and cursed, and was beside herself with disappointment and anger. First she thought she would not go to the wedding; but then she felt she should have no peace until she went and saw the bride. And when she saw her she knew her for Snow White, and could not stir from the place for anger and terror. For they had ready red-hot iron shoes, in which she had to dance until she fell down dead.

The Worn-Out Dancing Shoes

There was once upon a time a King who had twelve daughters, each one more beautiful than the other. They all slept together in one chamber, in which their beds stood side by side, and every night when they were in them the King locked the door, and bolted it. But in the morning when he unlocked the door, he saw that their shoes were worn out with dancing, and no one could find out how that had come to pass. Then the King caused it to be proclaimed that whosoever could discover where they danced at night, should choose one of them for his wife and be King after his death; but that whosoever came forward and had not discovered it within three days and nights, should have forfeited his life.

It was not long before a King's son presented himself, and offered to undertake the enterprise. He was well received, and in the evening was led into a room adjoining the Princesses' sleeping-chamber. His bed was placed there, and he was to observe where they went and danced, and in order that they might do nothing secretly or go away to some other place, the door of their room was left open.

But the eyelids of the Prince grew heavy as lead, and he fell asleep, and when he awoke in the morning, all twelve had been to the dance, for their shoes were standing there with holes in the soles. On the second and third nights it fell out just the same, and then his head was struck off without mercy. Many others came after this and undertook the enterprise, but all forfeited their lives.

Now it came to pass that a poor soldier who had a wound, and could serve no longer, found himself on the road to the town where the King lived. There he met an old woman, who asked him where he was going. "I hardly know myself," answered he, and added in jest, "I had half a mind to discover where the Princesses danced their shoes into holes, and thus become King." "That is not so difficult," said the old woman, "you must not drink the wine which will be brought to you at night, and must pretend to be sound asleep."

With that she gave him a little cloak, and said, "If you put on that, you will be invisible, and then you can steal after the twelve." When the soldier had received this good advice, he went into the thing in earnest, took heart, went to the King, and announced himself as a suitor. He was as well received as the others, and royal garments were put upon him. He was conducted that evening at bed-time into the ante-chamber, and as he was about to go to bed, the eldest came and brought him a cup of wine, but he had tied a sponge under his chin, and let the wine run down into it, without drinking a drop. Then he lay down and when he had lain a while, he began to snore, as if in the deepest sleep.

The twelve Princesses heard that, and laughed, and the eldest said, "He, too, might as well have saved his life." With that they got up, opened wardrobes, presses, cupboards, and brought out pretty dresses; dressed themselves before the mirrors, sprang about, and rejoiced at the prospect of the dance. Only the youngest said, "I know not how it is; you are very happy, but I feel very strange; some misfortune is certainly about to befall us." "You are a goose, who is always frightened," said the eldest. "Have you forgotten how many Kings' sons have already come here in vain? I had hardly any need to give the soldier a sleeping-draught; in any case the clown would not have awakened." When they were all ready they looked carefully at the soldier, but he had closed his eyes and did not move or stir, so they felt themselves quite secure. The eldest then went to her bed and tapped it; it immediately sank into the earth, and one after the other they descended through the opening, the eldest going first.

The soldier, who had watched everything, tarried no longer, put on his little cloak, and went down last with the youngest. Half-way down the steps, he just trod a little on her dress; she was terrified at that, and cried out, "What is that? who is pulling at my dress?" "Don't be so silly!" said the eldest, "you have caught it on a nail."

Then they went all the way down, and when they were at the bottom, they were standing in a wonderfully pretty avenue of trees, all the leaves of which were of silver, and shone and glistened. The soldier thought, "I must carry a token away with me," and broke off a twig from one of them, on which the tree cracked with a loud report. The youngest cried out again, "Something is wrong, did you hear the crack?" But the eldest said, "It is a gun fired for joy, because we have got rid of our Prince so quickly." After that they came into an avenue where all the leaves were of gold, and lastly into a third avenue where they were of bright diamonds. He broke off a twig from each, which made such a crack each time that the youngest started back in terror, but the eldest still maintained that they were salutes. They went on and came to a great lake whereon stood twelve little boats, and in every boat sat a handsome Prince, all of whom were waiting for the twelve, and each took one of them with him, but the soldier seated himself by the youngest. Then her Prince said, "I can't tell why the boat is so much heavier today; I shall have to row with all my strength, if I am to get it across." "What should cause that," said the youngest, "but the warm weather? I feel very warm too." On the opposite side of the lake stood a splendid, brightly lit castle, from whence resounded the joyous music of trumpets and kettle-drums. They rowed over there, entered, and each Prince danced with the girl he loved, but the soldier danced with them unseen, and when one of them had a cup of wine in her hand he drank it up, so that the cup was empty when she carried it to her mouth; the youngest was alarmed at this, but the eldest always made her be silent.

They danced there till three o'clock in the morning when all the shoes were danced into holes, and they were forced to leave off. The Princes rowed them back again over the lake, and this time the soldier seated himself by the eldest. On the shore they took leave of their Princes, and promised to return the following night. When they reached the stairs the soldier ran on in front and lay down in his bed, and when the twelve had come up slowly and wearily, he was already snoring so loudly that they could all hear him, and they said, "So far as he is concerned, we are safe." They took off their beautiful dresses, laid them away, put the worn-out shoes under the bed, and lay down. Next morning the soldier was resolved not to speak, but to watch the wonderful goings on, and again went with them.

Everything was done just as it had been done the first time, and each time they danced until their shoes were worn to pieces. But the third time he took a cup away with him as a token. When the hour had arrived for him to give his answer, he took the three twigs and the cup, and went to the King, but the twelve stood behind the door, and listened for what he was going to say. When the King put the question, "Where have my twelve daughters danced their shoes to pieces in the night?" he answered, "In an underground castle with twelve Princes," and related how it had come to pass, and brought out the tokens.

The King then summoned his daughters, and asked them if the soldier had told the truth, and when they saw that they were betrayed, and that falsehood would be of no avail, they were obliged to confess all. Thereupon the King asked which of them he would have to wife. He answered, "I am no longer young, so give me the eldest." Then the wedding was celebrated on the self-same day, and the kingdom was promised him after the King's death. But the Princes were bewitched for as many days as they had danced nights with the twelve.

The Six Swans

Once a King was hunting in a great wood, and he pursued a wild animal so eagerly that none of his people could follow him. When evening came he stood still, and looking round him he found that he had lost his way; and seeking a path, he found none. Then all at once he saw an old woman with a nodding head coming up to him; and it was a witch.

"My good woman," said he, "can you show me the way out of the wood?"

"Oh yes, my lord King," answered she, "certainly I can; but I must make a condition, and if you do not fulfill it, you will never get out of the wood again, but die there of hunger."

"What is the condition?" asked the King.

"I have a daughter," said the old woman, "who is as fair as any in the world, and if you will take her for your bride, and make her Queen, I will show you the way out of the wood."

The King consented, because of the difficulty he was in, and the old woman led him into her little house, and there her daughter was sitting by the fire.

She received the King just as if she had been expecting him, and though he saw that she was very beautiful, she did not please him, and he could not look at her without an inward shudder. Nevertheless, he took the maiden before him on his horse, and the old woman showed him the way, and soon he was in his royal castle again, where the wedding was held.

The King had been married before, and his first wife had left seven children, six boys and one girl, whom he loved better than all the world, and as he was afraid the step-mother might not behave well to them, and perhaps would do them some mischief, he took them to a lonely castle standing in the middle of a wood. There they remained hidden, for the road to it was so hard to find that the King himself could not have found it, had it not been for a clew of yarn, possessing wonderful properties, that a wise woman had given him; when he threw it down before him, it unrolled itself and showed him the way.

And the King went so often to see his dear children, that the Queen was displeased at his absence; and she became curious and wanted to know what he went out into the wood for so often alone. She bribed his servants with much money, and they showed her the secret, and told her of the clew of yarn, which alone could point out the way; then she gave herself no rest until she had found out where the King kept the clew, and then she made some little white silk shirts, and sewed a charm in each, as she had learned witchcraft of her mother. And once when the King had ridden to the hunt, she took the little shirts and went into the wood, and the clew of yarn showed her the way. The children seeing some one in the distance, thought it was their dear father coming to see them, and came jumping for joy to meet him. Then the wicked Queen threw one of the little shirts over each, and as soon as the shirts touched their bodies, they were changed into swans, and flew away through the wood. So the Queen went home very pleased to think she had got rid of her step-children; but the maiden had not run out with her brothers, and so the Queen knew nothing about her.

The next day the King went to see his children, but he found nobody but his daughter. "Where are thy brothers?" asked the King.

"Ah, dear father," answered she, "they are gone away and have left me behind," and then she told him how she had seen from her window her brothers in the guise of swans fly away through the wood, and she showed him the feathers which they had let fall in the court-yard, and which she had picked up. The King was grieved, but he never dreamt that it was the Queen who had done this wicked deed, and as he feared lest the maiden also should be stolen away from him, he wished to take her away with him. But she was afraid of the step-mother, and begged the King to let her remain one more night in the castle in the wood.

Then she said to herself, "I must stay here no longer, but go and seek for my brothers."

And when the night came, she fled away and went straight into the wood. She went on all that night and the next day, until she could go no longer for weariness. At last she saw a rude hut, and she went in and found a room with six little beds in it; she did not dare to lie down in one, but she crept under one and lay on the hard boards and wished for night. When it was near the time of sun-setting she heard a rustling sound, and saw six swans come flying in at the window. They alighted on the ground, and blew at one another until they had blown all their feathers off, and then they stripped off their swan-skin as if it had been a shirt. And the maiden looked at them and knew them for her brothers, and was very glad, and crept from under the bed. The brothers were not less glad when their sister appeared, but their joy did not last long.

"You must not stay here," said they to her; "this is a robbers' haunt, and if they were to come and find you here, they would kill you."

"And cannot you defend me?" asked the little sister.

"No," answered they, "for we can only get rid of our swan-skins and keep our human shape every evening for a quarter of an hour, but after that we must be changed again into swans."

Their sister wept at hearing this, and said, "Can nothing be done to set you free?"

"Oh no," answered they, "the work would be too hard for you. For six whole years you would be obliged never to speak or laugh, and make during that time six little shirts out of aster-flowers. If you were to let fall a single word before the work was ended, all would be of no good."

And just as the brothers had finished telling her this, the quarter of an hour came to an end, and they changed into swans and flew out of the window.

But the maiden made up her mind to set her brothers free, even though it should cost her her life. She left the hut, and going into the middle of the wood, she climbed a tree, and there passed the night. The next morning she set to work and gathered asters and began sewing them together: as for speaking, there was no one to speak to, and as for laughing, she had no mind to it; so she sat on and looked at nothing but her work.

When she had been going on like this for a long time, it happened that the King of that country went a-hunting in the wood, and some of his huntsmen came up to the tree in which the maiden sat. They called out to her, saying, "Who art thou?" But she gave no answer. "Come down," cried they; "we will do thee no harm." But she only shook her head. And when they tormented her further with questions she threw down to them her gold necklace, hoping they could be content with that. But they would not leave off, so she threw down to them her girdle, and when that was no good, her garters, and one after another everything she had on and could possibly spare, until she had nothing left but her smock. But all was no good, the huntsmen would not be put off any longer, and they climbed the tree, carried the maiden off, and brought her to the King.

The King asked, "Who art thou? What wert thou doing in the tree?" But she answered nothing. He spoke to her in all the languages he knew, but she remained dumb: but, being very beautiful, the King inclined to her, and he felt a great love rise up in his heart towards her; and casting his mantle round her, he put her before him on his horse and brought her to his castle. Then he caused rich clothing to be put upon her, and her beauty shone as bright as the morning, but no word would she utter. He seated her by his side at table, and her modesty and gentle mien so pleased him, that he said, "This maiden I choose for wife, and no other in all the world," and accordingly after a few days they were married.

But the King had a wicked mother, who was displeased with the marriage, and spoke ill of the young Queen. "Who knows where the maid can have come from?" said she, "and not able to speak a word! She is not worthy of a king!"

After a year had passed, and the Queen brought her first child into the world, the old woman carried it away, and marked the Queen's mouth with blood as she lay sleeping. Then she went to the King and declared that his wife was an eater of human flesh. The King would not believe such a thing, and ordered that no one should do her any harm. And the Queen went on quietly sewing the shirts and caring for nothing else.

The next time that a fine boy was born, the wicked step-mother used the same deceit, but the King would give no credence to her words, for he said, "She is too tender and good to do any such thing, and if she were only not dumb, and could justify herself, then her innocence would be as clear as day."

When for the third time the old woman stole away the new-born child and accused the Queen, who was unable to say a word in her defense, the King could do no other but give her up to justice, and she was sentenced to suffer death by fire.

The day on which her sentence was to be carried out was the very last one of the sixth year of the years during which she had neither spoken nor laughed, to free her dear brothers from the evil spell. The six shirts were ready, all except one which wanted the left sleeve. And when she was led to the pile of wood, she carried the six shirts on her arm, and when she mounted the pile and the fire was about to be kindled, all at once she cried out aloud, for there were six swans coming flying through the air; and she saw that her deliverance was near, and her heart beat for joy. The swans came close up to her with rushing wings, and stooped round her, so that she could throw the shirts over them; and when that had been done the swan-skins fell off them, and her brothers stood before her in their own bodies quite safe and sound; but as one shirt wanted the left sleeve, so the youngest brother had a swan's wing instead of a left arm.

They embraced and kissed each other, and the Queen went up to the King, who looked on full of astonishment, and began to speak to him and to say, "Dearest husband, now I may dare to speak and tell you that I am innocent, and have been falsely accused," and she related to him the treachery of the step-mother, who had taken away the three children and hidden them. And she was reconciled to the King with great joy, and the wicked step-mother was bound to the stake on the pile of wood and burnt to ashes.

And the King and Queen lived many years with their six brothers in peace and joy.

The Seven Ravens

A man had seven sons, but not a single daughter. This made both him and his wife very unhappy. At last a daughter was born, to their great joy; but the child was very small and slight, and so weak that they feared it would die. So the father sent his sons to the spring to fetch water that he might baptize her.

Each of the boys ran in great haste to be the first to draw the water for their little sister's baptism, but in the struggle to be first they let the pitcher fall into the well.

Then they stood still and knew not what to do; not one of them dared to venture home without the water. As the time went on and they did not return, the father became very impatient, and said, "I suppose in the midst of their play they have forgotten what I sent them for, the careless children."

He was in such an agony lest the child should die unbaptized that he exclaimed thoughtlessly, "I wish the youngsters were all turned into ravens!"

The words were scarcely uttered when there was heard a rushing of wings in the air over his head, and presently seven coal-black ravens flew over the house.

The father could not recall the dreadful words, and both parents grieved terribly over the loss of their seven sons; their only consolation now was the little daughter, who every day grew stronger and more beautiful.

For a long time the maiden was not told that she had brothers; her parents were most careful to avoid all mention of them. But one day she overheard some persons talking, and they said that no doubt the young girl was very beautiful, but that there must have been some strange cause for the misfortune which had happened to her seven brothers.

Oh, how surprised and sad she felt when she heard this! She went at once to her father and mother and asked them if she really had had any brothers, and what had become of them. Then her parents dared not any longer keep the secret from her. They told her, however, that it was the decree of Heaven, and that her birth was the innocent cause of all. As soon as she was alone she made a firm determination that she would try to break the enchantment in which her brothers were held.

She had neither rest nor peace till she had made up her mind to leave home and seek her brothers and set them free, cost what it might.

When at last she left home, she took nothing with her but a little ring, in memory of her parents, a loaf of bread, a jug of water, and a little stool, in case she felt tired.

So she went from her home, and traveled further and further, till she came to the end of the world, and there was the sun; but it was so hot and fierce that it scorched the little child, and she ran away in such a hurry that she ran into the moon. Here it was quite cold and dismal, and she heard a voice say, "I smell man's flesh," which made her escape from the moon as quickly as she could, and at last she reached the stars.

They were very kind and friendly to her. Each of the stars was seated on a wonderful chair, and the Morning Star stood up and said, "If you have not a key you will not be able to unlock the iceberg in which your brothers are shut up."

So the Morning Star gave the maiden the key, and told her to wrap it up carefully in her little handkerchief, and showed her the way to the iceberg. When she arrived the gate was closed; she opened her handkerchief to take out the key, but found it empty; she had forgotten the advice of the kind stars. What was she to do now? She wished to rescue her brothers and had no key to the iceberg.

At last the good little sister thought she would put her finger into the lock instead of a key. After twisting and turning it about, which hurt her very much, she happily succeeded in opening it, and immediately entered.

Presently a little dwarf came forward to meet her, and said, "My child, what are you seeking?" "I seek my brothers, the seven ravens," she said. "The seven ravens are not at home," replied the dwarf; "but if you would like to wait here till they return, pray step in."

Then the little dwarf took the maiden to the room where supper was prepared for the seven ravens, on seven little plates, by which stood seven little cups of water.

So the sister ate a few crumbs from each plate and drank a little draught from each cup, and into the last cup she let fall the ring that she brought from home.

Before she could get it out again she heard the rushing of wings in the air, and the little dwarf said, "Here come the seven Mr. Ravens flying home."

Then she hid herself behind the door to see and hear what they would do. They came in and were about to eat their supper, but as they caught sight of their little cups and plates, they said one to another: "Who has been eating from my little plate?" "Who has been drinking from my little cup?" "It has been touched by the mouth of a human being," cried one; "and, look here, what is this?" He took up his cup and turned it over, and out rolled the little ring, which they knew had once belonged to their father and mother.

Then said the eldest, "Oh, I remember that ring! Oh, if our sister would only come here, we should be free!" The maiden, who heard the wish from behind the door, came forth smiling, and stood before them.

In that same moment the seven ravens were freed from the enchantment, and became seven handsome young men. Oh, how joyfully they all kissed each other and their little sister, and started off at once in great happiness to their parents and their home!

The Twelve Brothers

Once upon a time there lived a King and Queen very peacefully together; they had twelve children, all boys.

Now the King said to the Queen one day, "If our thirteenth child should be a girl the twelve boys shall die, so that her riches may be the greater, and the kingdom fall to her alone."

Then he caused twelve coffins to be made; and they were filled with shavings, and a little pillow laid in each, and they were brought and put in a locked-up room; and the King gave the key to the Queen, and told her to say nothing about it to any one.

But the mother sat the whole day sorrowing, so that her youngest son, who never left her, and to whom she had given the Bible name Benjamin, said to her, "Dear mother, why are you so sad?" "Dearest child," answered she, "I dare not tell you."

But he let her have no peace until she went and unlocked the room, and showed him the twelve coffins with the shavings and the little pillows.

Then she said, "My dear Benjamin, your father has caused these coffins to be made for you and your eleven brothers, and if I bring a little girl into the world you are all to be put to death together and buried therein." And she wept as she spoke, and her little son comforted her and said, "Weep not, dear mother, we will save ourselves and go far away."

Then she answered, "Yes, go with your eleven brothers out into the world, and let one of you always sit on the top of the highest tree that can be found, and keep watch upon the tower of this castle. If a little son is born I will put out a white flag, and then you may safely venture back again; but if it is a little daughter I will put out a red flag, and then flee away as fast as you can, and the dear God watch over you. Every night will I arise and pray for you—in winter that you may have a fire to warm yourselves by, and in summer that you may not languish in the heat."

After that, when she had given her sons her blessing, they went away out into the wood. One after another kept watch, sitting on the highest oak tree, looking towards the tower. When eleven days had passed, and Benjamin's turn came, he saw a flag put out, but it was not white, but blood red, to warn them that they were to die. When the brothers knew this they became angry, saying, "Shall we suffer death because of a girl! We swear to be revenged; wherever we find a girl we will shed her blood."

Then they went deeper into the wood; and in the middle, where it was darkest, they found a little enchanted house, standing empty. Then they said, "Here will we dwell; and you, Benjamin, the youngest and weakest, shall stay at home and keep house; we others will go abroad and purvey food."

Then they went into the wood and caught hares, wild roes, birds, and pigeons, and whatever else is good to eat, and brought them to Benjamin for him to cook and make ready to satisfy their hunger. So they lived together in the little house for ten years, and the time did not seem long.

By this time the Queen's little daughter was growing up; she had a kind heart and a beautiful face, and a golden star on her forehead.

Once when there was a great wash she saw among the clothes twelve shirts, and she asked her mother, "Whose are these twelve shirts? they are too small to be my father's." Then the mother answered with a sore heart, "Dear child, they belong to your twelve brothers." The little girl said, "Where are my twelve brothers? I have never heard of them." And her mother answered, "God only knows where they are wandering about in the world."

Then she led the little girl to the secret room and unlocked it, and showed her the twelve coffins with the shavings and the little pillows. "These coffins," said she, "were intended for your twelve brothers, but they went away far from home when you were born," and she related how everything had come to pass. Then said the little girl, "Dear mother, do not weep, I will go and seek my brothers."

So she took the twelve shirts and went far and wide in the great forest. The day sped on, and in the evening she came to the enchanted house. She went in and found a youth, who asked, "Whence do you come, and what do you want?" and he marveled at her beauty, her royal garments, and the star on her forehead.

Then she answered, "I am a King's daughter, and I seek my twelve brothers, and I will go everywhere under the blue sky until I find them." And she showed him the twelve shirts which belonged to them. Then Benjamin saw that it must be his sister, and said, "I am Benjamin, your youngest brother."

And she began weeping for joy, and Benjamin also, and they kissed and cheered each other with great love. After a while he said, "Dear sister, there is still a hindrance; we have sworn that any maiden that we meet must die, as it was because of a maiden that we had to leave our kingdom."

Then she said, "I will willingly die, if so I may benefit my twelve brothers." "No," answered he, "you shall not die; sit down under this tub until the eleven brothers come, and I agree with them about it." She did so; and as night came on they returned from hunting, and supper was ready.

And as they were sitting at table and eating, they asked, "What news?" And Benjamin said, "Don't you know any?" "No," answered they. So he said, "You have been in the wood, and I have stayed at home, and yet I know more than you." "Tell us!" cried they.

He answered, "Promise me that the first maiden we see shall not be put to death." "Yes, we promise," cried they all, "she shall have mercy; tell us now."

Then he said, "Our sister is here," and lifted up the tub, and the King's daughter came forth in her royal garments with her golden star on her forehead, and she seemed so beautiful, delicate, and sweet, that they all rejoiced, and fell on her neck and kissed her, and loved her with all their hearts.

After this she remained with Benjamin in the house and helped him with the work. The others went forth into the woods to catch wild animals, does, birds, and pigeons, for food for them all, and their sister and Benjamin took care that all was made ready for them. She fetched the wood for cooking, and the vegetables, and watched the pots on the fire, so that supper was always ready when the others came in. She kept also great order in the house, and the beds were always beautifully white and clean, and the brothers were contented, and lived in unity.

One day the two got ready a fine feast, and when they were all assembled they sat down and ate and drank, and were full of joy.

Now there was a little garden belonging to the enchanted house, in which grew twelve lilies; the maiden, thinking to please her brothers, went out to gather the twelve flowers, meaning to give one to each as they sat at meat. But as she broke off the flowers, in the same moment the brothers were changed into twelve ravens, and flew over the wood far away, and the house with the garden also disappeared. So the poor maiden stood alone in the wild wood, and as she was looking around her she saw an old woman standing by her, who said, "My child, what hast thou done! why couldst thou not leave the twelve flowers standing? They were thy twelve brothers, who are now changed to ravens forever."

The maiden said, weeping, "Is there no means of setting them free?"

"No," said the old woman, "there is in the whole world no way but one, and that is difficult; thou canst not release them but by being dumb for seven years: thou must neither speak nor laugh; and wert thou to speak one single word, and it wanted but one hour of the seven years, all would be in vain, and thy brothers would perish because of that one word."

Then the maiden said in her heart, "I am quite sure that I can set my brothers free," and went and sought a tall tree, climbed up, and sat there spinning, and never spoke or laughed. Now it happened that a King, who was hunting in the wood, had with him a large greyhound, who ran to the tree where the maiden was, sprang up at it, and barked loudly. Up came the King and saw the beautiful Princess with the golden star on her forehead, and he was so charmed with her beauty that he prayed her to become his wife. She gave no answer, only a little nod of her head. Then he himself climbed the tree and brought her down, set her on his horse and took her home. The wedding was held with great splendor and rejoicing, but the bride neither spoke nor laughed.

After they had lived pleasantly together for a few years, the King's mother, who was a wicked woman, began to slander the young Queen, and said to the King, "She is only a low beggar-maid that you have taken to yourself; who knows what mean tricks she is playing? Even if she is really dumb and cannot speak she might at least laugh; not to laugh is the sign of a bad conscience."

At first the King would believe nothing of it, but the old woman talked so long, and suggested so many bad things, that he at last let himself be persuaded, and condemned the Queen to death.

Now a great fire was kindled in the courtyard, and she was to be burned in it; and the King stood above at the window, and watched it all with weeping eyes, for he had held her very dear. And when she was already fast bound to the stake, and the fire was licking her garments with red tongues, the last moment of the seven years came to an end. Then a rushing sound was heard in the air, and twelve ravens came flying and sank downwards; and as they touched the earth they became her twelve brothers that she had lost. They rushed through the fire and quenched the flames, and set their dear sister free, kissing and consoling her. And now that her mouth was opened, and that she might venture to speak, she told the King the reason of her dumbness, and why she had never laughed. The King rejoiced when he heard of her innocence, and they all lived together in happiness until their death.

But the wicked mother-in-law was very unhappy, and died miserably.

Iron John

Once upon a time there lived a King who had a great forest near his palace, full of all kinds of wild animals. One day he sent out a huntsman to shoot him a roe, but he did not come back. "Perhaps some accident has befallen him," said the King, and the next day he sent out two more huntsmen who were to search for him, but they too stayed away. Then on the third day, he sent for all his huntsmen, and said, "Scour the whole forest through, and do not give up until ye have found all three." But of these also, none came home again, and of the pack of hounds which they had taken with them, none were seen more. From that time forth, no one would any longer venture into the forest, and it lay there in deep stillness and solitude, and nothing was seen of it, but sometimes an eagle or a hawk flying over it.

This lasted for many years, when a strange huntsman announced himself to the King as seeking a situation, and offered to go into the dangerous forest. The King, however, would not give his consent, and said, "It is not safe in there; I fear it would fare with thee no better than with the others, and thou wouldst never come out again." The huntsman replied, "Lord, I will venture it at my own risk; I have no fear."

The huntsman therefore betook himself with his dog to the forest. It was not long before the dog fell in with some game on the way, and wanted to pursue it; but hardly had the dog run two steps when it stood before a deep pool, could go no farther, and a naked arm stretched itself out of the water, seized it, and drew it under. When the huntsman saw that, he went back and fetched three men to come with buckets and bail out the water. When they could see to the bottom there lay a wild man whose body was brown like rusty iron, and whose hair hung over his face down to his knees. They bound him with cords, and led him away to the castle. There was great astonishment over the wild man; the King, however, had him put in an iron cage in his court-yard, and forbade the door to be opened on pain of death, and the Queen herself was to take the key into her keeping. And from this time forth every one could again go into the forest with safety.

The King had a son eight years old, who was once playing in the court-yard, and while he was playing, his golden ball fell into the cage. The boy ran thither and said, "Give me my ball." "Not till thou hast opened the door for me," answered the man. "No," said the boy, "I will not do that; the King has forbidden it," and ran away. The next day he again went and asked for his ball; the wild man said, "Open my door," but the boy would not. On the third day the King had ridden out hunting, and the boy went once more and said, "I cannot open the door even if I wished, for I have not the key." Then the wild man said, "It lies under thy mother's pillow, thou canst get it there." The boy, who wanted to have his ball back, cast all thought to the winds, and brought the key. The door opened with difficulty, and the boy pinched his fingers. When it was open the wild man stepped out, gave him the golden ball, and hurried away. The boy had become afraid; he called and cried after him, "Oh, wild man, do not go away, or I shall be beaten!" The wild man turned back, took him up, set him on his shoulder, and went with hasty steps into the forest.

When the King came home, he observed the empty cage, and asked the Queen how that had happened. She knew nothing about it, and sought the key, but it was gone. She called the boy, but no one answered. The King sent out people to seek for him in the fields, but they did not find him. Then he could easily guess what had happened, and much grief reigned in the royal court.

When the wild man had once more reached the dark forest, he took the boy down from his shoulder, and said to him, "Thou wilt never see thy father and mother again, but I will keep thee with me, for thou hast set me free, and I have compassion on thee. If thou dost all I bid thee, thou shalt fare well. Of treasure and gold I have enough, and more than any one in the world." He made a bed of moss for the boy on which he slept, and the next morning the man took him to a well, and said, "Behold, the gold well is as bright and clear as crystal; thou shalt sit beside it, and take care that nothing falls into it, or it will be polluted. I will come every evening to see if thou hast obeyed my order." The boy placed himself by the margin of the well, and often saw a golden fish or a golden snake show itself therein, and took care that nothing fell in. As he was thus sitting, his finger hurt him so violently that he involuntarily put it in the water. He drew it quickly out again, but saw that it was quite gilded, and whatsoever pains he took to wash the gold off again, all was to no purpose.

In the evening Iron John came back, looked at the boy, and said,

"What has happened to the well?" "Nothing, nothing," he answered, and held his finger behind his back, that the man might not see it. But he said, "Thou hast dipped thy finger into the water; this time it may pass, but take care thou dost not let anything go in." By daybreak the boy was already sitting by the well and watching it. His finger hurt him again and he passed it over his head, and then unhappily a hair fell down into the well. He took it quickly out, but it was already quite gilded. Iron John came, and already knew what had happened. "Thou hast let a hair fall into the well," said he. "I will allow thee to watch by it once more, but if this happens for the third time then the well is polluted, and thou canst no longer remain with me."

On the third day, the boy sat by the well, and did not stir his finger, however much it hurt him. But the time was long to him, and he looked at the reflection of his face on the surface of the water. And as he still bent down more and more while he was doing so, and trying to look straight into the eyes, his long hair fell down from his shoulders into the water. He raised himself up quickly, but the whole of the hair of his head was already golden and shone like the sun. You may imagine how terrified the poor boy was! He took his pocket-handkerchief and tied it round his head, in order that the man might not see it. When he came he already knew everything, and said, "Take the handkerchief off." Then the golden hair streamed forth, and let the boy excuse himself as he might, it was of no use. "Thou hast not stood the trial, and canst stay here no longer. Go forth into the world, there thou wilt learn what poverty is. But as thou hast not a bad heart, and as I mean well by thee, there is one thing I will grant thee; if thou fallest into any difficulty, come to the forest and cry, 'Iron John,' and then I will come and help thee. My power is great, greater than thou thinkest, and I have gold and silver in abundance."

Then the King's son left the forest, and walked by beaten and unbeaten paths ever onwards until at length he reached a great city. There he looked for work, but could find none, and he had learnt nothing by which he could help himself. At length he went to the palace, and asked if they would take him in. The people about court did not at all know what use they could make of him, but they liked him, and told him to stay. At length the cook took him into his service, and said he might carry food and water, and rake the cinders together. Once when it so happened that no one else was at hand, the cook ordered him to carry the food to the royal table, but as he did not like to let his golden hair be seen, he kept his little cap on.

Such a thing as that had never yet come under the King's notice, and he said, "When thou comest to the royal table thou must take thy hat off." He answered, "Ah, Lord, I cannot; I have a bad sore place on my head." Then the King had the cook called before him and scolded him, and asked how he could take such a boy as that into his service, and that he was to turn him off at once. The cook, however, had pity on him, and exchanged him for the gardener's boy.

Now the boy had to plant and water the garden, hoe and dig, and bear the wind and bad weather. Once in summer when he was working alone in the garden, the day was so warm he took his little cap off that the air might cool him. As the sun shone on his hair it glittered and flashed so that the rays fell into the bed-room of the King's daughter, and up she sprang to see what that could be. Then she saw the boy, and cried to him, "Boy, bring me a wreath of flowers." He put his cap on with all haste, and gathered wild field-flowers and bound them together. When he was ascending the stairs with them, the gardener met him, and said, "How canst thou take the King's daughter a garland of such common flowers? Go quickly, and get another, and seek out the prettiest and rarest." "Oh, no," replied the boy, "the wild ones have more scent, and will please her better."

When he got into the room, the King's daughter said, "Take thy cap off, it is not seemly to keep it on in my presence." He again said, "I may not, I have a sore head." She, however, caught at his cap and pulled it off, and then his golden hair rolled down on his shoulders, and it was splendid to behold. He wanted to run out, but she held him by the arm, and gave him a handful of ducats. With these he departed, but he cared nothing for the gold pieces. He took them to the gardener, and said, "I present them to thy children, they can play with them."

The following day the King's daughter again called to him that he was to bring her a wreath of field-flowers, and when he went in with it, she instantly snatched at his cap, and wanted to take it away from him, but he held it fast with both hands. She again gave him a handful of ducats, but he would not keep them, and gave them to the gardener for playthings for his children. On the third day things went just the same; she could not get his cap away from him, and he would not have her money.

Not long afterwards, the country was overrun by war. The King gathered together his people, and did not know whether or not he could offer any opposition to the enemy, who was superior in strength and had a mighty army. Then said the gardener's boy, "I am grown up, and will go to the wars also, only give me a horse." The others laughed, and said, "Seek one for thyself when we are gone, we will leave one behind us in the stable for thee." When they had gone forth, he went into the stable, and got the horse out; it was lame of one foot, and limped hobblety jig, hobblety jig; nevertheless he mounted it, and rode away to the dark forest. When he came to the outskirts, he called "Iron John" three times so loudly that it echoed through the trees. Thereupon the wild man appeared immediately, and said, "What dost thou desire?" "I want a strong steed, for I am going to the wars." "That thou shalt have, and still more than thou askest for."

Then the wild man went back into the forest, and it was not long before a stable-boy came out of it, who led a horse that snorted with its nostrils, and could hardly be restrained, and behind them followed a great troop of soldiers entirely equipped in iron, and their swords flashed in the sun. The youth made over his three-legged horse to the stable-boy, mounted the other, and rode at the head of the soldiers. When he got near the battle-field a great part of the King's men had already fallen, and little was wanting to make the rest give way. Then the youth galloped thither with his iron soldiers, broke like a hurricane over the enemy, and beat down all who opposed him. They began to fly, but the youth pursued, and never stopped, until there was not a single man left. Instead, however, of returning to the King, he conducted his troop by bye-ways back to the forest, and called forth Iron John. "What dost thou desire?" asked the wild man. "Take back thy horse and thy troops, and give me my three-legged horse again." All that he asked was done, and soon he was riding on his three-legged horse.

When the King returned to his palace, his daughter went to meet him, and wished him joy of his victory. "I am not the one who carried away the victory," said he, "but a stranger knight who came to my assistance with his soldiers." The daughter wanted to hear who the strange knight was, but the King did not know, and said, "He followed the enemy, and I did not see him again." She inquired of the gardener where his boy was, but he smiled, and said, "He has just come home on his three-legged horse, and the others have been mocking him, and crying, 'Here comes our hobblety jig back again!' They asked, too, 'Under what hedge hast thou been lying sleeping all the time?' He, however, said, 'I did the best of all, and it would have gone badly without me.' And then he was still more ridiculed."

The King said to his daughter, "I will proclaim a great feast that shall last for three days, and thou shalt throw a golden apple. Perhaps the unknown will come to it." When the feast was announced, the youth went out to the forest, and called Iron John. "What dost thou desire?" asked he. "That I may catch the King's daughter's golden apple." "It is as safe as if thou hadst it already," said Iron John. "Thou shalt likewise have a suit of red armor for the occasion, and ride on a spirited chestnut horse." When the day came, the youth galloped to the spot, took his place amongst the knights, and was recognized by no one. The King's daughter came forward, and threw a golden apple to the knights, but none of them caught it but he, only as soon as he had it he galloped away.

On the second day Iron John equipped him as a white knight, and gave him a white horse. Again he was the only one who caught the apple, and he did not linger an instant, but galloped off with it. The King grew angry, and said, "That is not allowed; he must appear before me and tell his name." He gave the order that if the knight who caught the apple should go away again they should pursue him, and if he did not come back willingly, they were to cut him down and stab him.

On the third day, he received from Iron John a suit of black armor and a black horse, and again he caught the apple. But when he was riding off with it, the King's attendants pursued him, and one of them got so near him that he wounded the youth's leg with the point of his sword. The youth nevertheless escaped from them, but his horse leapt so violently that the helmet fell from the youth's head, and they could see that he had golden hair. They rode back and announced this to the King.

The following day the King's daughter asked the gardener about his boy, "He is at work in the garden; the queer creature has been at the festival too, and only came home yesterday evening; he has likewise shown my children three golden apples which he has won."

The King had him summoned into his presence, and he came and again had his little cap on his head. But the King's daughter went up to him and took it off, and then his golden hair fell down over his shoulders, and he was so handsome that all were amazed. "Art thou the knight who came every day to the festival, always in different colors, and who caught the three golden apples?" asked the King. "Yes," answered he, "and here the apples are," and he took them out of his pocket, and returned them to the King. "If thou desirest further proof, thou mayest see the wound which thy people gave me when they followed me. But I am likewise the knight who helped thee to thy victory over thine enemies." "If thou canst perform such deeds as that, thou art no gardener's boy; tell me, who is thy father?" "My father is a mighty King, and gold have I in plenty as great as I require." "I well see," said the King, "that I owe thanks to thee; can I do anything to please thee?" "Yes," answered he, "that indeed thou canst. Give me thy daughter to wife."

The maiden laughed, and said, "He does not stand much on ceremony, but I have already seen by his golden hair that he was no gardener's boy," and then she went and kissed him. His father and mother came to the wedding, and were in great delight, for they had given up all hope of ever seeing their dear son again. And as they were sitting at the marriage-feast, the music suddenly stopped, the doors opened, and a stately King came in with a great retinue. He went up to the youth, embraced him and said, "I am Iron John, and was by enchantment a wild man, but thou hast set me free; all the treasures which I possess, shall be thy property."

The Singing, Soaring Lark

There was once a man who was about to set out on a long journey, and on parting he asked his three daughters what he should bring back with him for them. The eldest wished for pearls, the second wished for diamonds, but the third said, "Dear father, I should like a singing, soaring lark." The father said, "Yes, if I can get it, you shall have it," kissed all three, and set out.

When the time had come for him to be on his way home again, he brought pearls and diamonds for the two eldest; but he had sought everywhere in vain for a singing, soaring lark for the youngest, and he was very unhappy about it, for she was his favorite child. His road lay through a forest, and in the midst of it was a splendid castle, and near the castle stood a tree, but quite on the top of the tree, he saw a singing, soaring lark. "Aha, you come just at the right moment!" he said, quite delighted, and called to his servant to climb up and catch the little creature.

But as he approached the tree, a lion leapt from beneath it, shook himself, and roared till the leaves on the tree trembled. "He who tries to steal my singing, soaring lark," he cried, "will I devour." Then the man said, "I did not know that the bird belonged to thee. I will make amends for the wrong I have done and ransom myself with a large sum of money, only spare my life." The lion said, "Nothing can save thee, unless thou wilt promise to give me for mine own what first meets thee on thy return home; but if thou wilt do that, I will grant thee thy life, and thou shalt have the bird for thy daughter, into the bargain."

But the man hesitated and said, "That might be my youngest daughter, she loves me best, and always runs to meet me on my return home." The servant, however, was terrified and said, "Why should your daughter be the very one to meet you, it might as easily be a cat, or dog?" Then the man allowed himself to be persuaded, took the singing, soaring lark, and promised to give the lion whatsoever should first meet him on his return home.

When he reached home and entered his house, the first who met him was no other than his youngest and dearest daughter, who came running up, kissed and embraced him, and when she saw that he had brought with him a singing, soaring lark, she was beside herself with joy. The father, however, could not rejoice, but began to weep, and said, "My dearest child, I have bought the little bird dear. In return for it, I have been obliged to promise thee to a savage lion, and when he has thee he will tear thee in pieces and devour thee," and he told her all, just as it had happened, and begged her not to go there, come what might. But she consoled him and said, "Dearest father, indeed your promise must be fulfilled. I will go thither and soften the lion, so that I may return to thee safely."

Next morning she had the road pointed out to her, took leave, and went fearlessly out into the forest. The lion, however, was an enchanted Prince and was by day a lion, and all his people were lions with him, but in the night they resumed their natural human shapes. On her arrival she was kindly received and led into the castle. When night came, the lion turned into a handsome man, and their wedding was celebrated with great magnificence. They lived happily together, remained awake at night, and slept in the daytime.

One day he came and said, "Tomorrow there is a feast in thy father's house, because thy eldest sister is to be married, and if thou art inclined to go there, my lions shall conduct thee." She said, "Yes, I should very much like to see my father again," and went thither, accompanied by the lions. There was great joy when she arrived, for they had all believed that she had been torn in pieces by the lion, and had long ceased to live. But she told them what a handsome husband she had, and how well off she was, remained with them while the wedding-feast lasted, and then went back again to the forest.

When the second daughter was about to be married, and she was again invited to the wedding, she said to the lion, "This time I will not be alone, thou must come with me." The lion, however, said that it was too dangerous for him, for if when there a ray from a burning candle fell on him, he would be changed into a dove, and for seven years long would have to fly about with the doves. She said, "Ah, but do come with me, I will take great care of thee, and guard thee from all light." So they went away together, and took with them their little child as well. She had a chamber built there, so strong and thick that no ray could pierce through it; in this he was to shut himself up when the candles were lit for the wedding-feast. But the door was made of green wood which warped and left a little crack which no one noticed.

The wedding was celebrated with magnificence, but when the pro-cession with all its candles and torches came back from church, and passed by this apartment, a ray about the breadth of a hair fell on the King's son, and when this ray touched him, he was transformed in an instant, and when she came in and looked for him, she did not see him, but a white dove was sitting there. The dove said to her, "For seven years must I fly about the world, but at every seventh step that thou takest I will let fall a drop of red blood and a white feather, and these will show thee the way, and if thou followest the trace thou canst release me." Thereupon the dove flew out at the door, and she followed him, and at every seventh step a red drop of blood and a little white feather fell down and showed her the way.

So she went continually further and further in the wide world, never looking about her or resting, and the seven years were almost past; then she rejoiced and thought that they would soon be delivered; and yet they were so far from it! Once when they were thus moving onwards, no little feather and no drop of red blood fell, and when she raised her eyes the dove had disappeared. And as she thought to herself, "In this no man can help thee," she climbed up to the sun, and said to him, "Thou shinest into every crevice, and over every peak, hast not thou seen a white dove flying?" "No," said the sun, "I have seen none, but I present thee with a casket, open it when thou art in sorest need."

Then she thanked the sun, and went on until evening came and the moon appeared; she then asked her, "Thou shinest the whole night through, and on every field and forest, hast thou not seen a white dove flying?" "No," said the moon, "I have seen no dove, but here I give thee an egg, break it when thou art in great need." She thanked the moon, and went on until the night wind came up and blew on her, then she said to it, "Thou blowest over every tree and under every leaf, hast thou not seen a white dove flying?" "No," said the night wind, "I have seen none, but I will ask the three other winds, perhaps they have seen it."

The east wind and the west wind came, and had seen nothing, but the south wind said, "I have seen the white dove, it has flown to the Red Sea; there it has become a lion again, for the seven years are over, and the lion is there fighting with a dragon; the dragon, however, is an enchanted Princess." The night wind then said to her, "I will advise thee; go to the Red Sea, on the right bank are some tall reeds, count them, break off the eleventh, and strike the dragon with it, then the lion will be able to subdue it, and both then will regain their human form. After that, look round and thou wilt see the griffin which is by the Red Sea; swing thyself, with thy beloved, on to his back, and the bird will carry thee over the sea to thine own home. Here is a nut for thee, when thou art above the center of the sea, let the nut fall, it will immediately shoot up, and a tall nut tree will grow out of the water, on which the griffin may rest; for if he cannot rest, he will not be strong enough to carry thee across, and if thou forgettest to throw down the nut, he will let thee fall into the sea."

Then she went thither, and found everything as the night wind had said. She counted the reeds by the sea, and cut off the eleventh, struck the dragon therewith, whereupon the lion overcame it, and immediately both of them regained their human shapes. But when the Princess, who had before been the dragon, was delivered from enchantment, she took the youth by the arm, seated herself on the griffin, and carried him off with her.

There stood the poor maiden who had wandered so far and was again forsaken. She sat down and cried, but at last she took courage and said, "Still I will go as far as the wind blows and as long as the cock crows, until I find him," and she went forth by long, long roads, until at last she came to the castle where both of them were living together. There she heard that soon a feast was to be held, in which they would celebrate their wedding, but she said, "God still helps me," and opened the casket that the sun had given her. A dress lay therein as brilliant as the sun itself. So she took it out and put it on, and went up into the castle, and every one, even the bride herself, looked at her with astonishment.

The dress pleased the bride so well that she thought it might do for her wedding-dress, and asked if it was for sale. "Not for money or land," answered she, "but for flesh and blood." The bride asked her what she meant by that, then she said, "Let me sleep a night in the chamber where the bridegroom sleeps." The bride would not, yet wanted very much to have the dress; at last she consented, but the page was to give the Prince a sleeping-draught.

When it was night, therefore, and the youth was already asleep, she was led into the chamber; she seated herself on the bed and said, "I have followed after thee for seven years. I have been to the sun and the moon, and the four winds, and have inquired for thee, and have helped thee against the dragon; wilt thou, then, quite forget me?" But the Prince slept so soundly that it only seemed to him as if the wind were whistling outside in the fir trees.

When therefore day broke, she was led out again, and had to give up the golden dress. And as even that had been of no avail, she was sad, went out into a meadow, sat down there, and wept. While she was sitting there, she thought of the egg which the moon had given her; she opened it, and there came out a clucking hen with twelve chickens all of gold, and they ran about chirping, and crept again under the old hen's wings; nothing more beautiful was ever seen in the world! Then she arose, and drove them through the meadow before her, until the bride looked out of the window. The little chickens pleased her so much that she immediately came down and asked if they were for sale. "Not for money or land, but for flesh and blood; let me sleep another night in the chamber where the bridegroom sleeps." The bride said, "Yes," intending to cheat her as on the former evening. But when the Prince went to bed he asked the page what the murmuring and rustling in the night had been. On this the page told all; that he had been forced to give him a sleeping-draught, because a poor girl had slept secretly in the chamber, and that he was to give him another that night. The Prince said, "Pour out the draught by the bed-side."

At night, she was again led in, and when she began to relate how ill all had fared with her, he immediately recognized his beloved wife by her voice, sprang up and cried, "Now I really am released! I have been as it were in a dream, for the strange Princess has bewitched me so that I have been compelled to forget thee, but God has delivered me from the spell at the right time." Then they both left the castle secretly in the night, for they feared the father of the Princess, who was a sorcerer, and they seated themselves on the griffin, which bore them across the Red Sea, and when they were in the midst of it, she let fall the nut. Immediately a tall nut tree grew up, whereon the bird rested, and then carried them home, where they found their child, who had grown tall and beautiful, and they lived thenceforth happily until their death.

The Nixie in the Pond

Once upon a time there was a miller who lived with his wife in great contentment. They had money and land, and their prosperity increased year by year more and more. But ill-luck comes like a thief in the night; as their wealth had increased so did it again decrease, year by year, and at last the miller could hardly call the mill in which he lived, his own. He was in great distress, and when he lay down after his day's work, found no rest, but tossed about in his bed, full of care.

One morning he rose before daybreak and went out into the open air, thinking that perhaps there his heart might become lighter. As he was stepping over the mill-dam the first sunbeam was just breaking forth, and he heard a rippling sound in the pond. He turned round and perceived a beautiful woman, rising slowly out of the water. Her long hair, which she was holding off her shoulders with her soft hands, fell down on both sides, and covered her white body. He soon saw that she was the Nixie of the Mill-pond, and in his fright did not know whether he should run away or stay where he was. But the nixie made her sweet voice heard, called him by his name, and asked him why he was so sad. The miller was at first struck dumb, but when he heard her speak so kindly, he took heart, and told her how he had formerly lived in wealth and happiness, but that now he was so poor that he did not know what to do. "Be easy," answered the nixie, "I will make thee richer and happier than thou hast ever been before, only thou must promise to give me the young thing which has just been born in thy house."

"What else can that be," thought the miller, "but a young puppy or kitten?" and he promised her what she desired. The nixie descended into the water again, and he hurried back to his mill, consoled and in good spirits. He had not yet reached it, when the maid-servant came out of the house, and cried to him to rejoice, for his wife had given birth to a little boy. The miller stood as if struck by lightning; he saw very well that the cunning nixie had been aware of it, and had cheated him. Hanging his head, he went up to his wife's bed-side and when she said, "Why dost thou not rejoice over the fine boy?" he told her what had befallen him, and what kind of a promise he had given to the nixie. "Of what use to me are riches and prosperity?" he added, "if I am to lose my child; but what can I do?" Even the relations, who had come thither to wish them joy, did not know what to say.

In the meantime prosperity again returned to the miller's house. All that he undertook succeeded, it was as if presses and coffers filled themselves of their own accord, and as if money multiplied nightly in the cupboards. It was not long before his wealth was greater than it had ever been before. But he could not rejoice over it untroubled, the bargain which he had made with the nixie tormented his soul. Whenever he passed the mill-pond, he feared she might ascend and remind him of his debt. He never let the boy himself go near the water. "Beware," he said to him, "if thou dost but touch the water, a hand will rise, seize thee, and draw thee down." But as year after year went by and the nixie did not show herself again, the miller began to feel at ease.

The boy grew up to be a youth and was apprenticed to a huntsman. When he had learnt everything, and had become an excellent hunts-man, the lord of the village took him into his service. In the village lived a beautiful and true-hearted maiden, who pleased the huntsman, and when his master perceived that, he gave him a little house, the two were married, lived peacefully and happily, and loved each other with all their hearts.

One day the huntsman was chasing a roe; and when the animal turned aside from the forest into the open country, he pursued it and at last shot it. He did not notice that he was now in the neighborhood of the dangerous mill-pond, and went, after he had disembowelled the stag, to the water, in order to wash his blood-stained hands. Scarcely, however, had he dipped them in than the nixie ascended, smilingly wound her dripping arms around him, and drew him quickly down under the waves, which closed over him.

When it was evening, and the huntsman did not return home, his wife became alarmed. She went out to seek him, and as he had often told her that he had to be on his guard against the snares of the nixie and dared not venture into the neighborhood of the millpond, she already suspected what had happened. She hastened to the water, and when she found his hunting-pouch lying on the shore, she could no longer have any doubt of the misfortune. Lamenting her sorrow, and wringing her hands, she called on her beloved by name, but in vain.

She hurried across to the other side of the pond, and called him anew; she reviled the nixie with harsh words, but no answer followed. The surface of the water remained calm, only the crescent moon stared steadily back at her. The poor woman did not leave the pond. With hasty steps, she paced round and round it, without resting a moment, sometimes in silence, sometimes uttering a loud cry, sometimes softly sobbing. At last her strength came to an end, she sank down to the ground and fell into a heavy sleep.

Presently a dream took possession of her. She was anxiously climbing upwards between great masses of rock; thorns and briars caught her feet, the rain beat in her face, and the wind tossed her long hair about. When she had reached the summit, quite a different sight presented itself to her; the sky was blue, the air soft, the ground sloped gently downwards, and on a green meadow, gay with flowers of every color, stood a pretty cottage. She went up to it and opened the door; there sat an old woman with white hair, who beckoned to her kindly.

At that very moment, the poor woman awoke, day had already dawned, and she at once resolved to act in accordance with her dream. She laboriously climbed the mountain; everything was exactly as she had seen it in the night. The old woman received her kindly, and pointed out a chair on which she might sit. "Thou must have met with a misfortune," she said, "since thou hast sought out my lonely cottage." With tears, the woman related what had befallen her. "Be comforted," said the old woman, "I will help thee. Here is a golden comb for thee. Tarry till the full moon has risen, then go to the mill-pond, seat thyself on the shore, and comb thy long black hair with this comb. When thou hast done, lay it down on the bank, and thou wilt see what will happen."

The woman returned home, but the time till the full moon came, passed slowly. At last the shining disc appeared in the heavens, then she went out to the mill-pond, sat down and combed her long black hair with the golden comb, and when she had finished, she laid it down at the water's edge. It was not long before there was a movement in the depths, a wave rose, rolled to the shore, and bore the comb away with it. In not more than the time necessary for the comb to sink to the bottom, the surface of the water parted, and the head of the huntsman arose. He did not speak, but looked at his wife with sorrowful glances. At the same instant, a second wave came rushing up, and covered the man's head. All had vanished, the mill-pond lay peaceful as before, and nothing but the face of the full moon shone on it.

Full of sorrow, the woman went back, but again the dream showed her the cottage of the old woman. Next morning she again set out and complained of her woes to the wise woman. The old woman gave her a golden flute, and said, "Tarry till the full moon comes again, then take this flute; play a beautiful air on it, and when thou hast finished, lay it on the sand; then thou wilt see what will happen." The wife did as the old woman told her. No sooner was the flute lying on the sand than there was a stirring in the depths, and a wave rushed up and bore the flute away with it. Immediately afterwards the water parted, and not only the head of the man, but half of his body also arose. He stretched out his arms longingly towards her, but a second wave came up, covered him, and drew him down again. "Alas, what does it profit me?" said the unhappy woman, "that I should see my beloved, only to lose him again!"

Despair filled her heart anew, but the dream led her a third time to the house of the old woman. She set out, and the wise woman gave her a golden spinning-wheel, consoled her and said, "All is not yet fulfilled, tarry until the time of the full moon, then take the spinning-wheel, seat thyself on the shore, and spin the spool full, and when thou hast done that, place the spinning-wheel near the water, and thou wilt see what will happen." The woman obeyed all she said exactly; as soon as the full moon showed itself, she carried the golden spinning-wheel to the shore, and spun industriously until the flax came to an end, and the spool was quite filled with the threads. No sooner was the wheel standing on the shore than there was a more violent movement than before in the depths of the pond, and a mighty wave rushed up, and bore the wheel away with it. Immediately the head and the whole body of the man rose into the air, in a water-spout. He quickly sprang to the shore, caught his wife by the hand and fled. But they had scarcely gone a very little distance, when the whole pond rose with a frightful roar, and streamed out over the open country. The fugitives already saw death before their eyes, when the woman in her terror implored the help of the old woman, and in an instant they were transformed, she into a toad, he into a frog. The flood which had overtaken them could not destroy them, but it tore them apart and carried them far away.

When the water had dispersed and they both touched dry land again, they regained their human form, but neither knew where the other was; they found themselves among strange people, who did not know their native land. High mountains and deep valleys lay between them. In order to keep themselves alive, they were both obliged to tend sheep. For many long years they drove their flocks through field and forest and were full of sorrow and longing. When spring had once more broken forth on the earth, they both went out one day with their flocks, and as chance would have it, they drew near each other. They met in a valley, but did not recognize each other; yet they rejoiced that they were no longer so lonely. Henceforth they each day drove their flocks to the same place; they did not speak much, but they felt comforted.

One evening when the full moon was shining in the sky, and the sheep were already at rest, the shepherd pulled the flute out of his pocket, and played on it a beautiful but sorrowful air. When he had finished he saw that the shepherdess was weeping bitterly. "Why are thou weeping?" he asked. "Alas," answered she, "thus shone the full moon when I played this air on the flute for the last time, and the head of my beloved rose out of the water." He looked at her, and it seemed as if a veil fell from his eyes, and he recognized his dear wife, and when she looked at him, and the moon shone in his face she knew him also. They embraced and kissed each other, and no one need ask if they were happy.

Hans the Hedgehog

There once was a countryman who had money and land in plenty, but no matter how rich he was, one thing was still wanting to complete his happiness—he had no children. Often when he went into the town with the other peasants they mocked him and asked why he had no children. At last he became angry, and when he got home he said, "I will have a child, even if it be a hedgehog." Then his wife had a child, that was a hedgehog in the upper part of his body, and a boy in the lower, and when she saw the child, she was terrified, and said, "See, there thou hast brought ill-luck on us." Then said the man, "What can be done now? The boy must be christened, but we shall not be able to get a godfather for him." The woman said, "And we cannot call him anything else but Hans the Hedgehog."

When he was christened, the parson said, "He cannot go into any ordinary bed because of his spikes." So a little straw was put behind the stove, and Hans the Hedgehog was laid on it. His mother could not suckle him, for he would have pricked her with his quills. So he lay there behind the stove for eight years, and his father was tired of him and thought, "If he would but die!" He did not die, however, but remained lying there.

Now it happened that there was a fair in the town, and the peasant was about to go to it, and asked his wife what he should bring back with him for her. "A little meat and a couple of white rolls which are wanted for the house," said she. Then he asked the servant, and she wanted a pair of slippers and some stockings with clocks. At last he said also, "And what wilt thou have, Hans my Hedgehog?" "Dear father," he said, "do bring me bagpipes."

When, therefore, the father came home again, he gave his wife what he had bought for her—meat and white rolls, and then he gave the maid the slippers, and the stockings with clocks; and lastly, he went behind the stove, and gave Hans the Hedgehog the bagpipes. And when Hans the Hedgehog had the bagpipes, he said, "Dear father, do go to the forge and get the cock shod, and then I will ride away, and never come back again." On this, the father was delighted to think that he was going to get rid of him, and had the cock shod for him, and when it was done, Hans the Hedgehog got on it, and rode away, but took swine and asses with him which he intended to keep in the forest.

When they got there he made the cock fly on to a high tree with him, and there he sat for many a long year, and watched his asses and swine until the herd was quite large, and his father knew nothing about him. While he was sitting in the tree, however, he played his bagpipes, and made music which was very beautiful. Once a King came traveling by who had lost his way and heard the music. He was astonished at it, and sent his servant forth to look all round and see from whence this music came. He spied about, but saw nothing but a little animal sitting up aloft on the tree, which looked like a cock with a hedgehog on it which made this music. Then the King told the servant he was to ask why he sat there, and if he knew the road which led to his kingdom.

So Hans the Hedgehog descended from the tree, and said he would show the way if the King would write a bond and promise him whatever he first met in the royal courtyard as soon as he arrived at home. Then the King thought, "I can easily do that, Hans the Hedgehog understands nothing, and I can write what I like." So the King took pen and ink and wrote something, and when he had done it, Hans the Hedgehog showed him the way, and he got safely home. But his daughter, when she saw him from afar, was so over-joyed that she ran to meet him, and kissed him. Then he remembered Hans the Hedgehog, and told her what had happened, and that he had been forced to promise whatsoever first met him when he got home, to a very strange animal which sat on a cock as if it were a horse, and made beautiful music, but that instead of writing that he should have what he wanted, he had written that he should not have it. Thereupon the Princess was glad, and said he had done well, for she never would have gone away with the Hedgehog.

Hans the Hedgehog, however, looked after his asses and pigs, and was always merry and sat on the tree and played his bagpipes.

Now it came to pass that another King came journeying by with his attendants and runners, and he also had lost his way, and did not know how to get home again because the forest was so large. He likewise heard the beautiful music from a distance, and asked his runner what that could be, and told him to go and see. Then the runner went under the tree, and saw the cock sitting at the top of it, and

Hans the Hedgehog on the cock. The runner asked him what he was about up there. "I am keeping my asses and my pigs; but what is your desire?" The messenger said that they had lost their way, and could not get back into their own kingdom, and asked if he would not show them the way. Then Hans the Hedgehog got down the tree with the cock, and told the aged King that he would show him the way, if he would give him for his own whatsoever first met him in front of his royal palace. The King said, "Yes," and wrote a promise to Hans the Hedgehog that he should have this. That done, Hans rode on before him on the cock, and pointed out the way, and the King reached his kingdom again in safety.

When he got to the courtyard, there were great rejoicings. The King had an only daughter who was very beautiful; she ran to meet him, threw her arms round his neck, and was delighted to have her old father back again. She asked him where in the world he had been so long. So he told her how he had lost his way, and had very nearly not come back at all, but that as he was traveling through a great forest, a creature, half hedgehog, half man, who was sitting astride a cock in a high tree, and making music, had shown him the way and helped him to get out; but that in return he had promised him whatsoever first met him in the royal courtyard, and how that was she herself, which made him unhappy now. But on this she promised that, for love of her father, she would willingly go with this Hans if he came.

Hans the Hedgehog, however, took care of his pigs, and the pigs multiplied until they became so many in number that the whole forest was filled with them. Then Hans the Hedgehog resolved not to live in the forest any longer, and sent word to his father to have every sty in the village emptied, for he was coming with such a great herd that all might kill who wished to do so. When his father heard that he was troubled, for he thought Hans the Hedgehog had died long ago. Hans the Hedgehog, however, seated himself on the cock, and drove the pigs before him into the village, and ordered the slaughter to begin. Ha!—but there was a killing and a chopping that might have been heard two miles off! After this Hans the Hedgehog said, "Father, let me have the cock shod once more at the forge, and then I will ride away and never come back as long as I live." Then the father had the cock shod once more, and was pleased that Hans the Hedgehog would never return again.

Hans the Hedgehog rode away to the first kingdom. There the King had commanded that whosoever came mounted on a cock and had bagpipes with him should be shot at, cut down, or stabbed by every one, so that he might not enter the palace. When, therefore, Hans the Hedgehog came riding thither, they all pressed forward against him with their pikes, but he spurred the cock and it flew up over the gate in front of the King's window and lighted there, and Hans cried that the King must give him what he had promised, or he would take both his life and his daughter's.

Then the King began to speak softly to his daughter and beg her to go away with Hans in order to save her own life and her father's. So she dressed herself in white, and her father gave her a carriage with six horses and magnificent attendants together with gold and possessions. She seated herself in the carriage, and placed Hans the Hedgehog beside her with the cock and the bagpipes, and then they took leave and drove away, and the King thought he should never see her again. He was, however, deceived in his expectation, for when they were at a short distance from the town, Hans the Hedgehog took her pretty clothes off, and pierced her with his hedgehog's skin until she bled all over. "That is the reward of your falseness," said he, "go your way, I will not have you!" and on that he chased her home again, and she was disgraced for the rest of her life.

Hans the Hedgehog, however, rode on further on the cock, with his bagpipes, to the dominions of the second King to whom he had shown the way. This one, however, had arranged that if any one resembling Hans the Hedgehog should come, they were to present arms, give him safe conduct, cry long life to him, and lead him to the royal palace.

But when the King's daughter saw him she was terrified, for he looked quite too strange. She remembered, however, that she could not change her mind, for she had given her promise to her father. So Hans the Hedgehog was welcomed by her, and married to her, and had to go with her to the royal table, and she seated herself by his side, and they ate and drank. When the evening came and they wanted to go to sleep, she was afraid of his quills, but he told her she was not to fear, for no harm would befall her, and he told the old King that he was to appoint four men to watch by the door of the chamber, and light a great fire, and when he entered the room and was about to get into bed, he would creep out of his hedgehog's skin and leave it lying there by the bed-side, and that the men were to run nimbly to it, throw it in the fire, and stay by it until it was consumed.

When the clock struck eleven, he went into the chamber, stripped off the hedgehog's skin, and left it lying by the bed. Then came the men and fetched it swiftly, and threw it in the fire; and when the fire had consumed it, he was delivered, and lay there in bed in human form, but he was coal-black as if he had been burnt. The King sent for his physician who washed him with precious salves, and anointed him, and he became white, and was a handsome young man. When the King's daughter saw that she was glad, and the next morning they arose joyfully, ate and drank, and then the marriage was properly solemnized, and Hans the Hedgehog received the kingdom from the aged King.

When several years had passed he went with his wife to his father, and said that he was his son. The father, however, declared he had no son—he had never had but one, and he had been born like a hedgehog with spikes, and had gone forth into the world. Then Hans made himself known, and the old father rejoiced and went with him to his kingdom.

The Golden Bird

In times gone by there was a King who had at the back of his castle a beautiful pleasure-garden, in which stood a tree that bore golden apples. As the apples ripened they were counted, but one morning one was missing. Then the King was angry, and he ordered that watch should be kept about the tree every night. Now the King had three sons, and he sent the eldest to spend the whole night in the garden: so he watched till midnight, and then he could keep off sleep no longer, and in the morning another apple was missing. The second son had to watch the following night; but it fared no better, for when twelve o'clock had struck he went to sleep, and in the morning another apple was missing. Now came the turn of the third son to watch, and he was ready to do so; but the King had less trust in him, and believed he would acquit himself still worse than his brothers, but in the end he consented to let him try. So the young man lay down under the tree to watch, and resolved that sleep should not be master. When it struck twelve something came rushing through the air, and he saw in the moonlight a bird flying towards him, whose feathers glittered like gold. The bird perched upon the tree, and had already pecked off an apple, when the young man let fly an arrow at it. The bird flew away, but the arrow had struck its target, and one of its golden feathers fell to the ground. The young man picked it up, and taking it next morning to the King, told him what had happened in the night.

The King called his council together, and all declared that such a feather was worth more than the whole kingdom. "Since the feather is so valuable," said the King, "one is not enough for me; I must and will have the whole bird."

So the eldest son set off, and relying on his own cleverness he thought he should soon find the golden bird. When he had gone some distance he saw a fox sitting at the edge of a wood, and he pointed his gun at him.

The fox cried out, "Do not shoot me, and I will give you good counsel. You are on your way to find the golden bird, and this evening you will come to a village, in which two taverns stand facing each

other. One will be brightly lighted up, and there will be plenty of merriment going on inside; do not mind about that, but go into the other
one, although it will look to you very uninviting."

"How can a silly beast give one any rational advice?" thought the
King's son, and let fly at the fox, but missed him, and he stretched out
his tail and ran quickly into the wood. Then the young man went on
his way, and towards evening he came to the village, and there stood
the two taverns; in one singing and dancing was going on, the other
looked quite dull and wretched. "I should be a fool," said he, "to go
into that dismal place, while there is anything so good close by." So
he went into the merry inn, and there lived in clover, quite forgetting
the bird and his father, and all good counsel.

As time went on, and the eldest son never came home, the second
son set out to seek the golden bird. He met with the fox, just as the
eldest did, and received good advice from him without attending to
it. And when he came to the two taverns, his brother was standing
and calling to him at the window of one of them, out of which came
sounds of merriment; so he could not resist, but went in and reveled
to his heart's content.

And then, as time went on, the youngest son wished to go forth,
and to try his luck, but his father would not consent. "It would be useless," said he; "he is much less likely to find the bird than his brothers,
and if any misfortune were to happen to him he would not know how
to help himself; his wits are none of the best."

But at last, as there was no peace to be had, he let him go. By the
side of the wood sat the fox, begged him to spare his life, and gave him
good counsel. The young man was kind, and said, "Be easy, little fox,
I will do you no harm."

"You shall not repent of it," answered the fox, "and that you may
get there all the sooner, get up and sit on my tail."

And no sooner had he done so than the fox began to run, and
off they went over stock and stone, so that the wind whistled in their
hair. When they reached the village the young man got down, and,
following the fox's advice, went into the mean-looking tavern, without
hesitating, and there he passed a quiet night.

The next morning, when he went out into the field, the fox, who
was sitting there already, said, "I will tell you further what you have
to do. Go straight on until you come to a castle, before which a great
band of soldiers lie, but do not trouble yourself about them, for they
will be all asleep and snoring; pass through them and forward into

the castle, and go through all the rooms, until you come to one where there is a golden bird hanging in a wooden cage. Near at hand will stand, empty, a golden cage of state, but you must beware of taking the bird out of his ugly cage and putting him into the fine one; if you do so you will come to harm."

After he had finished saying this the fox stretched out his tail again, and the King's son sat him down upon it; then away they went over stock and stone, so that the wind whistled through their hair. And when the King's son reached the castle he found everything as the fox had said, and he at last entered the room where the golden bird was hanging in a wooden cage, while a golden one was standing by; the three golden apples too were in the room. Then, thinking it foolish to let the beautiful bird stay in that mean and ugly cage, he opened the door of it, took hold of it, and put it in the golden one. In the same moment the bird uttered a piercing cry. The soldiers awaked, rushed in, seized the King's son and put him in prison. The next morning he was brought before a judge, and, as he confessed everything, condemned to death. But the King said he would spare his life on one condition, that he should bring him the golden horse whose paces were swifter than the wind, and that then he should also receive the golden bird as a reward.

So the King's son set off to find the golden horse, but he sighed, and was very sad, for how should it be accomplished? And then he saw his old friend the fox sitting by the roadside.

"Now, you see," said the fox, "all this has happened because you would not listen to me. But be of good courage, I will bring you through, and will tell you how you are to get the golden horse. You must go straight on until you come to a castle, where the horse stands in his stable; before the stable-door the grooms will be lying, but they will all be asleep and snoring; and you can go and quietly lead out the horse. But one thing you must mind—take care to put upon him the plain saddle of wood and leather, and not the golden one, which will hang close by; otherwise it will go badly with you."

Then the fox stretched out his tail, and the King's son seated himself upon it, and away they went over stock and stone until the wind whistled through their hair. And everything happened just as the fox had said, and he came to the stall where the golden horse was, and as he was about to put on him the plain saddle, he thought to himself, "Such a beautiful animal would be disgraced were I not to put on him the good saddle, which becomes him so well."

However, no sooner did the horse feel the golden saddle touch him than he began to neigh. And the grooms all awoke, seized the King's son and threw him into prison. The next morning he was delivered up to justice and condemned to death, but the King promised him his life, and also to bestow upon him the golden horse, if he could convey thither the beautiful Princess of the golden castle.

With a heavy heart the King's son set out, but by great good luck he soon met with the faithful fox.

"I ought now to leave you to your own ill-luck," said the fox, "but I am sorry for you, and will once more help you in your need. Your way lies straight up to the golden castle. You will arrive there in the evening, and at night when all is quiet, the beautiful Princess goes to the bath. And as she is entering the bathing-house, go up to her and give her a kiss, then she will follow you, and you can lead her away; but do not suffer her first to go and take leave of her parents, or it will go ill with you."

Then the fox stretched out his tail, the King's son seated himself upon it, and away they went over stock and stone, so that the wind whistled through their hair. And when he came to the golden castle all was as the fox had said. He waited until midnight, when all lay in deep sleep, and then as the beautiful Princess went to the bathing-house he went up to her and gave her a kiss, and she willingly promised to go with him, but she begged him earnestly, and with tears, that he would let her first go and take leave of her parents. At first he denied her prayer, but as she wept so much the more, and fell at his feet, he gave in at last. And no sooner had the Princess reached her father's bedside than he, and all who were in the castle, waked up, and the young man was seized and thrown into prison.

The next morning the King said to him, "Thy life is forfeit, but thou shalt find grace if thou canst level that mountain that lies before my windows, and over which I am not able to see; and if this is done within eight days thou shalt have my daughter for a reward."

So the King's son set to work, and dug and shoveled away without ceasing, but when, on the seventh day, he saw how little he had accomplished, and that all his work was as nothing, he fell into great sadness, and gave up all hope. But on the evening of the seventh day the fox appeared, and said, "You do not deserve that I should help you, but go now and lie down to sleep, and I will do the work for you."

The next morning when he awoke, and looked out of the window, the mountain had disappeared. The young man hastened full of joy to the

King, and told him that his behest was fulfilled, and, whether the King liked it or not, he had to keep to his word, and let his daughter go.

So they both went away together, and it was not long before the faithful fox came up to them.

"Well, you have got the best first," said he; "but you must know the golden horse belongs to the Princess of the golden castle."

"But how shall I get it?" asked the young man.

"I am going to tell you," answered the fox. "First, go to the King who sent you to the golden castle, and take to him the beautiful Princess. There will then be very great rejoicing; he will willingly give you the golden horse, and they will lead him out to you; then mount him without delay, and stretch out your hand to each of them to take leave, and last of all to the Princess, and when you have her by the hand swing her up on the horse behind you, and off you go! nobody will be able to overtake you, for that horse goes swifter than the wind."

And so it was all happily done, and the King's son carried off the beautiful Princess on the golden horse. The fox did not stay behind, and he said to the young man, "Now, I will help you to get the golden bird. When you draw near the castle where the bird is, let the lady alight, and I will take her under my care; then you must ride the golden horse into the castle-yard, and there will be great rejoicing to see it, and they will bring out to you the golden bird. As soon as you have the cage in your hand, you must start off back to us, and then you shall carry the lady away."

The plan was successfully carried out; and when the young man returned with the treasure, the fox said, "Now, what will you give me for my reward?"

"What would you like?" asked the young man.

"When we are passing through the wood, I desire that you should slay me, and cut my head and feet off."

"That were a strange sign of gratitude," said the King's son, "and I could not possibly do such a thing."

Then said the fox, "If you will not do it, I must leave you; but before I go let me give you some good advice. Beware of two things: buy no gallows-meat, and sit at no brook-side." With that the fox ran off into the wood.

The young man thought to himself, "That is a wonderful animal, with most singular ideas. How should any one buy gallows-meat? and I am sure I have no particular fancy for sitting by a brook-side."

So he rode on with the beautiful Princess, and their way led them through the village where his two brothers had stayed. There they heard great outcry and noise, and when he asked what it was all about, they told him that two people were going to be hanged. And when he drew near he saw that it was his two brothers, who had done all sorts of evil tricks, and had wasted all their goods. He asked if there were no means of setting them free.

"Oh yes! if you will buy them off," answered the people; "but why should you spend your money in redeeming such worthless men?"

But he persisted in doing so; and when they were let go they all went on their journey together.

After a while they came to the wood where the fox had met them first, and there it seemed so cool and sheltered from the sun's burning rays that the two brothers said, "Let us rest here for a little by the brook, and eat and drink to refresh ourselves."

The young man consented, quite forgetting the fox's warning, and he seated himself by the brook-side, suspecting no evil. But the two brothers thrust him backwards into the brook, seized the Princess, the horse, and the bird, and went home to their father.

"Is not this the golden bird that we bring?" said they; "and we have also the golden horse, and the Princess of the golden castle."

Then there was great rejoicing in the royal castle, but the horse did not feed, the bird did not chirp, and the Princess sat still and wept.

The youngest brother, however, had not perished. The brook was, by good fortune, dry, and he fell on soft moss without receiving any hurt, but he could not get up again. But in his need the faithful fox was not lacking; he came up running, and reproached him for having forgotten his advice.

"But I cannot forsake you all the same," said he; "I will help you back again into daylight." So he told the young man to grasp his tail, and hold on to it fast, and so he drew him up again.

"Still you are not quite out of all danger," said the fox; "your brothers, not being certain of your death, have surrounded the wood with sentinels, who are to put you to death if you let yourself be seen."

A poor beggar-man was sitting by the path, and the young man changed clothes with him, and went in that disguise into the King's courtyard. Nobody knew him, but the bird began to chirp, and the horse began to feed, and the beautiful Princess ceased weeping.

"What does this mean?" said the King, astonished.

The Princess answered, "I cannot tell, except that I was sad, and now I am joyful; it is to me as if my rightful bridegroom had returned."

Then she told him all that happened, although the two brothers had threatened to put her to death if she let out anything. The King then ordered every person who was in the castle to be brought before him, and with the rest came the young man like a beggar in his wretched garments; but the Princess knew him, and greeted him well, falling on his neck and kissing him. The wicked brothers were seized and put to death, and the youngest brother was married to the Princess, and succeeded to the inheritance of his father.

But what became of the poor fox? Long afterwards the King's son was going through the wood, and the fox met him and said, "Now, you have everything that you can wish for, but my misfortunes never come to an end, and it lies in your power to free me from them." And once more he prayed the King's son earnestly to slay him, and cut off his head and feet. So, at last, he consented, and no sooner was it done than the fox was changed into a man, and was no other than the brother of the beautiful Princess; and thus he was set free from a spell that had bound him for a long, long time.

And now, indeed, there lacked nothing to their happiness as long as they lived.

The Fisherman and His Wife

There was once a fisherman and his wife who lived together in a hovel by the sea-shore, and the fisherman went out every day with his hook and line to catch fish, and he angled and angled.

One day he was sitting with his rod and looking into the clear water, and he sat and sat.

At last down went the line to the bottom of the water, and when he drew it up he found a great flounder on the hook. And the flounder said to him, "Fisherman, listen to me; let me go. I am not a real fish but an enchanted Prince. What good shall I be to you if you land me? I shall not taste well; so put me back into the water again, and let me swim away."

"Well," said the fisherman, "no need of so many words about the matter; as you can speak I had much rather let you swim away."

Then he put him back into the clear water, and the flounder sank to the bottom, leaving a long streak of blood behind him. Then the fisherman got up and went home to his wife in their hovel.

"Well, husband," said the wife, "have you caught nothing today?" "No," said the man—"that is, I did catch a flounder, but as he said he was an enchanted Prince, I let him go again." "Then, did you wish for nothing?" said the wife. "No," said the man; "what should I wish for?"

"Oh dear!" said the wife; "and it is so dreadful always to live in this evil-smelling hovel; you might as well have wished for a little cottage. Go again and call him; tell him we want a little cottage, I daresay he will give it us; go, and be quick."

And when he went back, the sea was green and yellow, and not nearly so clear. So he stood and said,

> "O man, O man!—if man you be,
> Or flounder, flounder, in the sea—
> Such a tiresome wife I've got,
> For she wants what I do not."

Then the flounder came swimming up, and said, "Now then, what does she want?"

"Oh," said the man, "you know when I caught you my wife says I ought to have wished for something. She does not want to live any longer in the hovel, and would rather have a cottage." "Go home with you," said the flounder, "she has it already."

So the man went home, and found, instead of the hovel, a little cottage, and his wife was sitting on a bench before the door. And she took him by the hand, and said to him, "Come in and see if this is not a great improvement."

So they went in, and there was a little house-place and a beautiful little bed-room, a kitchen and larder, with all sorts of furniture, and iron and brass ware of the very best. And at the back was a little yard with fowls and ducks, and a little garden full of green vegetables and fruit.

"Look," said the wife, "is not that nice?" "Yes," said the man, "if this can only last we shall be very well contented." "We will see about that," said the wife. And after a meal they went to bed.

So all went well for a week or fortnight, when the wife said, "Look here, husband, the cottage is really too confined, and the yard and garden are so small; I think the flounder had better get us a larger house; I should like very much to live in a large stone castle; so go to your fish and he will send us a castle."

"Oh my dear wife," said the man, "the cottage is good enough; what do we want a castle for?" "We want one," said the wife; "go along with you; the flounder can give us one."

"Now, wife," said the man, "the flounder gave us the cottage; I do not like to go to him again, he may be angry." "Go along," said the wife, "he might just as well give us it as not; do as I say!"

The man felt very reluctant and unwilling; and he said to himself, "It is not the right thing to do"; nevertheless he went.

So when he came to the sea-side, the water was purple and dark blue and gray and thick, and not green and yellow as before. And he stood and said,

> "O man, O man!—if man you be,
> Or flounder, flounder, in the sea—
> Such a tiresome wife I've got,
> For she wants what I do not."

"Now then, what does she want?" said the flounder.

"Oh," said the man, half frightened, "she wants to live in a large stone castle." "Go home with you, she is already standing before the door," said the flounder.

Then the man went home, as he supposed, but when he got there, there stood in the place of the cottage a great castle of stone, and his wife was standing on the steps, about to go in; so she took him by the hand, and said, "Let us enter."

With that he went in with her, and in the castle was a great hall with a marble pavement, and there were a great many servants, who led them through large doors, and the passages were decked with tapestry, and the rooms with golden chairs and tables, and crystal chandeliers hanging from the ceiling; and all the rooms had carpets. And the tables were covered with eatables and the best wine for any one who wanted them. And at the back of the house was a great stable-yard for horses and cattle, and carriages of the finest; besides, there was a splendid large garden, with the most beautiful flowers and fine fruit trees, and a pleasance full half a mile long, with deer and oxen and sheep, and everything that heart could wish for.

"There!" said the wife, "is not this beautiful?" "Oh yes," said the man, "if it will only last we can live in this fine castle and be very well contented." "We will see about that," said the wife, "in the meanwhile we will sleep upon it." With that they went to bed.

The next morning the wife was awake first, just at the break of day, and she looked out and saw from her bed the beautiful country lying all round. The man took no notice of it, so she poked him in the side with her elbow, and said, "Husband, get up and just look out of the window. Look, just think if we could be King over all this country! Just go to your fish and tell him we should like to be King."

"Now, wife," said the man, "what should we be Kings for? I don't want to be King." "Well," said the wife, "if you don't want to be King, I will be King."

"Now, wife," said the man, "what do you want to be King for? I could not ask him such a thing." "Why not?" said the wife, "you must go directly all the same; I must be King."

So the man went, very much put out that his wife should want to be King.

"It is not the right thing to do—not at all the right thing," thought the man. He did not at all want to go, and yet he went all the same.

And when he came to the sea the water was quite dark gray, and rushed far inland, and had an ill smell. And he stood and said,

> "O man, O man!—if man you be,
> Or flounder, flounder, in the sea—
> Such a tiresome wife I've got,
> For she wants what I do not."

"Now then, what does she want?" said the fish. "Oh dear!" said the man, "she wants to be King." "Go home with you, she is King already," said the fish.

So the man went back, and as he came to the palace he saw it was very much larger, and had great towers and splendid gateways; the herald stood before the door, and a number of soldiers with kettle-drums and trumpets.

And when he came inside everything was of marble and gold, and there were many curtains with great golden tassels. Then he went through the doors of the saloon to where the great throne-room was, and there was his wife sitting upon a throne of gold and diamonds, and she had a great golden crown on, and the scepter in her hand was of pure gold and jewels, and on each side stood six pages in a row, each one a head shorter than the other. So the man went up to her and said, "Well, wife, so now you are King!" "Yes," said the wife, "now I am King."

So then he stood and looked at her, and when he had gazed at her for some time he said, "Well, wife, this is fine for you to be King! Now there is nothing more to wish for." "Oh husband!" said the wife, seeming quite restless, "I am tired of this already. Go to your fish and tell him that now I am King I must be Emperor."

"Now, wife," said the man, "what do you want to be Emperor for?" "Husband," said she, "go and tell the fish I want to be Emperor."

"Oh dear!" said the man, "he could not do it—I cannot ask him such a thing. There is but one Emperor at a time; the fish can't possibly make any one Emperor—indeed he can't."

"Now, look here," said the wife, "I am King, and you are only my husband, so will you go at once? Go along! for if he was able to make me King he is able to make me Emperor; and I will and must be Emperor, so go along!"

So he was obliged to go; and as he went he felt very uncomfortable about it, and he thought to himself, "It is not at all the right thing to do; to want to be Emperor is really going too far; the flounder will soon be beginning to get tired of this."

With that he came to the sea, and the water was quite black and thick, and the foam flew, and the wind blew, and the man was terrified. But he stood and said,

> "O man, O man!—if man you be,
> Or flounder, flounder, in the sea—
> Such a tiresome wife I've got,
> For she wants what I do not."

"What is it now?" said the fish. "Oh dear!" said the man, "my wife wants to be Emperor." "Go home with you," said the fish, "she is Emperor already."

So the man went home, and found the castle adorned with polished marble and alabaster figures, and golden gates. The troops were being marshaled before the door, and they were blowing trumpets and beating drums and cymbals; and when he entered he saw barons and earls and dukes waiting about like servants; and the doors were of bright gold. And he saw his wife sitting upon a throne made of one entire piece of gold, and it was about two miles high; and she had a great golden crown on, which was about three yards high, set with brilliants and carbuncles; and in one hand she held the scepter, and in the other the globe; and on both sides of her stood pages in two rows, all arranged according to their size, from the most enormous giant of two miles high to the tiniest dwarf of the size of my little finger; and before her stood earls and dukes in crowds.

So the man went up to her and said, "Well, wife, so now you are Emperor." "Yes," said she, "now I am Emperor."

Then he went and sat down and had a good look at her, and then he said, "Well now, wife, there is nothing left to be, now you are Emperor." "What are you talking about, husband?" said she; "I am Emperor, and next I will be Pope! so go and tell the fish so."

"Oh dear!" said the man, "what is it that you don't want? You can never become Pope; there is but one Pope in Christendom, and the fish can't possibly do it." "Husband," said she, "no more words about it; I must and will be Pope; so go along to the fish."

"Now, wife," said the man, "how can I ask him such a thing? It is too bad—it is asking a little too much; and, besides, he could not do it." "What rubbish!" said the wife; "if he could make me Emperor he can make me Pope. Go along and ask him; I am Emperor, and you are only my husband, so go you must."

So he went, feeling very frightened, and he shivered and shook, and his knees trembled; and there arose a great wind, and the clouds flew by, and it grew very dark, and the sea rose mountains high, and the ships were tossed about, and the sky was partly blue in the middle, but at the sides very dark and red, as in a great tempest. And he felt very despondent, and stood trembling and said,

> "O man, O man!—if man you be,
> Or flounder, flounder, in the sea—
> Such a tiresome wife I've got,
> For she wants what I do not."

"Well, what now?" said the fish. "Oh dear!" said the man, "she wants to be Pope." "Go home with you, she is Pope already," said the fish.

So he went home, and he found himself before a great church, with palaces all round. He had to make his way through a crowd of people; and when he got inside he found the place lighted up with thousands and thousands of lights; and his wife was clothed in a golden garment, and sat upon a very high throne, and had three golden crowns on, all in the greatest priestly pomp; and on both sides of her there stood two rows of lights of all sizes—from the size of the longest tower to the smallest rushlight, and all the Emperors and Kings were kneeling before her and kissing her foot.

"Well, wife," said the man, and sat and stared at her, "so you are Pope." "Yes," said she, "now I am Pope!"

And he went on gazing at her till he felt dazzled, as if he were sitting in the sun. And after a little time he said, "Well, now, wife, what is there left to be, now you are Pope?" And she sat up very stiff and straight, and said nothing.

And he said again, "Well, wife, I hope you are contented at last with being Pope; you can be nothing more."

"We will see about that," said the wife. With that they both went to bed; but she was as far as ever from being contented, and she could not get to sleep for thinking of what she should like to be next.

The husband, however, slept as fast as a top after his busy day; but the wife tossed and turned from side to side the whole night through, thinking all the while what she could be next, but nothing would occur to her; and when she saw the red dawn she slipped off the bed, and sat before the window to see the sun rise, and as it came up she said, "Ah, I have it! Cannot I make the sun and moon to rise? Husband!" she cried, and stuck her elbow in his ribs, "wake up, and go to your fish, and tell him I want to be God."

The man was so fast asleep that when he started up he fell out of bed. Then he shook himself together, and opened his eyes and said, "Oh wife, what did you say?"

"Husband," said she, "if I cannot get the power of making the sun and moon rise when I want them, I shall never have another quiet hour. Go to the fish and tell him so."

"Oh wife!" said the man, and fell on his knees to her, "the fish can really not do that for you. I grant you he could make you Emperor and Pope. Do be contented with that, I beg of you."

And she became wild with impatience, and screamed out, "I can wait no longer, go at once! I want to be God!"

And so off he went as well as he could for fright. And a dreadful storm arose, so that he could hardly keep his feet; and the houses and trees were blown down, and the mountains trembled, and rocks fell in the sea; the sky was quite black, and it thundered and lightninged; and the waves, crowned with foam, ran mountains high. So he cried out, without being able to hear his own words,

> "O man, O man!—if man you be,
> Or flounder, flounder, in the sea—
> Such a tiresome wife I've got,
> For she wants what I do not."

"Well, what now?" said the flounder.

"Oh dear!" said the man, "she wants to be God!" "Go home with you!" said the flounder, "you will find her the way she was—in the old hovel."

And there they are sitting to this very day.

The Youth Who Could Not
Shiver and Shake

A father had two sons. The elder was smart and could do anything. But the younger was so stupid that he could neither learn nor understand a thing, and people would say, "What a burden that stupid boy must be to his father."

Whatever the father wanted done, Jack, the elder boy, was obliged to do, even to take messages, for his brother was too stupid to understand or remember. But Jack was a terrible coward, and if his father wished him to go anywhere late in the evening, and the road led through the churchyard, he would say, "Oh, no, father, I can't go there, it makes me tremble and shake so."

Sometimes when they sat round the fire in the evening, while someone told stories that frightened him, he would say, "Please don't go on, it makes me shake all over."

The younger boy, seated in his corner among the listeners, would open his eyes quite wide and say, "I can't think what he means by saying it makes him shiver and shake. It must be something very wonderful that could make me shiver and shake."

At last one day the father spoke to his younger son very plainly and said, "Listen, you there in the corner; you are growing tall and strong, you must learn very soon to earn your own living. See how your brother works, while you do nothing but run and jump about all day."

"Well, father," he replied, "I am quite ready to earn my own living when you like, if I may only learn to shiver and shake, for I don't know how to do that at all."

His brother laughed at this speech, and said to himself, "What a simpleton my brother is! He will have to sweep the streets by and by or else starve."

His father sighed and said, "You will never get your living by that, boy, but you will soon learn to shiver and shake, no doubt."

Just at this moment the sexton of the church came in, and the father related the trouble he was in about his younger son who was so silly and unable to learn. "What do you think he said to me when I told him he must learn to earn his own living?" asked the father. "Something silly, I suppose," answered the sexton. "Silly, indeed! he said he wished he could learn to shiver and shake." "Oh!" cried the sexton, "let him come to me, I'll soon manage that for him; he won't be long learning to shiver and shake if I have him with me."

The father was delighted with this proposal; it was really a good beginning for his stupid son. So the sexton took the youth in hand at once, led him to the church tower, and made him help ring the bells. For the first two days he liked it very well, but on the third at midnight the sexton roused him out of his sleep to toll the passing bell; he had to mount to the highest part of the church tower. "You will soon learn what it is to shiver and shake now, young man," thought the sexton, but he did not go home, as we shall hear later on.

The youth walked through the churchyard and mounted the steps to the belfry without feeling the least fear, but just as he reached the bell rope, he saw a figure in white standing on the steps. "Who's there?" he cried. But the figure neither moved nor spoke. "Answer me," he said, "or take yourself off; you have no business here."

But the sexton, who had disguised himself to frighten the boy, remained immovable, for he wished to be taken for a ghost, but Hans was not to be frightened. He exclaimed, for the second time, "What do you want here? Speak, if you are an honest man, or I will throw you down the steps."

The sexton, thinking he could not intend to do anything so dreadful, answered not a word, but stood still, as if he were made of stone. "Once more, I ask you what you want," said Hans; and as there was still no answer, he sprung upon the sham ghost, and giving him a push, he rolled down ten steps, and falling into a corner, there remained.

Thereupon Hans went back to the bell, tolled it for the proper number of minutes, then went home, laid himself down without saying a word, and went fast asleep.

The sexton's wife waited a long time for her husband, and finding he did not come home she became alarmed, and going to Hans, woke him and said, "Do you know why my husband is staying out so late—he was with you in the tower I suppose?"

"There was someone dressed in white standing on the top of the steps when I went into the belfry, and as he would not answer a word when I spoke to him, I took him for a thief and kicked him down-stairs. We will go and see who it is; if it should be your husband I shall be sorry, but of course I did not know."

The wife ran out to the tower and found her husband lying in a corner groaning, for he had broken his leg. Then she went to the father of Hans with a loud outcry against the boy. "Your son," cried she, "has brought bad luck to the house; he has thrown my husband down the steps and broken his leg; he shan't stay with us any longer, send for him home."

Then the father was terribly vexed, sent for his son, and scolded him. "What do you mean, you wretched boy," he said, "by these wicked tricks?" "Father," answered the boy, "hear what I have to say. I never meant to do wrong, but when I saw a white figure standing there in the night, of course I thought it was there for some bad pur-pose. I did not know it was the sexton, and I warned him three times what I would do, if he did not answer."

"Ah! yes, you are the plague of my life," said his father. "Now get out of my sight, and never let me see you again." "Yes, father, I will go right willingly tomorrow, and then if I learn to shiver and shake, I shall acquire knowledge that will enable me to earn my living at all events."

"Learn what you like," said his father, "it's all the same to me. There are fifty dollars, take them and go out into the world when you please; but don't tell any one where you come from, or who is your father, for I am ashamed to own you." "Father," said Hans, "I will do just as you tell me; your orders are very easy to perform."

At daybreak the next morning, the youth put the fifty dollars into his pocket, and went out into the highroad, saying to himself as he walked on, "When shall I learn to shiver and shake—when shall I learn to be afraid?"

Presently a man met him on the road, overheard what he said, and saw at once that the young man was fearless. He quickly joined him, and they walked a little way together till they came to a spot where they could see a gallows.

"Look," he said, "there is a tree where seven men have been mar-ried with the ropemaker's daughter, and have learned how to swing; if you only sit down here and watch them till night comes on, I'll answer for it you will shiver and shake before morning." "I never had a better opportunity," answered the youth. "That is very easily done. You come to me again early tomorrow morning, and if it teaches me to shiver and shake, you shall have my fifty dollars."

Then the young man went and seated himself under the gallows and waited till the evening, and feeling cold he lighted a fire; but at midnight the wind rose and blew so fiercely and chill, that even a large fire could not warm him.

The high cold wind made the bodies of the murderers swing to and fro, and he thought to himself, if I am so cold down here by the fire, they must be frozen up there; and after pitying them for some time he climbed up, untied the ropes and brought down all the seven bodies, stirred the fire into a blaze, and seated them round it so close, that their clothes caught fire. Finding they did not move, he said to them, "Sit farther back, will you, or I will hang you up again." But the dead could not hear him, they only sat silent and let their rags burn.

Then Hans became angry, and said, "If you will not move, there is no help for it; I must not let you burn, I must hang you up." So he hung the seven bodies up again all in a row, then laid himself down by the fire and fell fast asleep.

In the morning the man came, according to his promise, hoping to get the fifty dollars. "Well, I suppose you know now what it is to shiver and shake?" he said.

"No, indeed," he replied. "Why should I? Those men up there have not opened their mouths once; and when I seated them round the fire, they allowed their old rags to burn without moving, and if I had not hung the bodies up again, they would have been burned also." The man looked quite scared when he heard this, and went away without attempting to ask for the fifty dollars.

Then Hans continued his journey, and again said aloud to himself, "I wonder what this shivering and shaking can be."

A wagoner walking along the road by his horses overtook him, and asked who he was. "I don't know," he replied. The wagoner asked again, "Why are you here?" "I can't tell," said Hans. "Who is your father?" "I dare not say." "What were you grumbling about just now, when I came up with you?" "I want to learn to shiver and shake," said Hans.

"Don't talk nonsense," said the wagoner. "Come with me, I will show you a little of the world, and find you something to do better than that."

So the young man went with the wagoner, and about evening they arrived at an inn, where they put up for the night. No sooner, however, did Hans enter the room than he muttered to himself, "Oh! if I could only learn to shiver and shake." The landlord heard him, and said with a laugh, "If that is all you wish to learn, I can tell you of a splendid opportunity in this part of the world."

"Ah! be silent now," said the landlady. "You know how many people have already lost their lives through their curiosity. It would be a pity for a nice young man like this, with such fine blue eyes, never to see daylight again."

But Hans spoke for himself at once. "If it is so bad as you say," he cried, "I should like to try as soon as possible; all I want is to learn how to shiver and shake, so tell me what I am to do." And the youth gave the landlord no rest till he had explained the matter to him.

"Well," he said at last, "not far from here stands an enchanted castle, where you could easily learn to shiver and shake, if you remain in it. The King of the country has promised to give his daughter in marriage to any one who will venture to sleep in the castle for three nights, and she is as beautiful a young lady as the sun ever shone upon. Rich and valuable treasures in the castle are watched over by wicked spirits, and any one who could destroy these goblins and demons, and set free the treasures which are rotting in the castle, would be made a rich and lucky man. Lots of people have gone into the castle full of hope that they should succeed, but they have not been heard of since."

Hans was not in the least alarmed by this account, and the next morning he started off early to visit the King.

When he was admitted to the palace the King looked at him earnestly, and seemed much pleased with his appearance; then he said, "Do you really wish to be allowed to remain for three nights in the enchanted castle?" "Yes," replied Hans, "I do request it."

"You can take no living creature with you," said the King; "what else will you have?" "I only ask for a fire, a turning lathe, a cutting board, and a knife," he replied.

To this the King readily agreed, and these articles Hans was permitted to take into the castle during the day. When night came, he took up his abode in one of the rooms, lighted a fire which soon burned brightly, placed the turning lathe and the cutting board near it, and sat down on the cutting board, determined to make himself comfortable. Presently he exclaimed, "Oh, when shall I learn to shiver and shake? Not here, I am certain, for I am feeling too comfortable."

But at midnight, just as he had stirred the fire into a blaze, he suddenly heard in a corner the cry of a cat: "Miou, miou; how cold it is!"

"What a fool you must be, then," cried Hans, "to stay out there in the cold; come and seat yourself by the fire, and get warm if you will."

As he spoke, two very large black cats sprang forward furiously, seated themselves on each side of the fire, and stared at him with wild, fiery eyes. After a while, when the cats became thoroughly warm, they spoke, and said, "Comrade, will you have a game of cards?" "With all my heart," answered Hans; "but first stretch out your feet, and let me examine your claws."

The cats stretched out their paws. "Ah!" said he, "what long nails you have, and now that I have seen your fingers, I would rather be excused from playing cards with you."

Then he killed them both, and threw them out of the window into the moat. As soon as he had settled these two intruders, he seated himself again by the fire, hoping to have a little rest; but in a few moments there rushed out from every corner of the room black cats and black dogs with fiery chains one after another, till there seemed no end to them. They mewed, and barked, and growled, and at length jumped on his fire and scattered it about the room, as if they wished to put it out.

For a while he watched them in silence, till at last he got angry, and seizing his cutting board, exclaimed, "Be off! you horrid creatures!" and then rushing after them, he chased them round the room. Some few escaped in the clamor, but the rest he killed with his cutting-knife, and threw into the moat.

As soon as he had cleared the room, he rekindled his fire, by gathering the sparks together, and sat down to warm himself in the blaze. After a time he began to feel so sleepy that his eyes would not keep open any longer; so he looked round the room, and espied in a corner a large bed. "That is the very place for me," he said, rising, and laying himself upon it; but just as he was closing his eyes to sleep, the bed began to move about the room, and at last increased its speed, and went off at a gallop through the castle.

"All right," cried Hans, "now, go on again." At this the bed started off, as if six horses were harnessed to it, through the doorway, down the steps, to the great gates of the castle, against which it came with a great bump, and tumbled, legs uppermost, throwing all the pillows and blankets on Hans, who lay underneath, as if a mountain were upon him. He struggled out from the load, and said, "Anyone may travel in that fashion who likes, but I don't." So he laid himself down again by the fire, and slept till the daybreak.

In the morning the King came to the castle, and, as he caught sight of Hans lying by the fire asleep, he thought the evil spirits had killed him, and that he was dead. "Alas!" said the King, "I am very sorry; it is a great pity that such a fine youth should lose his life in this manner."

But Hans, who heard, sprang up in a moment and exclaimed, "No, King, I am not dead yet." The King, quite astonished and joyful at finding him unhurt, asked him how he had passed the night. "Oh, very pleasantly indeed," replied Hans; and then he related to the King all that had passed, which amused him very much.

On returning to the inn, the landlord stared at him with wide open eyes: "I never expected to see you again alive; but I suppose you have learned to shiver and shake by this time." "Not I," he replied; "I believe it is useless for me to try, for I never shall learn to be afraid."

The second night came, and he again went up to the old castle, and seated himself by the fire, singing the burden of his old song, "When shall I learn to shiver and shake?"

At midnight he heard a noise, as of something falling. It came nearer; then for a little while all was quiet; at last, with a tremendous scream, half the body of a man came tumbling down the chimney, and fell right in front of Hans.

"Holloa!" he cried, "all that noise, and only half a man; where's the other half?" At this, the noise and tumult began again, and, amid yellings and howlings, the other half of the man fell on the hearth.

"Wait," said Hans, rising; "I will stir the fire into a blaze first." But when he turned to sit down again, he found that the two halves of the man had joined, and there sat an ugly-looking object in his place. "Stay," cried the young man. "I did not bargain for this; that seat is mine."

The ugly man tried to push Hans away; but he was too quick for him, and putting out all his strength, he dislodged the creature from his seat, and placed himself again upon it.

Immediately there came tumbling down the chimney nine more of these horrid men, one after the other; each of them held a human thigh-bone in his hand, and the first who appeared brought out two skulls, and presently they set up the nine bones like skittles, and began to play, with the skulls for balls.

"Shall I play with you?" asked Hans, after he had looked on for some time. "Yes, willingly," they replied, "if you have any money." "Plenty," he said. "But your balls are not quite round." So he took the skulls and turned them on his lathe. "Now they will roll better; come on, let us set to work."

The strange men played with great spirit, and won a few of his dollars; but all at once the cock crowed, and they vanished from his eyes. After they were gone he laid himself down and slept peacefully till the King arrived, and asked him what had happened, and how it had fared with him during the night.

"Well," said Hans, "I played a game of skittles with some horrid-looking fellows who had bones and skulls for skittles and balls. I won sometimes, and I lost a couple of dollars." "Did you not shiver and shake?" asked the King, in surprise. "Not I, indeed! I wish I could! Oh, if I only knew how to shiver and shake."

The third night came, and found our hero once more seated on his bench by the fire, and saying quite mournfully, "When shall I ever learn to shiver and shake?"

As he spoke there came into the room six tall men, bearing a coffin containing a dead man. "Ah!" said Hans, "I know what you have there, it is the body of my cousin. He has been dead two days." Then he beckoned with his finger and said, "Come here, little cousin, I should like to see you!"

The men placed the coffin on the ground before him, and took off the lid. Hans touched the face, and it felt as cold as ice. "Wait," he said, "I will soon warm it!" so he went to the fire, and warming his hand, laid it on the face of the dead man, which remained as cold as ever.

At last he took him out of the coffin, carried him to the fire, and placed him on his lap, while he rubbed the hands and chest that he might cause the blood to circulate, but all to no purpose; the body remained as cold as before. Presently he remembered that when two lie in bed together they warm each other, so he placed the dead man in bed, covered him over, and lay down beside him. After a while this seemed to produce warmth in the body, the blood began to circulate, and at last the dead man moved and spoke.

"There, now, dear cousin," said Hans, "see, I have warmed you into life again, as I said I could." But the dead man sprang up and cried, "Yes, and now I will strangle you."

"What!" cried Hans, "is that your gratitude? You may as well go back into your coffin again." He leaped out of bed as he spoke, and, seizing the body, he threw it into the coffin and shut the lid down closely upon it. Then the six tall men walked in, lifted up the coffin and carried it away.

"That's over," said Hans. "Oh! I am sure nothing will ever teach me to shiver and shake."

As he spoke a man walked in who was taller and larger than any of the others, and the look of his eyes was frightful; he was old, and wore a long white beard.

"You wretched creature," cried the man, "I will soon teach you what it is to shiver and shake, for you shall die." "Not so fast, friend," answered Hans. "You cannot kill me without my own consent." "I will soon have you on the ground," replied the monster. "Softly, softly, do not boast; you may be strong, but you will find that I am stronger than you." "That is to be proved," said the old man. "If you are stronger than I am, I will let you go. Come, we will try."

The old man, followed by Hans, led the way through long dark passages and cellars, till they saw the reflection of a smith's fire, and presently came to a forge. Then the old man took an axe, and with one blow cut through the anvil right down to the ground.

"I can do better than that," said Hans, taking up the axe and going towards another anvil. The monster was so surprised at this daring on the part of Hans that he followed him closely, and as he leaned over to watch what the youth was going to do, his long white beard fell on the anvil.

Hans raised his axe, split the anvil at one blow, wedging the old man's beard in the opening at the same time.

"Now I have got you, old fellow," cried Hans, "prepare for the death you deserve." Then he took up an iron bar and beat the old man till he cried for mercy, and promised to give him all the riches that were hidden in the castle.

At this Hans drew out the axe from the anvil, and set the old man's beard free, while he watched him closely. He kept his word, however, and leading the young man back to the castle, pointed out to him a cellar in which were three immense chests full of gold. "There is one for the poor," said he; "another for the King, and the third for yourself."

Hans was about to thank him, when the cock crowed, and the old man vanished, leaving the youth standing in the dark.

"I must find my way out of this place," he said, after groping about for some time, but at last daylight penetrated into the vaults, and he succeeded in reaching his old room, and lying down by the fire, slept soundly till he was aroused by the King's arrival.

"Well," he said, in a glad voice when he saw the young man alive, "have you learned to shiver and shake yet?" "No!" replied Hans, "what was there to make me fear? My dead cousin came to see me, and a bearded old man tried to conquer me, but I managed him, and he has shown me where to find hidden treasures of gold, and how could I shiver and shake at these visitors?"

"Then," said the King, "you have released the castle from enchantment. I will give you, as I promised, my daughter in marriage."

"That is good news," cried Hans. "But I have not learned to shiver and shake after all."

The gold was soon after brought away from the castle, and the marriage celebrated with great pomp. Young Prince Hans, as he was now called, did not seem quite happy after all. Not even the love of his bride could satisfy him. He was always saying: "When shall I learn to shiver and shake?"

This troubled the Princess very much, till her lady's-maid said, "I will help you in this matter; I will show you how to make the Prince shiver and shake, that you may depend upon." So the Princess agreed to do what the lady's-maid advised.

First she went out to a brook that flowed through the gardens of the palace, and brought in a whole pailful of water, containing tiny fish, which she placed in the room.

"Remember," said the lady's-maid, "when the Prince is asleep in bed, you must throw this pail of water over him; that will make him shiver and shake, I am quite certain, and then he will be contented and happy."

So that night while Hans was in bed and asleep, the Princess drew down the bedclothes gently, and threw the cold water with the gudgeons all over him. The little fish wriggled about as they fell on the bed, and the Prince, waking suddenly, exclaimed, "Oh! dear, how I do shiver and shake, what can it be?" Then seeing the Princess standing by his bed, he guessed what she had done.

"Dear wife," he said, "now I am satisfied, you have taught me to shiver and shake at last," and from that hour he lived happily and contented with his wife, for he had learned to shiver and shake—but not to fear.

The Spindle, the Shuttle,
and the Needle

There was once a girl whose father and mother died while she was still
a little child. All alone, in a small house at the end of the village, dwelt
her godmother, who supported herself by spinning, weaving, and sewing. The old woman took the forlorn child to live with her, kept her
to her work, and educated her in all that is good. When the girl was
fifteen years old, the old woman became ill, called the child to her
bedside, and said, "Dear daughter, I feel my end drawing near. I leave
you the little house, which will protect you from wind and weather;
and my spindle, shuttle, and needle, with which you can earn your
bread." Then she laid her hands on the girl's head, blessed her, and
said, "Only preserve the love of God in your heart, and all will go well
with you." Thereupon she closed her eyes, and when she was laid in
the earth, the maiden followed the coffin, weeping bitterly, and paid
her the last mark of respect.

And now the maiden lived quite alone in the little house, and was
industrious, and span, wove, and sewed, and the blessing of the good
old woman was on all that she did. It seemed as if the flax in the room
increased of its own accord, and whenever she wove a piece of cloth
or carpet, or had made a shirt, she at once found a buyer who paid
her amply for it, so that she was in want of nothing, and even had
something to share with others.

About this time, the son of the King was traveling about the country looking for a bride. He was not to choose a poor one, and did not
want to have a rich one. So he said, "She shall be my wife who is the
poorest, and at the same time the richest." When he came to the village where the maiden dwelt, he inquired, as he did wherever he went,
who was the richest and also the poorest girl in the place. They first
named the richest; the poorest, they said, was the girl who lived in the
small house quite at the end of the village.

The rich girl was sitting in all her splendor before the door of her
house, and when the Prince approached her, she got up, went to meet

him, and made him a low curtsey. He looked at her, said nothing, and rode on. When he came to the house of the poor girl, she was not standing at the door, but sitting in her little room. He stopped his horse, and saw through the window, on which the bright sun was shining, the girl sitting at her spinning-wheel, busily spinning. She looked up, and when she saw that the Prince was looking in, she blushed all over her face, let her eyes fall, and went on spinning. I do not know whether, just at that moment, the thread was quite even; but she went on spinning until the King's son had ridden away again. Then she went to the window, opened it, and said, "It is so warm in this room!" But she still looked after him as long as she could distinguish the white feathers in his hat.

Then she sat down to work again in her own room and went on with her spinning, and a saying which the old woman had often repeated when she was sitting at her work, came into her mind, and she sang these words to herself:

> "Spindle, my spindle, haste, haste thee away,
> And here to my house bring the wooer, I pray."

And what do you think happened? The spindle sprang out of her hand in an instant, and out of the door, and when, in her astonishment, she got up and looked after it, she saw that it was dancing out merrily into the open country, and drawing a shining golden thread after it. Before long, it had entirely vanished from her sight. As she had now no spindle, the girl took the weaver's shuttle in her hand, sat down to her loom, and began to weave.

The spindle, however, danced continually onwards, and just as the thread came to an end, reached the Prince. "What do I see?" he cried; "the spindle certainly wants to show me the way!" He turned his horse about, and rode back with the golden thread. The girl was, however, sitting at her work singing,

> "Shuttle, my shuttle, weave well this day,
> And guide the wooer to me, I pray."

Immediately the shuttle sprang out of her hand and out by the door. Before the threshold, however, it began to weave a carpet which was more beautiful than the eyes of man had ever yet beheld. Lilies and roses blossomed on both sides of it, and on a golden ground in the center green branches ascended, under which bounded hares and rabbits; stags and deer stretched their heads in between them, brightly colored birds were sitting in the branches above; they lacked nothing but the gift of song. The shuttle leapt hither and thither, and everything seemed to grow of its own accord.

As the shuttle had run away, the girl sat down to sew. She held the needle in her hand and sang,

"Needle, my needle, sharp-pointed and fine,
Prepare for a wooer this house of mine."

Then the needle leapt out of her fingers, and flew everywhere about the room as quick as lightning. It was just as if invisible spirits were working; they covered tables and benches with green cloth in an instant, and the chairs with velvet, and hung the windows with silken curtains. Hardly had the needle put in the last stitch than the maiden saw through the window the white feathers of the Prince, whom the spindle had brought thither by the golden thread. He alighted, stepped over the carpet into the house, and when he entered the room, there stood the maiden in her poor garments, but she shone out from within them like a rose surrounded by leaves. "You are the poorest and also the richest," said he to her. "Come with me; you shall be my bride." She did not speak, but she gave him her hand. Then he gave her a kiss, led her forth, lifted her on to his horse, and took her to the royal castle, where the wedding was solemnized with great rejoicings. The spindle, shuttle, and needle were preserved in the treasure-chamber, and held in great honor.

The Master-Thief

One day an old man and his wife were sitting in front of a dilapidated house resting a while from their work. Suddenly a splendid carriage with four black horses came driving up, and a richly-dressed man descended from it. The peasant stood up, went to the great man, and asked what he wanted, and in what way he could be useful to him. The stranger stretched out his hand to the old man, and said, "I want nothing but to enjoy for once a country dish. Cook me some potatoes, in the way you always have them, and then I will sit down at your table and eat them with pleasure." The peasant smiled and said, "You are a count or a Prince, or perhaps even a duke; noble gentlemen often have such fancies, but you shall have your wish." The wife went into the kitchen, and began to wash and rub the potatoes, and to make them into balls, as they are eaten by the country-folks.

While she was busy with this work, the peasant said to the stranger, "Come into my garden with me for a while, I have still something to do there." He had dug some holes in the garden, and now wanted to plant some trees in them. "Have you no children," asked the stranger, "who could help you with your work?" "No," answered the peasant, "I had a son, it is true, but it is long since he went out into the world. He was a ne'er-do-well; sharp, and knowing, but he would learn nothing and was full of bad tricks; at last he ran away from me, and since then I have heard nothing of him."

The old man took a young tree, put it in a hole, drove in a post beside it, and when he had shoveled in some earth and had trampled it firmly down, he tied the stem of the tree above, below, and in the middle, fast to the post by a rope of straw. "But tell me," said the stranger, "why you don't tie that crooked knotted tree, which is lying in the corner there, bent down almost to the ground, to a post also that it may grow straight, as well as these?" The old man smiled and said, "Sir, you speak according to your knowledge, it is easy to see that you are not familiar with gardening. That tree there is old, and misshapen, no one can make it straight now. Trees must be trained while they are young."

"That is how it was with your son," said the stranger, "if you had trained him while he was still young, he would not have run away; now he too must have grown hard and misshapen." "Truly it is a long time since he went away," replied the old man, "he must have changed." "Would you know him again if he were to come to you?" asked the stranger. "Hardly by his face," replied the peasant, "but he has a mark about him, a birth-mark on his shoulder, that looks like a bean." When he had said that the stranger pulled off his coat, bared his shoulder, and showed the peasant the bean. "Good God!" cried the old man, "you are really my son!" and love for his child stirred in his heart. "But," he added, "how can you be my son? You have become a great lord and live in wealth and luxury. How have you contrived to do that?" "Ah, father," answered the son, "the young tree was bound to no post and has grown crooked; now it is too old, it will never be straight again. How have I got all that? I have become a thief, but do not be alarmed, I am a master-thief. For me there are neither locks nor bolts, whatsoever I desire is mine. Do not imagine that I steal like a common thief! I only take some of the superfluity of the rich. Poor people are safe! I would rather give to them than take anything from them. It is the same with anything which I can have without trouble, cunning and dexterity—I never touch it." "Alas, my son," said the father, "it still does not please me, a thief is still a thief, I tell you it will end badly." He took him to his mother, and when she heard that was her son, she wept for joy, but when he told her that he had become a master-thief, two streams flowed down over her face. At length she said, "Even if he has become a thief, he is still my son, and my eyes have beheld him once more." They sat down to table, and once again he ate with his parents the wretched food which he had not eaten for so long. The father said, "If our Lord, the count up there in the castle, learns who you are and what trade you follow, he will not take you in his arms and cradle you in them as he did when he held you at the font, but will cause you to swing from a halter." "Be easy, father, he will do me no harm, for I understand my trade. I will go to him myself this very day."

When evening drew near, the master-thief seated himself in his carriage, and drove to the castle. The count received him civilly, for he took him for a distinguished man. When, however, the stranger made himself known, the count turned pale and was quite silent for some time. At length he said, "You are my godson, and on that account mercy shall take the place of justice, and I will deal leniently with you.

Since you pride yourself on being a master-thief, I will put your art to the proof, but if you do not stand the test, you must marry the rope-maker's daughter, and the croaking of the raven must be your music on the occasion." "Lord count," answered the master-thief, "Think of three things as difficult as you like, and if I do not perform your tasks, do with me what you will." The count reflected for some minutes, and then said, "Well, then, in the first place, you shall steal the horse I keep for my own riding, out of the stable; in the next, you shall steal the sheet from beneath the bodies of my wife and myself when we are asleep, without our observing it, and the wedding-ring of my wife as well; thirdly and lastly, you shall steal away out of the church, the parson and clerk. Mark what I am saying, for your life depends on it."

The master-thief went to the nearest town; there he bought the clothes of an old peasant woman, and put them on. Then he stained his face brown, and painted wrinkles on it as well, so that no one could have recognized him. Then he filled a small cask with old Hungary wine in which was mixed a powerful sleeping-drink. He put the cask in a basket, which he took on his back, and walked with slow and tottering steps to the count's castle. It was already dark when he arrived. He sat down on a stone in the court-yard and began to cough, like an asthmatic old woman, and to rub his hands as if he were cold.

In front of the door of the stable some soldiers were lying round a fire; one of them observed the woman, and called out to her, "Come nearer, old mother, and warm yourself beside us. After all, you have no bed for the night, and must take one where you can find it." The old woman tottered up to them, begged them to lift the basket from her back, and sat down beside them at the fire. "What have you got in the little cask, old lady?" asked one. "A good mouthful of wine," she answered. "I live by trade; for money and fair words I am quite ready to let you have a glass." "Let us have it here, then," said the soldier, and when he had tasted one glass he said, "When wine is good, I like another glass," and had another poured out for himself, and the rest followed his example. "Hallo, comrades," cried one of them to those who were in the stable, "here is an old goody who has wine that is as old as herself; take a draught, it will warm your stomachs far better than our fire." The old woman carried her cask into the stable. One of the soldiers had seated himself on the saddled riding-horse, another held its bridle in his hand, a third had laid hold of its tail. She poured out as much as they wanted until the spring ran dry.

It was not long before the bridle fell from the hand of the one, and he fell down and began to snore, the other left hold of the tail, lay down and snored still louder. The one who was sitting in the saddle, did remain sitting, but bent his head almost down to the horse's neck, and slept and blew with his mouth like the bellows of a forge. The soldiers outside had already been asleep for a long time, and were lying on the ground motionless, as if dead. When the master-thief saw that he had succeeded, he gave the first a rope in his hand instead of the bridle, and the other who had been holding the tail, a wisp of straw, but what was he to do with the one who was sitting on the horse's back? He did not want to throw him down, for he might have awakened and have uttered a cry. He had a good idea; he unbuckled the girths of the saddle, tied a couple of ropes which were hanging to a ring on the wall fast to the saddle, and drew the sleeping rider up into the air on it, then he twisted the rope round the posts, and made it fast. He soon unloosed the horse from the chain, but if he had ridden over the stony pavement of the yard they would have heard the noise in the castle. So he wrapped the horse's hoofs in old rags, led him carefully out, leapt upon him, and galloped off.

When day broke, the master galloped to the castle on the stolen horse. The count had just got up, and was looking out of the window. "Good morning, Sir Count," he cried to him, "here is the horse, which I have got safely out of the stable! Just look, how beautifully your soldiers are lying there sleeping; and if you will but go into the stable, you will see how comfortable your watchers have made it for themselves." The count could not help laughing, then he said, "For once you have succeeded, but things won't go so well the second time, and I warn you that if you come before me as a thief, I will handle you as I would a thief."

When the countess went to bed that night, she closed her hand with the wedding-ring tightly together, and the count said, "All the doors are locked and bolted, I will keep awake and wait for the thief, but if he gets in by the window, I will shoot him." The master-thief, however, went in the dark to the gallows, cut a poor sinner who was hanging there down from the halter, and carried him on his back to the castle. Then he set a ladder up to the bedroom, put the dead body on his shoulders, and began to climb up. When he had got so high that the head of the dead man showed at the window, the count, who was watching in his bed, fired a pistol at him, and immediately the master let the poor sinner fall down, and hid himself in one corner.

The night was sufficiently lighted by the moon, for the master to see distinctly how the count got out of the window on to the ladder, came down, carried the dead body into the garden, and began to dig a hole in which to lay it.

"Now," thought the thief, "the favorable moment has come," stole nimbly out of his corner, and climbed up the ladder straight into the countess's bedroom. "Dear wife," he began in the count's voice, "the thief is dead, but, after all, he is my godson, and has been more of a scapegrace than a villain. I will not put him to open shame. Besides, I am sorry for the parents. I will bury him myself before daybreak, in the garden that the thing may not be known, so give me the sheet, I will wrap up the body in it, and bury him as a dog buries things by scratching." The countess gave him the sheet. "I tell you what," continued the thief, "I have a fit of magnanimity on me; give me the ring too—the unhappy man risked his life for it, so he may take it with him into his grave." She would not gainsay the count, and although she did it unwillingly she drew the ring from her finger, and gave it to him. The thief made off with both these things, and reached home safely before the count in the garden had finished his work of burying.

What a long face the count did pull when the master came next morning, and brought him the sheet and the ring. "Are you a wizard?" said he, "who has fetched you out of the grave in which I myself laid you, and brought you to life again?" "You did not bury me," said the thief, "but the poor sinner on the gallows." And he told him exactly how everything had happened, and the count was forced to own to him that he was a clever, crafty thief. "But you have not reached the end yet," he added. "You still have to perform the third task, and if you do not succeed in that, all is of no use." The master smiled and returned no answer.

When night had fallen he went with a long sack on his back, a bundle under his arms, and a lantern in his hand to the village-church. In the sack he had some crabs, and in the bundle short wax-candles. He sat down in the churchyard, took out a crab, and stuck a wax-candle on his back. Then he lighted the little light, put the crab on the ground, and let it creep about. He took a second out of the sack, and treated it in the same way, and so on until the last was out of the sack. Hereupon he put on a long black garment that looked like a monk's cowl, and stuck a gray beard on his chin. When at last he was quite unrecognizable, he took the sack in which the crabs had been, went into the church, and ascended the pulpit. The clock in the tower was just striking twelve; when the last stroke had sounded, he cried with a loud and piercing voice, "Hearken, sinful men, the end of all things has come! The last day is at hand! Hearken! Hearken! Whosoever wishes to go to heaven with me must creep into the sack. I am Peter, who opens and shuts the gate of heaven. Behold how the dead outside there in the churchyard, are wandering about collecting their bones. Come, come, and creep into the sack; the world is about to be destroyed!"

The cry echoed through the whole village. The parson and clerk who lived nearest to the church, heard it first, and when they saw the lights which were moving about the churchyard, they observed that something unusual was going on, and went into the church. They listened to the sermon for a while, and then the clerk nudged the parson and said, "It would not be amiss if we were to use the opportunity together, and before the dawning of the last day, find an easy way of getting to heaven." "To tell the truth," answered the parson, "that is what I myself have been thinking, so if you are inclined, we will set out on our way." "Yes," answered the clerk, "but you, the pastor, have the precedence, I will follow." So the parson went first, and ascended the pulpit where the master opened his sack. The parson crept in first, and then the clerk.

The master immediately tied up the sack tightly, seized it by the middle, and dragged it down the pulpit-steps, and whenever the heads of the two fools bumped against the steps, he cried, "We are going over the mountains." Then he drew them through the village in the same way, and when they were passing through puddles, he cried, "Now we are going through wet clouds," and when at last he was dragging them up the steps of the castle, he cried, "Now we are on the steps of heaven, and will soon be in the outer court." When he had got to the top, he pushed the sack into the pigeon-house, and when the pigeons fluttered about, he said, "Hark how glad the angels are, and how they are flapping their wings!" Then he bolted the door upon them, and went away.

Next morning he went to the count, and told him that he had performed the third task also, and had carried the parson and clerk out of the church. "Where have you left them?" asked the lord. "They are lying upstairs in a sack in the pigeon-house, and imagine that they are in heaven." The count went up himself, and convinced himself that the master had told the truth. When he had delivered the parson and clerk from their captivity, he said, "You are an arch-thief, and you have won the wager. For once you escape with a whole skin, but leave my land; for if you ever set foot on it again, you may count on your elevation to the gallows." The arch-thief took leave of his parents, once more went forth into the wide world, and no one has ever heard of him since.

Godfather Death

A poor man had twelve children and was forced to work night and day to give them even bread. When therefore the thirteenth came into the world, he knew not what to do in his trouble, but ran out into the great highway, and resolved to ask the first person whom he met to be godfather.

The first to meet him was the good God who already knew what filled his heart, and said to him, "Poor man, I pity you. I will hold your child at its christening, and will take charge of it and make it happy on earth." The man said, "Who are you?" "I am God." "Then I do not desire to have you for a godfather," said the man; "you give to the rich, and leave the poor to hunger."

Thus spoke the man, for he did not know how wisely God apportions riches and poverty. He turned therefore away from the Lord, and went farther.

Then the Devil came to him and said, "What do you seek? If you will take me as a godfather for your child, I will give him gold in plenty and all the joys of the world as well." The man asked, "Who are you?" "I am the Devil." "Then I do not desire to have you for godfather," said the man; "you deceive men and lead them astray."

He went onward, and then came Death striding up to him with withered legs, and said, "Take me as godfather." The man asked, "Who are you?" "I am Death, and I make all equal." Then said the man, "You are the right one, you take the rich as well as the poor, without distinction; you shall be godfather." Death answered, "I will make your child rich and famous, for he who has me for a friend can lack nothing." The man said, "Next Sunday is the christening; be there at the right time." Death appeared as he had promised, and stood godfather quite in the usual way.

When the boy had grown up, his godfather one day appeared and bade him go with him. He led him forth into a forest, and showed him a herb which grew there, and said, "Now shall you receive your godfather's present. I make you a celebrated physician. When you are called to a patient, I will always appear to you. If I stand by the head of the sick man, you may say with confidence that you will make him well again, and if you give him of this herb he will recover; but if I stand by the patient's feet, he is mine, and you must say that all remedies are in vain, and that no physician in the world could save him. But beware of using the herb against my will, or it might fare ill with you."

It was not long before the youth was the most famous physician in the whole world. He had only to look at the patient and he knew his condition at once, and if he would recover, or must needs die. From far and wide people came to him, sent for him when they had anyone ill, and gave him so much money that he soon became a rich man.

Now it befell that the King became ill, and the physician was summoned, and was to say if recovery were possible. But when he came to the bed, Death was standing by the feet of the sick man, and the herb did not grow which could save him.

"If I could but cheat Death for once," thought the physician, "he is sure to take it ill if I do, but, as I am his godson, he will shut one eye; I will risk it." He therefore took up the sick man, and laid him the other way, so that now Death was standing by his head. Then he gave the King some of the herb, and he recovered and grew healthy again. But Death came to the physician, looking very black and angry, threatened him with his finger, and said, "You have overreached me. This time I will pardon it, as you are my godson; but if you venture it again, it will cost you your neck, for I will take you yourself away with me."

Soon afterwards the King's daughter fell into a severe illness. She was his only child, and he wept day and night, so that he began to lose the sight of his eyes, and he caused it to be made known that whosoever rescued her from death should be her husband and inherit the crown. When the physician came to the sick girl's bed, he saw Death by her feet. He ought to have remembered the warning given by his godfather, but he was so infatuated by the great beauty of the King's daughter, and the happiness of becoming her husband, that he flung all thought to the winds. He did not see that Death was casting angry glances on him, that he was raising his hand in the air, and threatening him with his withered fist. He raised up the sick girl, and placed her head where her feet had lain. Then he gave her some of the herb, and instantly her cheeks flushed red, and life stirred afresh in her.

When Death saw that for a second time he was defrauded of his own property, he walked up to the physician with long strides, and said, "All is over with you, and now the lot falls on you," and seized him so firmly with his ice-cold hand, that he could not resist, and led him into a cave below the earth. There he saw how thousands and thousands of candles were burning in countless rows, some large, others half-sized, others small. Every instant some were extinguished, and others again burned up, so that the flames seemed to leap hither and thither in perpetual change.

"See," said Death, "these are the lights of men's lives. The large ones belong to children, the half-sized ones to married people in their prime; the little ones belong to old people; but children and young folks likewise have often only a tiny candle."

"Show me the light of my life," said the physician, and he thought that it would be still very tall. Death pointed to a little end which was just threatening to go out, and said, "Behold, it is there."

"Ah, dear godfather," said the horrified physician, "light a new one for me, do it for love of me, that I may enjoy my life, be King, and the husband of the King's beautiful daughter."

"I cannot," answered Death, "one must go out before a new one is lighted." "Then place the old one on a new one, that will go on burning at once when the old one has come to an end," pleaded the physician. Death behaved as if he were going to fulfill his wish, and took hold of a tall new candle; but as he desired to revenge himself, he purposely made a mistake in fixing it, and the little piece fell down and was extinguished. Immediately the physician fell on the ground. And now he himself was in the hands of Death.

Bearskin

A young fellow enlisted as a soldier and conducted himself so bravely that he was always the foremost when it rained bullets. As long as the war lasted, all went well, but when peace was made, he received his dismissal, and the captain said he might go where he liked. His parents were dead, and he had no longer a home, so he went to his brothers and begged them to take him in, and keep him until war broke out again. The brothers, however, were hardhearted and said, "What can we do with thee? Thou art of no use to us; go and make a living for thyself." The soldier had nothing left but his gun; he took that on his shoulder, and went forth into the world.

He came to a wide heath, on which nothing was to be seen but a circle of trees; under these he sat sorrowfully down, and began to think over his fate. "I have no money," thought he, "I have learnt no trade but that of fighting, and now that they have made peace they don't want me any longer; so I see beforehand that I shall have to starve." All at once he heard a rustling, and when he looked round, a strange man stood before him, who wore a green coat and looked right stately, but had a hideous cloven foot. "I know already what thou art in need of," said the man; "gold and possessions shalt thou have, as much as thou canst make away with, do what thou wilt, but first I must know if thou art fearless, that I may not bestow my money in vain." "A soldier and fear—how can those two things go together?" he answered; "thou canst put me to the proof." "Very well, then," answered the man, "look behind thee."

The soldier turned round, and saw a large bear, which came growling towards him. "Oho!" cried the soldier, "I will tickle thy nose for thee, so that thou shalt soon lose thy fancy for growling," and he aimed at the bear and shot it through the muzzle; it fell down and never stirred again. "I see quite well," said the stranger, "that thou art not wanting in courage, but there is still another condition which thou wilt have to fulfill." "If it does not endanger my salvation," replied the soldier, who knew very well who was standing by him. "If it does,

I'll have nothing to do with it." "Thou wilt look to that for thyself," answered Greencoat; "thou shalt for the next seven years neither wash thyself, nor comb thy beard, nor thy hair, nor cut thy nails, nor say one paternoster. I will give thee a coat and a cloak, which during this time thou must wear. If thou diest during these seven years, thou art mine; if thou remainest alive, thou art free, and rich to boot, for all the rest of thy life."

The soldier thought of the great extremity in which he now found himself, and as he so often had gone to meet death, he resolved to risk it now also, and agreed to the terms. The Devil took off his green coat, gave it to the soldier, and said, "If thou hast this coat on thy back and puttest thy hand into the pocket, thou wilt always find it full of money." Then he pulled the skin off the bear and said, "This shall be thy cloak, and thy bed also, for thereon shalt thou sleep, and in no other bed shalt thou lie, and because of this apparel shalt thou be called Bearskin." After this the Devil vanished.

The soldier put the coat on, felt at once in the pocket, and found that the thing was really true. Then he put on the bearskin and went forth into the world, and enjoyed himself, refraining from nothing that did him good and his money harm. During the first year his appearance was passable, but during the second he began to look like a monster. His hair covered nearly the whole of his face, his beard was like a piece of coarse felt, his fingers had claws, and his face was so covered with dirt that if cress had been sown on it, it would have come up. Whosoever saw him, ran away, but as he everywhere gave the poor money to pray that he might not die during the seven years, and as he paid well for everything, he still always found shelter. In the fourth year, he entered an inn where the landlord would not receive him, and would not even let him have a place in the stable, because he was afraid the horses would be scared. But as Bearskin thrust his hand into his pocket and pulled out a handful of ducats, the host let himself be persuaded and gave him a room in an outhouse. Bearskin was, however, obliged to promise not to let himself be seen, lest the inn should get a bad name.

As Bearskin was sitting alone in the evening, and wishing from the bottom of his heart that the seven years were over, he heard a loud lamenting in a neighboring room. He had a compassionate heart, so he opened the door, and saw an old man weeping bitterly, and wringing his hands. Bearskin went nearer, but the man sprang to his feet and tried to escape from him. At last when the man perceived that Bearskin's voice was human he let himself be prevailed on, and by kind words Bearskin succeeded so far that the old man revealed the cause of his grief. His property had dwindled away by degrees, he and his daughters would have to starve, and he was so poor that he could not pay the innkeeper, and was to be put in prison. "If that is thy only trouble," said Bearskin, "I have plenty of money." He caused the innkeeper to be brought thither, paid him and put a purse full of gold into the poor old man's pocket besides.

When the old man saw himself set free from all his troubles he did not know how to be grateful enough. "Come with me," said he to Bearskin; "my daughters are all miracles of beauty; choose one of them for thyself as a wife. When she hears what thou hast done for me, she will not refuse thee. Thou dost in truth look a little strange, but she will soon put thee to rights again." This pleased Bearskin well, and he went. When the eldest saw him she was so terribly alarmed at his face that she screamed and ran away. The second stood still and looked at him from head to foot, but then she said, "How can I accept a husband who no longer has a human form? The shaven bear that once was here and passed itself off for a man pleased me far better, for at any rate it wore a hussar's dress and white gloves. If it were nothing but ugliness, I might get used to that." The youngest, however, said, "Dear father, that must be a good man to have helped you out of your trouble, so if you have promised him a bride for doing it, your promise must be kept."

It was a pity that Bearskin's face was covered with dirt and with hair, for if not they might have seen how delighted he was when he heard these words. He took a ring from his finger, broke it in two, and gave her one half, the other he kept for himself. He wrote his name, however, on her half, and hers on his, and begged her to keep her piece carefully, and then he took his leave and said, "I must still wander about for three years, and if I do not return then, thou art free, for I shall be dead. But pray to God to preserve my life."

The poor betrothed bride dressed herself entirely in black, and when she thought of her future bridegroom tears came into her eyes. Nothing but contempt and mockery fell to her lot from her sisters. "Take care," said the eldest, "if thou givest him thy hand, he will strike his claws into it." "Beware!" said the second. "Bears like sweet things, and if he takes a fancy to thee, he will eat thee up." "Thou must always do as he likes," began the eldest again, "or else he will growl." And the second continued, "but the wedding will be a merry one, for bears dance well." The bride was silent, and did not let them vex her. Bearskin, however, traveled about the world from one place to another, did good where he was able, and gave generously to the poor that they might pray for him.

At length, as the last day of the seven years dawned, he went once more out on to the heath, and seated himself beneath the circle of trees. It was not long before the wind whistled, and the Devil stood before him and looked angrily at him; then he threw Bearskin his old coat, and asked for his own green one back. "We have not got so far as that yet," answered Bearskin, "thou must first make me clean." Whether the Devil liked it or not, he was forced to fetch water, and wash Bearskin, comb his hair, and cut his nails. After this, he looked like a brave soldier, and was much handsomer than he had ever been before.

When the Devil had gone away, Bearskin was quite light-hearted. He went into the town, put on a magnificent velvet coat, seated himself in a carriage drawn by four white horses, and drove to his bride's house. No one recognized him, the father took him for a distinguished general, and led him into the room where his daughters were sitting. He was forced to place himself between the two elder ones; they helped him to wine, gave him the best pieces of meat, and thought that in all the world they had never seen a handsomer man. The bride, however, sat opposite to him in her black dress, and never raised her eyes, nor spoke a word.

When at length he asked the father if he would give him one of his daughters to wife, the two eldest jumped up, ran into their bedrooms to put on splendid dresses, for each of them fancied she was the chosen one. The stranger, as soon as he was alone with his bride, brought out his half of the ring, and threw it in a glass of wine which he reached across the table to her. She took the wine, but when she had drunk it, and found the half ring lying at the bottom, her heart began to beat. She got the other half, which she wore on a ribbon round her neck, joined them, and saw that the two pieces fitted exactly together. Then said he, "I am thy betrothed bridegroom, whom thou sawest as Bearskin, but through God's grace I have again received my human form, and have once more become clean." He went up to her, embraced her, and gave her a kiss.

In the meantime the two sisters came back in full dress, and when they saw that the handsome man had fallen to the share of the youngest, and heard that he was Bearskin, they ran out full of anger and rage. One of them drowned herself in the well, the other hanged herself on a tree. In the evening, some one knocked at the door, and when the bridegroom opened it, it was the Devil in his green coat, who said, "Seest thou, I have now got two souls in the place of thy one!"

The Spirit in the Glass Bottle

There was once a poor woodcutter who toiled from early morning till late night. When at last he had laid by some money he said to his boy, "Thou art my only child, I will spend the money which I have earned with the sweat of my brow on thy education; if thou learnest some honest trade thou canst support me in my old age, when my limbs have grown stiff and I am obliged to stay at home."

Then the boy went to a High School and learned diligently so that his masters praised him, and he remained there a long time. When he had worked through two classes, but was still not yet perfect in everything, the little pittance which the father had earned was all spent, and the boy was obliged to return home to him. "Ah," said the father, sorrowfully, "I can give thee no more, and in these hard times I cannot earn a farthing more than will suffice for our daily bread."

"Dear father," answered the son, "do not trouble thyself about it, if it is God's will, it will turn to my advantage. I shall soon accustom myself to it." When the father wanted to go into the forest to earn money by helping to pile and stack wood and also to chop it, the son said, "I will go with thee and help thee." "Nay, my son," said the father, "that would be hard for thee; thou art not accustomed to rough work, and wilt not be able to bear it, besides I have only one axe and no money left wherewith to buy another." "Just go to the neighbor," answered the son, "he will lend thee his axe until I have earned one for myself."

The father then borrowed an axe of the neighbor, and next morning at break of day they went out into the forest together. The son helped his father and was quite merry and brisk about it. But when the sun was right over their heads, the father said, "We will rest, and have our dinner, and then we shall work as well again." The son took his bread in his hands, and said, "Rest thou, father, I am not tired; I will walk up and down a little in the forest, and look for birds' nests." "Oh, thou fool," said the father, "why shouldst thou want to run about there? Afterwards thou wilt be tired, and no longer able to raise thy arm; stay here, and sit down beside me." The son, however, went into the forest, ate his bread, was very merry and peered in among the green branches to see if he could discover a bird's nest anywhere.

So he went up and down to see if he could find a bird's nest, until at last he came to a great dangerous-looking oak, which certainly was already many hundred years old, and which five men could not have spanned. He stood still and looked at it, and thought, "Many a bird must have built its nest in that." Then all at once it seemed to him that he heard a voice. He listened and became aware that some one was crying in a very smothered voice, "Let me out, let me out!" He looked around, but could discover nothing; nevertheless, he fancied that the voice came out of the ground. Then he cried, "Where art thou?" The voice answered, "I am here down among the roots of the oak tree. Let me out! Let me out!"

The scholar began to loosen the earth under the tree, and search among the roots, until at last he found a glass bottle in a little hollow. He lifted it up and held it against the light, and then saw a creature shaped like a frog springing up and down in it. "Let me out! Let me out!" it cried anew, and the scholar, thinking no evil, drew the cork out of the bottle. Immediately a spirit ascended from it, and began to grow, and grew so fast that in a very few moments he stood before the scholar, a terrible fellow as big as half the tree by which he was standing.

"Knowest thou," he cried in an awful voice, "what thy wages are for having let me out?" "No," replied the scholar fearlessly, "how should I know that?" "Then I will tell thee," cried the spirit; "I must strangle thee for it." "Thou shouldst have told me that sooner," said the scholar, "for I should then have left thee shut up, but my head shall stand fast for all thou canst do; more persons than one must be consulted about that." "More persons here, more persons there," said the spirit. "Thou shalt have the wages thou hast earned. Dost thou think that I was shut up there for such a long time as a favor? No, it was a punishment for me. I am the mighty Mercurius. Whoso releases me, him must I strangle." "Softly," answered the scholar, "not so fast. I must first know that thou wert shut up in that little bottle, and that thou art the right spirit. If, indeed, thou canst get in again, I will believe, and then thou mayst do as thou wilt with me." The spirit said haughtily, "That is a very trifling feat," drew himself together, and made himself as small and slender as he had been at first, so that he crept through the same opening, and right through the neck of the bottle in again. Scarcely was he within than the scholar thrust the cork he had drawn back into the bottle, and threw it among the roots of the oak into its old place, and the spirit was betrayed.

And now the scholar was about to return to his father, but the spirit cried very piteously, "Ah, do let me out! ah, do let me out!" "No," answered the scholar, "not a second time! He who has once tried to take my life shall not be set free by me, now that I have caught him again." "If thou wilt set me free," said the spirit, "I will give thee so much that thou wilt have plenty all the days of thy life." "No," answered the scholar, "thou wouldst cheat me as thou didst the first time." "Thou art playing away thy own good luck," said the spirit; "I will do thee no harm, but will reward thee richly." The scholar thought, "I will venture it, perhaps he will keep his word, and anyhow he shall not get the better of me."

Then he took out the cork, and the spirit rose up from the bottle as he had done before, stretched himself out and became as big as a giant. "Now thou shalt have thy reward," said he, and handed the scholar a little bag just like a plaster, and said, "If thou spreadest one end of this over a wound it will heal, and if thou rubbest steel or iron with the other end it will be changed into silver." "I must just try that," said the scholar, and went to a tree, tore off the bark with his axe, and rubbed it with one end of the plaster. It immediately closed together and was healed. "Now, it is all right," he said to the spirit, "and we can part." The spirit thanked him for his release, and the scholar thanked the spirit for his present, and went back to his father.

"Where hast thou been racing about?" said the father; "why hast thou forgotten thy work? I said at once that thou wouldst never get on with anything." "Be easy, father, I will make it up." "Make it up indeed," said the father angrily, "there's no art in that." "Take care, father, I will soon hew that tree there, so that it will split." Then he took his plaster, rubbed the axe with it, and dealt a mighty blow, but as the iron had changed into silver, the edge turned. "Hollo, father, just look what a bad axe thou hast given me, it has become quite crooked." The father was shocked and said, "Ah, what hast thou done? Now I shall have to pay for that, and have not the wherewithal, and that is all the good I have got by thy work." "Don't get angry," said the son, "I will soon pay for the axe." "Oh, thou blockhead," cried the father, "wherewith wilt thou pay for it? Thou hast nothing but what I give thee. These are students' tricks that are sticking in thy head, but thou hast no idea of woodcutting." After a while the scholar said, "Father, I can really work no more, we had better take a holiday." "Eh, what!" answered he. "Dost thou think I will sit with my hands lying in my lap like thee? I must go on working, but thou mayst take thyself home." "Father, I am here in this wood for the first time, I don't know my way alone. Do go with me."

As his anger had now abated, the father at last let himself be persuaded and went home with him. Then he said to the son, "Go and sell thy damaged axe, and see what thou canst get for it, and I must earn the difference, in order to pay the neighbor." The son took the axe, and carried it into town to a goldsmith, who tested it, laid it in the scales, and said, "It is worth four hundred thalers; I have not so much as that by me." The son said, "Give me what you have, I will lend you the rest." The goldsmith gave him three hundred thalers, and remained a hundred in his debt. The son thereupon went home and said, "Father, I have got the money, go and ask the neighbor what he wants for the axe." "I know that already," answered the old man, "one thaler six groschen." "Then give him two thalers, twelve groschen, that is double and enough; see, I have money in plenty," and he gave the father a hundred thalers, and said, "You shall never know want; live as comfortably as you like." "Good heavens!" said the father, "how hast thou come by these riches?"

The scholar then told how all had come to pass, and how he, trusting in his luck, had made such a good hit. But with the money that was left, he went back to the High School and went on learning more, and as he could heal all wounds with his plaster, he became the most famous doctor in the whole world.

AMERICAN LITERATURE

Little Women — Louisa May Alcott
The Last of the Mohicans — James Fenimore Cooper
The Red Badge of Courage and *Maggie* — Stephen Crane
Selected Poems — Emily Dickinson
Narrative of the Life and Other Writings — Frederick Douglass
The Scarlet Letter — Nathaniel Hawthorne
The Call of the Wild and *White Fang* – Jack London
Moby-Dick — Herman Melville
Major Tales and Poems — Edgar Allan Poe
The Jungle — Upton Sinclair
Uncle Tom's Cabin — Harriet Beecher Stowe
Walden and *Civil Disobedience* — Henry David Thoreau
Adventures of Huckleberry Finn — Mark Twain
The Complete Adventures of Tom Sawyer — Mark Twain
Ethan Frome and *Summer* — Edith Wharton
Leaves of Grass — Walt Whitman

WORLD LITERATURE

Tales from the 1001 Nights — Sir Richard Burton
Don Quixote — Miguel de Cervantes
The Divine Comedy — Dante Alighieri
Crime and Punishment — Fyodor Dostoevsky
The Count of Monte Cristo — Alexandre Dumas
The Three Musketeers — Alexandre Dumas
Selected Tales of the Brothers Grimm — Jacob and Wilhelm Grimm
The Iliad — Homer
The Odyssey — Homer
The Hunchback of Notre-Dame — Victor Hugo
Les Misérables — Victor Hugo
The Metamorphosis and *The Trial* — Franz Kafka
The Phantom of the Opera — Gaston Leroux
The Prince — Niccolò Machiavelli
The Art of War — Sun Tzu
The Death of Ivan Ilych and Other Stories — Leo Tolstoy
Around the World in Eighty Days — Jules Verne
Candide and *The Maid of Orléans* — Voltaire
The Bhagavad Gita — Vyasa

BRITISH LITERATURE

Beowulf — Anonymous
Emma — Jane Austen
Persuasion — Jane Austen
Pride and Prejudice — Jane Austen
Sense and Sensibility — Jane Austen
Peter Pan — J. M. Barrie
Jane Eyre — Charlotte Brontë
Wuthering Heights — Emily Brontë
Alice in Wonderland — Lewis Carroll
The Canterbury Tales — Geoffrey Chaucer
Heart of Darkness and Other Tales — Joseph Conrad
Robinson Crusoe — Daniel Defoe
A Christmas Carol and Other Holiday Tales — Charles Dickens
Great Expectations — Charles Dickens
Oliver Twist — Charles Dickens
A Tale of Two Cities — Charles Dickens
The Waste Land and Other Writings — T. S. Eliot
A Passage to India — E. M. Forster
The Jungle Books — Rudyard Kipling
Paradise Lost and *Paradise Regained* — John Milton
The Sonnets and Other Love Poems — William Shakespeare
Three Romantic Tragedies — William Shakespeare
Frankenstein — Mary Shelley
Dr. Jekyll and Mr. Hyde and Other Strange Tales — Robert Louis Stevenson
Kidnapped — Robert Louis Stevenson
Treasure Island — Robert Louis Stevenson
Dracula — Bram Stoker
Gulliver's Travels — Jonathan Swift
The Time Machine and *The War of the Worlds* — H. G. Wells
The Picture of Dorian Gray — Oscar Wilde

ANTHOLOGIES

Four Centuries of Great Love Poems

BORDERS®
CLASSICS

The text of this book is set in 11 point Goudy Old Style, designed by American printer and typographer Frederic W. Goudy (1865–1947).

The archival-quality, natural paper is composed of recyclable products made from wood grown in sustainable forests; the manufacturing processes conform to the environmental regulations of the country of origin.

The finished volume demonstrates the convergence of Old-World craftsmanship and modern technology that exemplifies books manufactured by Edwards Brothers, Inc. Established in 1893, the family-owned business is a well-respected leader in book manufacturing, recognized the world over for quality and attention to detail.

In addition, Ann Arbor Media Group's editorial and design services provide full-service book publication to business partners.